The Truth

Love and lies - 1

Addison Carter

J A Publishing

Copyright © 2021 J A Publishing

All rights reserved

The characters and events portrayed in this book are fictitious. Any similarity to real persons, living or dead, is coincidental and not intended by the author.

No part of this book may be reproduced, or stored in a retrieval system, or transmitted in any form or by any means, electronic, mechanical, photocopying, recording, or otherwise, without express written permission of the publisher.

ISBN: 9798758354926

For Emma,
My ultimate cheerleader.
You're a boss bitch, don't you ever forget it.

1
Meg

Who the hell was that guy? It isn't exactly shocking that more than one person would want that piece of shit dead. Except *I* was the one who should have been pulling the trigger.

This was supposed to be a nice simple job, I'd be calling in for a clean up right now, and then giving my boss a quick run down as I made my way home to fill my painfully empty stomach with Chinese food.

But that won't be happening. No, because some arsehole decided to come waltzing into the carpark where Mr Baxter had been stood, fumbling with his keys, and shot him in the back of the head before my finger could tighten around my own trigger.

Fuck, I really wish I hadn't skipped lunch today.

I kept my sight on the shooter, maybe I could take him out too. It's not what I had planned for, but what's one more body?

He isn't leaving in any kind of rush, in fact he's casually leaning against the black BMW that Rob Baxter was about to climb into. I watch as he shrugs off his black leather jacket, slings it over his shoulder and slides his gun into a holster. Then proceeds to pull a phone from his trouser pocket, and bring it to his ear.

I watch as he talks, my lip reading is good, not perfect, but maybe Ill be able to gain some valuable information. Maybe find out something about who he is, who he works for, anything. My boss will be a lot happier about the screw up to my plan if I can at least give him something useful about this guy. Something better than *'he dressed well and radiated big dick energy'*.

I pulled all of my focus on to his lips. *Its done.* Well that's not much to go on. *Are you doubting my skills? He's not coming back from this. One shot is all I need.* Arrogant ass! A tiny part of me now wants Rob Baxter to survive this – he absolutely won't, but wouldn't it be funny if he did - just to stomp all over this arsehole's ego. There's nothing worse than thinking someone's dead when they aren't, and that kind of fuck up doesn't go down well in our world. That is presuming he's from my world. He's definitely not one of ours though. My boss likes to keep our circle small. So unless someone has been bought in in the fifteen minutes that have passed since my last call with Boss, this guy is not a Brother.

Im being watched. As I watch the words leave his mouth his eyes shoot up to mine. I know he cant see me. Not really. But that doesn't stop my mouth going suddenly drier than the Sahara. How did he know I was still up here? Was it just a lucky guess that he pinpointed my exact location? *Hey beautiful,* he raises a hand and waggles his fingers in a lazy wave. Is he? Was that aimed at me? *Oh calm down. I'm behaving myself.* I'm certain that he can't really see me, and he absolutely cannot tell that the sniper on this roof is female. Can he? No, but that's not the kind of thing that you presume.

A sudden realisation hits me, followed by a rush of dread, this guy doesn't just know that I'm female, he knows *exactly* who is up here. How. The. Fuck.

He hung up and put his phone away, but his eyes remained locked on my location, a deadly smirk playing on his lips. Everything about this guy is pissing me off.

The feeling of dread began to slowly disappear from my body the longer I looked at him and I found myself being overpowered by intense irritation.

He isn't moving. He *knows* I'm here, and he's made himself an easy target. He is either the cockiest man I have ever laid eyes on, or he's just plain stupid. Unfortunately I get the feeling it's the former.

My attention is pulled by the buzz of my phone. *Fuck.* I don't have to look at the screen to know who it is. I should have called him by now. He knows something has gone wrong.

"Get your ass back here now." the command comes through my phone like a whip.

"Boss, I need to take care -." he cuts me off before I can tell him about the guy in the carpark.

"No M, get here. Now." With that he hangs up.

Of course he already knows that Rob Baxter has been taken care of, he will be sat at his beautiful mahogany desk watching the cameras from the carpark. He's always watching.

I let out a long breath and tuck my phone away, I notice that the dark eyes of the mysterious arsehole are still staring up at me.

I could... No, Boss would know. He gave me an order, he's angry already. I'm not dumb enough to piss him off even more. Not by doing something like this anyway.

With a growl of frustration I force my attention away from the arsehole below and gather my things together and drop down the buildings fire escape, careful to not be noticed by any of the residents going about their evenings. Slipping through dark alleys to reach my silver Mercedes, I wonder what fate will be waiting for me when I face my Boss.

The Boss usually conducts business from one of his venues, but this evening is different. This evening he will be hosting an intimate dinner for his trusted circle and their families.

I hate socialising with the guys' families. The wives don't ever attempt to hide how they feel about The Brotherhood's only female member, and if any of their sons are around my ass becomes the main topic of conversation.

The Boss had invited me, one of the lucky five. But I turned it down, telling him I'd be his eyes for the night. Staying home and handling business for him. I don't really want to do that either, but I know I can't just refuse him without giving him a decent trade off.

It doesn't take long for me to reach my destination on the outskirts of Westeroak, and I only have to wait at the gate for a few short moments. The guard has likely been told to allow me in without calling up to the house first.

The driveway is long and allows me a small amount of time to swallow down the nervous energy that I can feel bubbling inside me. There is only one man who has ever been able to bring that emotion to my surface, but I will never let him see that. His ego is already dangerously big. When I emerge from this car my mask will be firmly in place.

I pull up to the left of the front door next to a black Cadillac. Grey is already here. I quickly check my face in the mirror and run a finger under one eye to remove a small smudge of mascara. Then step out and make my way to the front door. It opens as I approach, "In the office please M" the tall member of staff tells me as I pause in the foyer. "Thank you, Clive" I reply and offer him a genuine smile. Most of the men who frequent this building ignore the staff, I hate that.

 The office is just past the double doors to the dining room, as I walk past, I look in through the open doors and am met with the hard glare of Greys' wife. No doubt she isn't happy that she has been dragged here half an hour earlier than expected and now has to sit alone while her husband handles business. I scan her from head to toe in a bitchy manner, it's a low move, but always has the desired effect, she already hates me, so why not push her buttons too.

 I knock twice on the closed office door and wait for a response.

 "Enter." *Great,* he sounds even angrier than he did on the phone.

 I push open the door and stride towards the huge desk, stopping between two empty chairs and placing my hands on the backs of them both as I hold eye contact with the man sat on the other side waiting for me.

2

Lorenzo

She doesn't back down easily. This is what drew me to her when we first met. This girl had bigger balls than most of the guys I knew. She was strong in so many ways. It wasn't hard for her to fit into my life. My first female member. So many idiots tried to argue with me over that decision, until they met her.

As she stands between the two chairs, I force myself to resist the urge to run my gaze slowly over her body. She knows *exactly* what she is doing.

"Pick a fucking seat M" I snap. I've never felt comfortable calling her by her name. Megan, I'm not sure why, but it doesn't suit her. M caught and stuck. In fact the only people who I have ever heard call her by her name are the wives.

She lowers herself into one of the chairs, crossing her legs over each other and adopting a comfortable, casual position. I lean forward, resting my elbows on the desk, and steepling my fingers below my chin. She knows what this means. This isn't to say I am predictable. No, never predictable. But those who are close to me understand these cues. This is my favourite power play, if you misinterpret, you're fucked. She rarely gets it wrong, she knows she has to explain herself.

She finally breaks eye contact, glancing to the computer screen to my left.

"You saw what happened." Her jaw tenses then she lets out a loud sigh, "Whoever that guy was, he knew I was there. He knew *exactly* where I was."

"What makes you think that?" Grey spoke from behind me. A little out of character for him, he usually stays quiet through meetings like this. Debbie must have lost her shit with him when I had asked him to be here early, he's probably pissed that he's now in the dog house, or maybe he just didn't like M. Regardless, the way he spat the words at her made it clear he needed to let some anger out. I'll remember that for later, I'm sure I can find him a better outlet. Maybe we should take a nice afternoon trip to the shooting range tomorrow, it's been too long since I last fired a gun.

She looked up at him, then returned her eyes to mine. "My lip reading skills aren't bad, he told whoever he called that he was being watched, then he looked directly at me." she paused and ran her fingers through her hair, "obviously he couldn't actually see me, but I don't for one second think it was just a lucky guess. Boss, you sent me because I was the best person for that job, I'm not saying he's better, he fucking isn't. But this guy clearly knows what he's doing. Do we know who he is?" her brows furrowed with the question, like she was trying to place his face, "a new member of The Wolves maybe?" she followed up.

"Its being handled." I respond. Intending for my words to be firm and final. But she pushes. No surprise there.

"Boss," she said softly, then hesitates, clearly debating if she should continue. "why didn't you let me take care of him there and then?" Not many people would question my choices. Most wouldn't receive a response if they did.

"You are aware of who you are speaking to, aren't you M? do you really think it's wise to question *me*?" and those that did get a response, well they usually didn't like it.

Her entire body tenses as if she didn't expect that response. I watch her as she forces herself to relax, it's subtle, and amusing as hell to me.

"Sorry Boss" she said in an even tone. Clever girl. Never stepping too far out of line. Pushing just enough to only mildly piss me off. It made me wonder why I'd chosen Grey as my second instead of her.

Deep down I know though. Someone like her would become far too dangerous with that level of power. Best to keep her where she is for now.

"You will do better next time M, I don't think my expectations of you are unreasonable," I relax back into my chair, now feeling comfortably in control. "are they?"

"Of course not Boss." She keeps her lips slightly parted after the words have left her mouth. *That perfect fucking mouth.*

"Grey, go find Cooper and make sure he is being thorough in his clean up, I'll join you in the main lounge once I have decided what to do with our girl here." I don't look up, I don't watch him leave, I don't react when the door closes behind him with far too much force. Instead I keep my focus on the captivating woman sat across from me. My eyes never leaving her mouth as it lifts in a slight smile and then falls as her expression fills with confusion.

"You may not have any blood on your hands M, but you were still there." I said simply, propping an ankle on top of the opposite knee.

Her eyes flicker with annoyance and she repositions herself to sit tall, but she's not mad about the reminder that she screwed up. No, she's mad that I've called her M when it's just the two of us.

I ignore it. "We don't need footage of your

perfect ass shimmying down a fire escape to fall into the wrong hands do we?" Of course I've already watched footage from the surrounding cameras and have let that image play over and over in my head up until now.

I know she wears those tight black leggings because they are practical, but part of me wonders if she also does it because she knows how she looks in them.

"No, we don't need that, *Sir*." she shakes her head. Not directly reacting to my sleezy compliment, but there is a layer of lust to her voice as the final word escapes her lips.

I turn my gaze to the wall, and she stays silent, waiting for me to speak again.

"Your fuck up won't go any further than the four of us," Myself, Her, Grey and Cooper. "but you *will* be punished." I look back at her and she sucks in a sharp intake of breath.

Placing both feet firmly back on the floor I push my chair back a little, "Come here." I demand.

A flicker of defiance crosses her face, but it doesn't linger, a second later she does as she's told, rising from her chair, rounding my desk and perching on it in front of me.

"Good girl." She bites down on her lower lip, "Now turn." She releases her lip and follows the command with no hesitation this time. "Jacket off." She removes the black leather jacket and I watch it drop to the floor.

I take a moment to admire her petite figure, the strappy sports bra, the exposed pale skin of her tiny waist. The way the curves of her body flow is close to perfection.

I cave to desire far too quickly, moving to stand behind her and trail my fingers softly up the sides of her body from her hips, then onto her back, gliding higher until I'm drawing small circles on her shoulders as I speak. "What am I going to do with you, *Il mio Tesoro?*" she leans back into me and lets out a satisfied groan at my words. My treasure, the rarest jewel. The sound makes my cock ache.

I bring my mouth down to her neck, pressing soft kisses from below her earlobe to her shoulder, dragging gentle, breathy moans from her. Hearing her desperation build as quickly as my own as my hands caress every inch of her body as they travel back down to her hips.

She grips the desk to steady herself as my thumbs slip into the waistband of her leggings, moving them down over her ass, leaving them sat at her mid thighs. I want her fully stripped down. Completely bare for me. but we don't have long, and I desperately need to bury myself inside her.

Of course her panties are black, does this girl own anything that isn't? If she doesn't, she will soon.

Sliding them to one side I realise that she's holding her breath in anticipation. I gently brush one finger along from her clit to her ass, barely touching her, then brush it back down again, repeating the torturous motion over and over until she lets out a trembling, slow breath and I stop, hovering over her soaked entrance.

I push my free hand into her hair and grasp a handful, then push her down over the table as my finger pushes deep inside her. A loud gasp escapes her and turns into a low moan as I slide in a second finger. *Fuck, she feels incredible.* Moans continue to fall from her lips as I twist and pump my fingers inside her. She controls her volume so well, she knows we can't get caught.

It doesn't take long to bring her to her first violent orgasm, her body writhing on my desk.

Untangling my hand from her hair and removing my fingers from her perfect pussy, I tell her not to move. But as I free my cock from my trousers, I notice her wiggle her ass. *Was that deliberate?* Even if it wasn't, it gives me an excuse to let out a small fragment of my carefully controlled rage.

I don't give her any warning. My hand comes down in a stinging blow on her ass cheek, causing her to yelp. *Fuck, I really hope no one is lurking outside of the door. Not that I would ever have to explain myself, but appearances and all that.* 'I told you not to move.'

"Sorry Boss." she never calls me by my name. I wonder how it would sound on her lips.

"That isn't good enough tesoro, If you want

me to continue now, you'll have to beg." I step back, stroking my dick and admiring the glowing print on her ass as I wait for her response.

"Please Boss, please fuck me." she whispers.

This is where I would usually walk away. I used to love walking away and leaving her desperate and filling with angry frustration. But now, she's become an addiction, and jerking myself off alone just to rile her up isn't satisfying anymore.

Instead I grab hold of her and fill her in one bruising thrust, her hips slamming against the hard wood that is supporting her body. She curses through a loud gasp and moves her hands from the edge of the desk to sit just under her chest, bracing herself in preparation. She knows I won't be gentle with her. I repeat the motion over and over, picking up pace as I mark her skin with my fingers and let out low groans as I feel myself drawing rapidly close to my release. The feeling of her slick pussy encasing me and the heavenly sounds of pleasure escaping her push me up to the very edge.

She tightens around me, her moans becoming frantic, "Come for me." I demand, and with those words she falls apart, the final rush of pleasure ripping through her and a gush of heat wraps around my cock, dragging me along for the ride.

I collapse back into my chair and work to steady my breathing. Smirking as she eventually stands and pulls her clothes back into place.

She turns to me, raking her fingers through

her deep red curls, and I notice that her face is holding the composed mask that she has perfected so well. The only hint of what we have just done being the slight flush on her cheeks, the same routine every damn time, "Can I go and clean up before I head off Boss?".

"You can go clean up M, but you're not leaving." She jolts, but this time I'm not sure if its due to the sudden switch back to *M,* or because I've told her she won't be going.

"Did you think you could just fuck your way out of this?" I let a wicked grin form on my mouth. "*This* is not your punishment. Go to the guest bedroom, Clive will find you something suitable to change into." her jaw drop's and she curses under her breath. "You're coming to dinner. and you're already late".

3

Meg

I make my way up the staircase that winds to the right of the building and down the corridor to the guest bedroom.

I'm extremely comfortable in this room, being intimate with the boss didn't mean I was welcome in his bed. I was a guest; *this* was my place.

I walk past the neatly made bed and head straight into the bathroom that I have become so familiar with, kick off my shoes, twist the knob on the shower and strip out of my clothes. I look down at my discarded clothes as the water heats up. I know that if I ask nicely Clive would take them to be cleaned, but that leaves me without panties all evening. This usually wouldn't bother me. But usually id be pulling on my leggings and driving straight home, not sitting in a room full of people -

half of whom I despise - wearing fuck knows what! I grab the black lace panties from the pile and examine them. No, no I cannot put these back on, they are soaked with evidence of the fun I had just been having with my boss.

I step into the shower, careful to not get my hair wet, and scrub myself with the lemon scented soap that I love so much.

Of course it wasn't going to be that easy! I curse myself for thinking that I could use our private relationship to my advantage like that. Of course he wouldn't just let it go because we're fucking. Of course he would have me doing something that gave me no enjoyment. He said punishment, not *funishment*.

But this dinner, *eugh*, he knows it's the perfect punishment. *Bastard.* Oh and that smug stupid grin on his face as he told me. If the consequences didn't scare me I'd have quite happily broken his perfect nose.

As I step out of the shower and switch off the flow of water my stomach makes a loud growl. At least I don't have to drive home, order and wait for my food to arrive. Every cloud and all that.

Grabbing a luxuriously fluffy towel and wrapping it tightly around myself I head back into the bedroom and perch on the edge of the bed. I need to get some of these for my place. I've never been that into fancy things, but these towels, I'd spend good money to wrap myself in these every morning.

A second later there is a gentle tap on the door, "Hey Clive," I start and he takes those words as permission to enter. "I'm sorry that the boss has you running around after me, I'm sure you have other things you'd rather be doing."

He walks over to the bed and gently lays down a slinky red dress, then places a pair of strappy black heels on the floor, "Ah its not a problem M." he looks at me with a soft smile on his kind face. I enjoy these brief moments with Clive, where he relaxes a little and lets the professionalism drop a fraction. It didn't take long for us to develop this connection. Its painfully clear that my 'Brothers' don't see past his job title, but I refuse to ever treat any of the 'staff' the way they do.

"Well, thank you, I really appreciate it." I run a finger over the silky fabric of the dress next to me, "was this…?" My words trail off, but Clive knows where my thoughts had gone.

"Yes, I managed to find one that was never worn, I hope that its ok?"

Clive is aware of mine and Lorenzo's relationship - if you can even stretch the term that far – and is very cautious when it comes to anything connected to Lorenzo's wife. I can tell that he liked her, that he misses her. I knew her. Not very well. But I can understand how hard it must be for him. She was this insanely kind ray of sunshine, she shouldn't have met her end in the way that she did.

She deserved better than a bullet to the head. And then here I am, about to wear one of her dresses and sit at her table. I don't want him to ever think that I am trying to replace her, that absolutely is not what this is.

"Its beautiful, Selene would have looked amazing in it." I inwardly cringe at my own words, why did I have to say that.

"That she would've M," I can sense that he wants to say more, but he doesn't, the smile drops from his face and is replaced with his usual unreadable expression. "Is there anything else I can do for you?"

"If I bring my clothes down to the laundry room would it be alright if I popped them in a machine?" I ask. He's already pulling a small white plastic bag from a draw when I finish speaking and tells me to pop them in the bag and he will do the rest.

After Clive leaves the room I drop the towel, step into the dress and stand in front of a full length mirror. *Holy shit.* This dress is amazing. The deep shade of red closely matching that of my hair. The plunging neckline and low drop of the back showing off soft, toned, pale skin. I turn and admire my reflection from as many angles as I can, feeling a whole new level of confidence.

My stomach growls at me again, pulling me from my brief obsession with my own reflection. I slide on the shoes, a size to big, but they are open toe and have straps that I can tighten enough for it to not be a huge issue.

I ruffle my hair and check my face for any smudges to my makeup. A red lip would look amazing with this dress, but there is not a chance in hell that I'd go snooping around to find a dead woman's makeup, if he had even kept that.

The satisfaction in my appearance had managed to distract me from the negative feelings I have about my punishment, but as I close the bedroom door behind me and head back to the staircase, I feel them pushing forward. My mood souring with every step, until I'm stood toe to toe with familiar Italian leather shoes, and cold fingers tip my chin up to meet my lovers hard, dark gaze.

"Exquisite." A single word, whispered in the empty foyer.

With a voice like silk, a jawline that could make the most beautiful model in the world jealous and that flawless olive complexion how could I not want this man.

Never getting too close to Selene had turned out to be a small blessing. For wholly selfish reasons. I'd never have fallen into his bed if me and her had been more than acquaintances.

On occasion I feel a rush of guilt, but then I remind myself that we don't need to deprive ourselves of physical desires. That's all it is, we close doors and become each other's release. He lifts me up, and I calm him down. When the doors open again its business as usual. I am not his little treasure anymore.

I try not to overthink that, the sinking feeling I get when that affectionate term is replaced with *M*.

I know I don't *really* want this to be more than it is, it's not like me to get attached. Neither does he. He only uses it to create a clear distinction between our two dynamics. That's all.

"Thank you, Boss," I force the words out, my bad mood spilling out into the air around us.

"Try amore mio," he whispers, still holding my chin, "try to hide how much you hate this. I might even reward you if you put on a good show." He smiles and drops his hand, turning to walk to the dining room door.

4

Meg

Inhaling deeply, I steady myself and follow Lorenzo into the room. Forcing my body to let go of the clenching sensation I feel between my legs from our brief exchange outside the door.

I plaster a fake smile on to my face and I make a decision quickly as I walk into the room and am met with the disgusted glares of 3 women scattered around the table, I *will* hide how much I hate this, but I will not play nice. He wants a good show, but he wasn't specific about my role.

I find an empty chair waiting for me halfway down one side of the table and seat myself between Cooper and Debbie.

Well at least one of them likes me.

Cooper's face lights up when he sees me, and I relax a fraction. He is here alone, as usual. He has a girlfriend, Samantha, but he keeps her away from all of us. Wise choice.

I hear Debbie quietly ask Grey to switch seats with her, telling him that she doesn't want to completely lose her appetite. I purse my lips to avoid laughing at the situation, earning me a stern look from Lorenzo.

His attention is drawn away from me as Grey hesitantly relays Debbie's request. He gives a sharp shake of his head and turns his focus to the woman next to me.

"Not a good start to our evening *Deb.*" He says sharply and the woman reaches for her husband's hand. Her face staying neutral, only that one movement hinting to the fear she feels around my boss.

"Sorry Boss." She says quietly and he turns his attention away from her.

"Buonasera, la mia famiglia" Lorenzo addresses the rest of the table in his native tongue. "I am thrilled that you are *all* here." I don't miss the emphasis he puts on the word all. A subtle dig in my direction. Neither does Cooper apparently, covering his snort of amusement with a cough. Smooth buddy.

I try so hard, but I can't resist shoving my elbow into his ribs. Scoring us both another deadly glare from our boss, and the rest of the table look at us like we are a pair of naughty children.

'Are you done.' Lorenzo says with a fierce

spark in his eyes. It is not a question. We both have the decency to look apologetic as we nod our heads.

After a long, tense moment he continues.

"This annual dinner has become one of my favourite evenings of the year, a tradition passed down through generations of Brothers, a time to reflect and celebrate. It has been quite a year, we have had many successes," he smiles, "the occasional fuck up," I feel Greys eyes burn into me from his spot next to Lorenzo, but I refuse to look at him. Instead I hold myself tall and keep my eyes fixed on a painting across the room.

"And sadly, we have experienced the loss of two people who meant a great deal to all of us, My wonderful wife Selene," he pauses, and my eyes reluctantly travel to find his, "and our loyal brother, Jason." My skin goes cold, and a lump forms in my throat as a tidal wave of emotion crashes over me.

Coopers hand finds mine under the table and squeezes gently. I squeeze back, thankful that I have him here with me right now, and blink hard, pushing back the tears that are threatening to fall as I remember what happened to Jase. *My* Jase. *My* brother. My big, brave, protective older brother. The only family that I had left. Now gone. It's been nine months. Some days I can think about him and smile, other days I hear his name and my heart breaks all over again.

Lorenzo keeps his focus on me, "What happened after was unfortunate," a sad expression briefly crosses his face, and his next words are just for me, "but we are healing together." He nods at me before he turns his attention back to the room.

Fuck, I hated being reminded of what had happened after we lost them both. Sure it had felt so good pulling that trigger, but it wasn't enough. Getting the call from Lorenzo telling me he had a 'very special treat' that might cheer me up - the current location of Jason's murderer. I didn't hesitate for a single second when I saw the face of that worthless piece of shit. The attempt to end Slash's life – *what a dumb name* – didn't fix how I felt, it didn't stop the pain I felt, but in that moment, it changed *something*.

I didn't linger after, shooting the prick in broad daylight had been risky as hell. He was a Wolf, a member of our biggest rival gang, I knew I had to get out of there before someone realised who had just put a bullet in Slash's head. Charon, the leader of The Westeroak Wolves, hadn't retaliated. That should have been great news. Except the shot had not been fatal, Slash had managed to survive, he was pretty messed up afterwards though. It didn't feel like enough, but I was under strict instruction to leave it be. So I had to accept that this was the closest I'd get to revenge for the family taken from me.

After we found out that he was still alive I had expected Charon to come for me, Slash had seen my face before I'd pulled the trigger, he knew who had done that to him. For weeks after I was a mess with anxiety, Lorenzo couldn't trust me to take on any serious business, *again,* too scared that I'd fuck it up. But Charon did nothing, somehow the whole thing had been buried. I asked Lorenzo how, but he refused to explain. I wanted to ask again, but I'd worry he would think that I was only sleeping with him to manipulate him into letting me in on one of the many things that he keeps to himself. I'm not stupid enough to piss him off like that.

"Together," he pauses, "we can get through anything." his stare is hard. I'm unsure if it's a mask to protect himself, or a mask to keep up the illusion that this man cannot be broken. Maybe both.

"Those responsible will pay. We are The Brotherhood, we will not give up. We will always have each other, so let us eat, drink, and enjoy each other's company." My stomach groans at those words, mostly from hunger, but also a little from the churning sensation that I've felt since Jase was mentioned.

The double doors of the room open and we are presented with a huge spread of Italian delights. The sight and smell snapping me from my little emotional spiral. I come back to the reality that I'm sat at this table, the one that I had tried so hard to avoid. In retaliation of my punishment, I plan on pissing off as many of the people in this room as possible. Subtly of course.

Next to me Debbie is now talking across the

table to Collette, Franks far-too-young wife. Its blindingly obvious that he's punching above his weight, she's in it for his status.

They are talking about their plans for Sunday brunch, drawing the other woman at the table, Rebecca, to their conversation. Rebecca hasn't been around for long; Michael and Rebecca have had a bit of a whirlwind romance. They met 8 months ago, then eloped after a month, it's kinda cute I guess, to be that sure of someone. I think I could've befriended her if those witches hadn't got their claws into her first, but now she's one of them.

Collette is directly opposite me, and with just one carefully planned, *accidental,* movement, I can very easily upset her.

She looks pristine, perfect makeup, not a single blonde curl out of place in its intricately styled updo, and her dress, *Oh Cole, was white ever going to be a good idea?* Immaculate.

If I lift my left leg just a little too high, with a smidge too much force, as I cross it over my right and turn to begin conversation with Cooper, I can knock the table, and the full glass of Pinot Noir sat just beyond my plate will topple over, flood over the tablecloth, and spill down into her lap. If I'm lucky it might even splash on to her husband too.

"So Coop," I start, "how's -." I'm instantly cut off by a high-pitched shriek and the scraping noise of a chair being pushed away from the table.

"My dress!" Collette's shrill voice is almost

painful to listen to. "Megan! You fucking bitch!" I turn my face up to meet her furious expression. At least, I think she's furious, Fuck that woman has had a lot of work done, do her eyebrows actually move?

I pull my brows – that have a fantastic range of motion by the way - into a confused frown then let my eyes widen in shock as I slowly skim my gaze down her dress, playing the innocent thing almost a little too well.

"Collette." Lorenzo snaps before I'm able to defend myself, pulling her attention away from me.

"My *dress*." She whines, and I have to bite down on the inside of my cheek to stop myself from laughing. Bloody hell she sounds pathetic.

"Go clean yourself up. And don't be so fucking disrespectful." He says sternly. She doesn't argue back, just dramatically storms out of the dining room.

Debbie is whispering to Grey, I can't hear the words, but from his face, I'd guess that she's defending Collette, probably complaining that its unfair that she was spoken to like that when she hadn't done anything wrong. Except she had, I *may* have provoked her, but in this room, I rank a hell of a lot higher than she does.

The wives' usual bitchy comments, subtle digs and low-key shade thrown towards me are usually ignored, but to be that blatantly rude to me, Cole fucked up. *That shit won't slide.*

I glance to Lorenzo and notice that he's eating

again and chatting away to Michael as though nothing had just happened. I think I find his ability to do that one of the scariest things about him.

"That was no accident, was it M?" Cooper whispers so quietly I almost don't hear him.

Turning back to him I smile and raise my brows, causing a low rumble of laughter to vibrate in his chest.

"How's Samantha doing?" I make pleasant small talk with him, but I can't help but notice out of the corner of my eye, the embarrassed look on Frank's face. He isn't speaking to anyone, just using his fork to push some pasta around his plate. Good, now for act 2.

"Mikey," I raise my voice a little to get his attention. "your sister came into my office earlier this week," I was going to mention this to him when I next saw him alone, but seeing as I'm here, and fully intent on causing more shit, ill drop this little nugget and hope it unravels a little string of drama. "don't worry, I didn't let anything slip, but when are you going to tell her about Rebecca? You know she's thinking of setting you up with some girl she went to college with right?"

Rebecca stiffens and her jaw tenses, turning herself fully in her chair to face Michael and inhaling deeply.

"You said you told your family" she grinds the words out, her hands shaking with rage. Michael's face pales a little before he tries to defend himself. Rebecca is having none of it, she never raises her voice, but the venom behind each word she spits at him is enough to satisfy me.

I catch Lorenzo's eye, his expression is unreadable, but he doesn't break eye contact with me until Rebecca stands and storms out, pushing past Collette, who is coming back through the doors in her dry, but stained, dress. I guess no one would help her clean up properly. What a shame.

Collette finds her seat and leans over to ask Frank what she's missed. Michael quickly excuses himself from the table and apologises profusely to Lorenzo for the disruption. I don't miss the furious look he throws my way as he walks past.

"What a show, I'm guessing you've saved the best for last?" Cooper asks quietly when conversations start to flow around the table again.

"You guessed right my friend." I reply and lean back in my chair as our dinner plates are replaced with mouth-watering desserts. A different item in front of each of us. In front of me, Tiramisu, my favourite.

I glance at Debbie, then to Lorenzo, who is now reclined in his chair at the head of the table. My boss simply raises his brows at me. Is that a warning or an invitation? For once I'm unsure what he's trying to say.

Oh well, I'm probably already in trouble. "Coop, can I borrow the item that's in your boot, please," I whisper, barely moving my lips before filling my mouth with a spoon full of creamy coffee flavoured dessert. Without hesitating he leans down and pretends to itch his ankle, then places the requested item on my lap before raising his hand above the table to continue eating. "Thanks."

"I'm sorry to have to do this to you all, but I have just been informed of some important business that I need to take care of," Lorenzo declares as he moves to stand and tucks his phone into his trouser pocket before straightening out his suit jacket. "Please, stay and finish your food and drinks. Buonanotte, amici miei."

Grey stands up as Lorenzo walks past his chair, "Sit, your presence in here is more important. M, you can join me." Grey shoots our boss a grateful look, and Debbie beams at her husband. *Fuck.* I guess that look was a warning after all. He's worked out what I'm doing and no doubt thinks I'd push things too far.

I grasp the item on my lap in one hand and pick up my half-eaten Tiramisu in the other hand. Lorenzo stops behind my chair, and I turn to meet his questioning stare.

"I'm hungry, and this is *really* good." I explain, and I swear he smiles, but he turns to continue towards the door in a movement to fast for me to be sure.

I get up to follow but Cooper stops me, gently grabbing my arm, but before he can speak, I pull out of his grip and lean in to place my mouth close to his ear, "I might still need it." I tell him. Then straighten up and head to the place by the door where our boss is waiting with a dangerous look in his eye.

"Finally, how do you all tolerate her? She reeks of desperation, the way she just came on to Cooper, and *that dress*, she just screams cheap whore, Jason would be disgusted by her if he was still with us!" Debbie's words stop me two steps before the place where Lorenzo is stood. My body tenses, and a rage begins to bubble deep inside of me. I don't look up at the man in front of me. I spin on my heels, and in one swift, skilled motion, I send Coopers blade from my left hand flying across the room, watching it sink deep into the dark wood of the chair that Debbie is sitting in, narrowly missing her shoulder.

She screams and almost jumps into her husband's lap. I turn back to see Lorenzo holding the door open, "Get in my office now!" he thunders.

"That psycho could have killed me." I hear Debbie sob from behind me. I flick my hair and look at her over my shoulder and murmur "If fucking only."

"Megan!" *Oh crap!* I quickly glide past Lorenzo, keeping my head down, and flinch as he slams the door behind us.

I hurry along to the door of his office, but he doesn't follow. Instead he leans against one of the dining room doors.

"That was quite a show amore." He says darkly. Then turns the opposite way and heads to the staircase. Pausing at the bottom step. "Well?" That's all he says. One word. Then ascends the steps. Leaving me grasping my dessert while my mouth drops open.

5

Don

"Wait there until they arrive this time." I let out a quiet huff of breath at his words and leaned more of my weight onto the BMW behind me and settle in for the wait. If I walked away before the clean-up team arrived this time I'd be out.

Being family meant fuck all. It pissed me off, but I guess the shit that I'd been pulling recently had been the kind of thing's that my boss couldn't just ignore. Fuck knows I wouldn't be standing for that shit if anyone tried it when I take over.

"I'm being watched" Remembering what he had said earlier when briefing me on this job my eyes snap up to the top of the building opposite me, spotting a tiny imperfection in the smooth line of the roof and holding that location in my gaze.

I wonder if she's reading my lips right now. I

know if the roles were reversed, I would be.

"Hey beautiful." I say, throwing a mocking little wave her way. I'm hopeful that the compliment has pissed her off just as much as its probably pissed off my boss. My guess is the girl up there is important to him in some weird way, I was told I'm not allowed to kill her if I ever come face to face with her. Seems a little unfair to me.

"Adonis, don't fu…" yep, he's pissed.

"Oh calm down," I cut across him, not caring that he had probably killed men for less than interrupting him, "I'm behaving myself."

He let out an aggravated growl and I could almost guarantee that it was taking a hell of a lot of willpower for him to not throw his phone into the wall. "Don't fucking push me Son. Remember your place." And with those lovely parting words the line went dead.

I'm calling this a successful evening. One wound up boss, one dead piece of shit, and one hopefully very irritated girl.

Megan Fields, the girl on the roof, has quite the reputation. The first female gang member in this town. Some believe she may be close to wriggling her way up to become Lorenzo D'Angelo's second. Knocking that arsehole Grey down a peg.

Finding out that she would be here tonight, a rival on the same job, well that was so damn exciting to me. Beating her to this kill, that was the kind of confidence knock the girl needed. And it did great things for my ego.

Keeping my eye trained on the spot where she was still sat I let my mouth curl into a smug smirk. Would she shoot me? Doubtful. She knows as well as I do that we are being watched. She knows that I know she's there, and that my boss knows it too, shooting me would not end well for her. If it truly is her goal to reach the top of The Brotherhood, she won't do anything reckless, D'Angelo isn't the type of man to tolerate insubordination from his men. Women. Whatever.

I'd honestly be pretty disappointed if she did decide to shoot me. What a boring way to go. And what a boring way to get back at the guy who just stole away your kill.

A few minutes later I notice that the view I'm staring up at has changed slightly, indicating that she has finally gone. Just in time, as a tall guy dressed all in black approaches me, "Don, we'll take it from here." He glances at the floor next to where I'm still leaning against the dead arsehole's car. "Dammit Adonis," he groans, "are you just a shit shot, or do you make these kinds of messes on purpose?"

Keeping my mouth twisted in that cruel smirk that falls so naturally on my face I push off of the car and silently stroll away, leaving a short trail of bloodied footprints behind me.

6

Meg

I wake to an unfamiliar noise. Snoring. Who the fuck is snoring in my ear?! I snap my eyes open, and it only takes a short moment for me to realise that I have royally fucked up. I should *not* be here.

Lorenzo is sleeping deeply next to me in his dark mahogany king size bed. The softest white sheets that I've ever felt are wrapped around my body and barely cover my boss's peachy ass. Looks like I still hog the sheets. *Fuck. I'm not alone.* Panic rises and sits like a heavy weight on my chest. The last time I woke up with someone else around was the last time I saw my brother. He was sitting on my bed. I'd woken up to him carrying a tray of pancakes and coffee to me, setting it down on my bedside table so he could present me with a card and a small black box. Three days late for my birthday, but I didn't care, he hadn't been able to get out of a 'business trip' to spend the actual day with me, but he had come over first thing in the morning when he arrived back home.

Two days later he was gone. Forever. The birthday card with the simple message still sat on my bedside table and the gold star shaped earrings hadn't left my ears once since that day. *His shooting-star.* A slightly twisted joke, Jase was a shit shot, unlike me. He had his own talents though. I touched a finger to my left lobe and gently stroked the earring, trying to pull any level of calm back into my body and finding a deep comfort in the motion. I'd started noticing myself do this more often recently, I made a mental note to put a stop to it, knowing that even the most subtle sign of weakness could be used against me. *What a life.*

When the panic subsided a little I rolled over and took in the unfamiliar room, it fit Lorenzo well, it was as neat and simple as I had expected his private space to be, mahogany furniture, a couple of photos but nothing too personal. There were two open doors, one appearing to lead to a bathroom and the other to a walk in wardrobe, the walls were a clean fresh white, except for the one opposite the bed that was covered entirely in floor to ceiling windows, showing off the most breath-taking view of the garden and Oak Lake shimmering under the morning sun just beyond the back wall. I've never been in here before. I'm a guest. Aren't I? This didn't mean anything. But still I couldn't dismiss the confusion that I was feeling.

Last night I had followed Lorenzo up the stairs and into the guest bedroom where he showed me *exactly* what he thought of my performance at dinner, punishing and praising me in equal measure. The last thing I recall was collapsing in a blissfully satisfied heap, thinking to myself that I'd allow myself five minutes to enjoy the feeling before finding my clothes and driving home. I guess I must have fallen asleep. So why am I in this bed instead? Did Lorenzo carry me here? When? Why?

"Good morning, il mio tesoro." His rough sleep filled voice rumbled next to me, pulling me back to the present. I looked over at him, watching the way his muscles flexed as he stretched his arms over his head and bought them down underneath his head. His dark eyes met mine, they resembled melted chocolate in this light, warm and inviting, they had never looked this way before. They were usually so cold and harsh, able to inflict intense fear with one simple glare.

"Morning," I replied.

He spoke again before I could voice any of me questions. "How did you sleep?"

What? He asked the question as though this was normal routine for us. I couldn't stop the confusion from showing on my face.

"Erm, I slept ok, this is a really lovely bed, but why am I here?" his features changed to mirror my own, his brows pinching together and eyes narrowing. But he did not speak. "I didn't think we would be doing sleepovers, its blurring lines a little isn't it?" the confusion dropped from his face and was quickly replaced with his usual flat expression, his eyes turning cold in a flash.

"I'm not having a valued asset ending up in the hospital because she was too tired to safely drive herself home, and my mattress is better for your back than the one in the guestroom. If you're feeling well rested, I will call Clive to bring your clothes up and you can leave, M." *fuck I'm an idiot.* His reasons made perfect sense. Of course it's nothing more. How could I be stupid enough to think he was suddenly wanting to change the relationship we have. I felt my body relax at his words; lines painted clearly in his tone.

"Thank you, Boss," I smiled at him, but he turned his back to me, reaching for the phone on the bedside table. After tapping out a quick message he got out of the bed and made his way to the en suite bathroom, pausing in the doorway to look down at the phone still in his hand.

"Are you in the office tomorrow?" he asked as he leaned into the doorframe, his back still to me.

"I am, do you need me for something?" Being self-employed had the lovely perk of being able to come and go as I please, but I always went into the office on Mondays, doing so felt like a reset button for a new week. Putting whatever had happened the previous week behind me. It helped me to keep a clear head and not dwell on the aspects of my role in The Brotherhood that would keep normal people up at night.

"Yes, 6pm, The Crown, I'll have details then. Come well equipped though M." Meaning he has no solid plan yet, but I know Lorenzo, he will have one, and numerous backups, mapped out in his head by the time he's stepped out of the shower. He was the boss for a reason.

"I'll be there. See you tomorrow then Boss." He nodded his head in one sharp movement and continued into the bathroom, closing the door behind himself and leaving me with a silent message. *Don't hang around here.*

There was a gentle knock at the bedroom door, but it did not open. "Clive?" I questioned, but there was no response. I wrapped the white sheet around my naked body and went to open the door. No one was there, on the floor sat a neat pile of clothes and my trainers. Was this room off limits to staff too? The thought made me feel as though every second longer I spent in Lorenzo's room was overstaying my welcome.

I threw my clothes on quickly and checked my reflection in the small mirror on one of the walls. I didn't look great. Makeup was smudged below my eyes and my lips were still puffy from the night before. My hair fortunately wasn't too bad, it was easily smoothed down with my fingers. I suppose it didn't really matter as I only planned on getting down to my car and heading straight home.

I made it to the front door without seeing another person, I had hoped to bump into Clive so that I could thank him for washing and delivering my clothes. I noticed a notepad and pen on a side table in the foyer, perfect. I wrote out a quick thank you message for him and headed out of the front door and climbed into my car to begin my journey home.

I reached my apartment half an hour later, parking my car in its reserved space in the garage of the building. Coffee. I am in desperate need of coffee. I checked my phone once I was inside the lift heading to my floor. Six new messages. One from Grey demanding I apologise to Debbie, one from my personal trainer requesting to push our session this evening back an hour, one from a client that I'll ignore until tomorrow, I don't reply outside of office hours anyway. The last three messages were from Cooper.

Coop
Holy shit Sunshine! Are you ok? I've never heard the boss use your full name. I think I may have slightly shit myself on your behalf.
Good luck.
Also, damn girl, sometimes I forget how insane your aim is!

Coop
Heads up, if Lorenzo hasn't murdered you yet then Grey will.
The man is livid.
It was nice knowing you. I'll try to look sad at your funeral.

Coop
Well no one has called to cover up your murder yet, so I'm presuming you're still alive, confirmation would be good though.

I chuckled to myself as I read over his messages. It was nice having Cooper around, I was starting to feel like he was one of the only real friends I had nowadays. I quickly fired off two messages, one to Grey rolling over and telling him I'd send flowers to Debbie, that should shut her up for a bit, and another to my trainer confirming the change of time. I then went back to the messages from Cooper and hit the call button on the top of the screen and put him on speaker as I exited the lift and headed to my door and let myself into my sanctuary.

"Well well well, she survived the wrath of Lorenzo D'Angelo. Or am I speaking to a ghost?" I barked a laugh in response to his greeting.

"Only just, I'm just as shocked as you are that I'm breathing right now." I lied, I liked having a friend, but I didn't need him knowing the truth about my night. I didn't need anyone making presumptions about my motive for fucking our boss, especially after Debbie's comments last night. I doubt any of the guys would believe it was purely for my own selfish enjoyment. "But it would take more than his wrath to end me Coop."

"Don't let him hear you say that, you know he'd just see it as a challenge." he wasn't wrong.

"Probably. You got plans? Fancy breakfast at Tate's? Fill me in on what happened when I left?" I desperately needed a shower first though.

"Sure thing. I'm not seeing Sam until this afternoon, Time?" he asked, and we agreed to meet in an hour.

The sun appeared to be holding out this morning, so I opted for a dark blue sundress for a change. My wardrobe was filled with various colours, but since losing Jase I mostly wore black, it was starting to feel like a shame to waste such nice clothes though.

I arrived at Tate's café ten minutes early, as usual. Cooper, shockingly, was already there, a menu holding his attention. He had chosen to sit outside, good choice. The café was on the edge of Oak Lake, on the opposite side to where our boss's home was.

I sat down opposite Cooper, and he lowered the menu revealing a wide grin that I couldn't help but mirror back to him. Coop was an attractive guy, not in an overly buff, in your face kind of way, he was pretty. Like Lorenzo, he had no scars, tattoos, or any other physical evidence of being in a gang. If you met him on the street, you wouldn't avoid him. He was smart as hell, the go to guy for all your tech related stuff, spending the majority of his time behind some kind of screen. Coop didn't need to be scary, he didn't need to intimidate, but he could. I'd only ever seen it once, but behind his nice guy exterior he was dangerous. Not in the same way as I am, dangerous doesn't even come close for me, but he could handle himself with ease.

"Good morning, Sunshine." He beamed at me and leaned across to plant a gentle kiss to the side of my head. *See, not even a little bit scary.*

"Morning Coops, you ordered?" I asked, quietly enjoying his little pet-name for me. He shook his head in response and pushed the menu across the table to me. I don't pick it up though, I already know what I want.

Gina came out to our table and greeted us in her usual friendly manner. "Meg, Coop, great to see you both! What are we having today?"

"Black coffee and a sausage and -."

"Bacon baguette? I don't know why I even ask you girl!" she smiles and turns her attention to Cooper, "Never changes her order this one!" she tells him, "Whereas you have never had the same order twice!"

"Variety is the spice of life Gina," he says, flashing her the same huge grin that I was met with a few minutes ago. "I'll have a cappuccino and eggs benedict please." She noted down his order and went back inside to make our drinks.

"You look cute, like a real girl, it's weird." Cooper declared as he flicked his gaze over my outfit.

"Shut up, I *am* a real girl." I shot back, without a single drop of venom in my words. He huffed a laugh in response and Gina came back out with our drinks.

When she left us again, I shifted to a comfortable position and dove straight into getting the details of the rest of the night.

Turns out Debbie had begun to genuinely cry when I'd left the room, she was hysterical and begging Grey to have me kicked out of The Brotherhood. Collette had agreed with her, and they had declared me a psychotic whore who belonged in an institution. I couldn't help but laugh. Apparently, they had tried to drag Coop into it all, telling him he should stay away from me, especially if he saw any future with Samantha. He had defended me, not that they had listened to him, but he had tried. In that moment I decided that Cooper was my favourite person in the world. His loyalty meant a lot to me.

We let conversation flow in other directions, discussing his relationship, my 'day job', and avoiding any sensitive subjects. A while later, once we were full from our breakfasts and a cheeky slice of cake each that Gina had unexpectedly bought out to us, we said our goodbyes.

I had planned on going back home and sorting

through paperwork for the morning, but the calming atmosphere by the lake on a Sunday morning made it so hard to leave. Instead I decided to take a walk around to an empty bench on a grassy area and sit and people watch. I stayed for another hour, enjoying my own company and for the first time in a long time not falling prey to the grief that consumed me and escaped to the forefront of my mind whenever I was alone.

 The rest of my day went by in a blur, my session at the gym in the evening with my trainer took the last morsel of energy from my body, and I collapsed on my bed fully clothed when I arrived back home.

***

Work was busy on Monday morning, I barely left my desk until mid-afternoon, relying on the kindness of people passing by my office door to bring me coffee.

 Eden came waltzing in and sat her ass down on a piece of paper that I was skimming over. "You haven't eaten Meg! I'm ordering from the café down the road, what are you having?"

 I looked up at her, the irritation that I felt at her interruption quickly fading as she glared down at me. I leaned back in my chair and let out a long sigh. "I'll just have whatever you're having." I told her and she got up, tapping at her phone, and sat down in the chair opposite me.

Eden was an accountant too; her office was a couple of doors down from mine. I was always polite to the people who worked from this building, but I tried to avoid getting close to anyone here, not wanting them to find out who I am outside of this job, but I couldn't avoid Eden. She badgered me daily, practically threw herself at me until she had eventually chipped away at my wall and become a friend. The girl was feisty, ambitious and overly confident, I loved all of those things about her.

"So Lukas decided to try this new thing with his tongue last night, some guy at work had suggested it, apparently his girlfriend goes crazy for it." She paused and looked up from her phone to meet my already amused face, I knew already where this was going, "That girl either has no idea what good head feels like, or she's faking." yep, Eden loved to tell me about Lukas' bedroom fuckups.

I let out a laugh and shook my head at her. "Lady, just tell him what you like! It's been six years!"

"That, my dear, is exactly the problem. How do I tell him he sucks in bed after *six years?!*" I gave her a sympathetic smile in return.

"Just be honest. He's crazy about you, he won't get mad." I tell her.

"No, but he might cry. I can't do that to him. Anyway, how are things with your mystery *lover?*" she waggled her eyebrows at me with the word *lover.*

"Mind blowing, as usual." I said, struggling to hide the smug grin on my face.

"Bitch!" she huffed, "so why are you not pinning that down?" the same question she asked me over and over for the last two months.

"Because I don't do relationships, and even if I did, it's complicated, and I don't know if I even like him, he's just a really good fuck." I told her the complete truth, minus ever telling her who he was. She didn't need to know I had anything to do with Lorenzo D'Angelo, sexually or professionally.

She dropped the subject and we discussed work and her life over our late lunch. She didn't go back to her office when we were done, apparently having a light workload today, and stayed with me sifting through some old files that needed sorting until it was past the end of my usual working day.

We took the lift down to the basement carpark of the office block and parted ways, agreeing to go for a drink together later in the week. I got into my Mercedes and drove the short distance to The Crown to meet Lorenzo. Arriving ten minutes early, but not walking in until 6pm.

I walked straight past the bar and to a booth at the back of the dimly lit room. Waiting for me, as I expected, were Lorenzo and Grey. My boss gave me a quick once over and a sharp nod. His second just glared. Thank god looks can't *actually* kill.

"M, I hope you were smart enough to bring a change of clothes." Lorenzo said as the bartender came and placed a glass of soda on the table in front of me. I never deliberately drink on the job.

"In the boot of my car, as always." I said and took a sip of the refreshingly cold drink. I was currently wearing a satin blouse, tight skirt, and black heels, my standard office attire. I could get away with wearing this outfit on some jobs, usually ones where it wasn't likely that I'd have to get physical.

"Good girl." *Bastard,* "I need you to go to this location." He slipped a piece of paper across the table to me. I knew the area well enough to not have to think too hard about where I needed to go.

Lorenzo filled me in on what he expected me to do. "Do we have a backup plan if this goes to shit Boss?" I asked.

"We do." He said and slid out of the booth and fixed me with a hard glare. "But it won't."

With that he left. Grey following obediently behind him.

7

Meg

I grabbed a bag from the boot of my car then climbed into the back seat. Having blacked out windows was a necessity with how often I had to get changed in my car.

I changed into a black t-shirt and leggings, then searched for my trainers. *Fuck.* The trainers I usually kept in my car were the ones I'd worn at the weekend and were currently discarded under a pile of clothes in my bedroom. I guess I'll be doing this in heels tonight. Not a first for me, but not ideal.

I sped through the city and down to the outskirts where the warehouse was based. The tip off that my boss had received stated that the deal would be going down here in ten minutes. Some sneaky little fucker who was believed to be looking to impress and get in with The Wolves had managed to break into one of our garages and had stolen a selection of items that have a questionable legality and a hefty price tag. Allegedly, Charon had told this little fucker that he wasn't interested in taking on any new initiates. Which then left him with a dodgy little loot, and it's not like he was going to just hand it all back. He had found himself a buyer. And said buyer just so happened to be a *friend* of Lorenzo D'Angelo. The first lesson this kid needed to learn was to check out your buyer, make sure he's not likely to double cross you. The second would be to not steal from The Brotherhood. I'd be the one teaching him that lesson.

It felt nice to be having a close-up confrontation for once. Being a damn good shot had put me at a distance from all of the action for a while now. Boss liked to play up to peoples strengths, put a rifle in my hand and I'll never let you down, so it made sense. But sometimes I craved the feeling of breaking bones. *Shit, that's kinda messed up isn't it.*

I parked my car out of sight and found a dark corner to wait in. I took the time to check my weapons. This guy was a nobody, not likely to actually be dangerous, but I still anticipated a fight. If stealing from us wasn't enough to impress Charon, taking down one of the elite would be. I know what I'd do if I was him and the opportunity presented itself.

Headlights reflected on the metal of the fence

to the far right of the warehouse. *Here he comes.* The dark van pulled up at one side of the building and a short guy dressed head to toe in dark denim stepped out. He looked shifty as hell as he paced around outside the front of the building. His eyes darting all over the place, poor kid had no idea what was coming for him. Another set of headlights appeared then abruptly turned off, the only hint that the vehicle was still heading this way was the low hum of its engine. *At least someone knew what they were doing.*

Giorgio walked across the forecourt; he knew that I was here somewhere. His involvement in Lorenzo's plan was minimal, exact details didn't matter to him. As long as he got paid, he didn't give a shit what anyone else did.

"What've you got for me kid." He asked, the low rumble of his voice and the way he towered menacingly over the sneaky fuck was enough to hint that he wasn't someone to be fucked with. Not one of us, but a scary bastard in his own right.

The little prick listed off all of the items he had stolen from us. Smirking as Giorgio's brows lifted higher as the list went on.

"Shit kid, how'd you come across all of that?" Giorgio asked.

"What does that matter! You want it or not." This kid had balls, he puffed his chest out, like that might make any difference to the obvious difference in strength the two men had.

"Only a halfwit would agree to a deal like this without weighing up the consequences first. I wanna know which scary fucker is gonna come after me if they follow the trail you've no doubt left." Giorgio took a step back, cocking his head to one side. *Oh come on man, stop dragging this out.*

"No one important." The kid lied. Giorgio knew it. I knew Giorgio knew it. The kid, he thought he was pulling the wool over his eyes. Giorgio was a great little actor. A smart man always knew when to play dumb.

"Good good, lets see it then pal, and then we can talk money." The kid led Giorgio over to his van, and pulled open a back door, grinning from ear to ear as light spilled in and revealed the contents of the van. Perfect.

Welcome to the stage, the one you've been waiting for, Megan Fields.

"My my, what do we have here?" My words rang out clear and smooth as velvet as I slowly emerged from the shadows. *Ok, the heels totally help with the drama here!* "You've been a naughty boy haven't you." I kept my focus on the kid, confusion etched over his features. No fear though, not yet.

"Oh you are *so* fucked kid." Giorgio chuckled and turned away from him to walk back towards his car.

"You set me up!" The kid shouted, shock and anger rippling through him as he lunged for Giorgio.

But our friend wasn't dumb, he swung back around before the kid could touch him and I smiled as a loud crack sounded in the air as Giorgio's fist connected with the kids jaw.

The kid cried out in pain and Giorgio continued back to his car without uttering another word, opening the window and saluting me before he drove off.

I kept walking, closing the gap between myself and the kid as he rubbed his jaw and spat blood onto the floor at my feet. "Ew," I sneered at the blood and stepped over it to place myself in his personal space.

He kept eye contact, *good boy*. "So," I ran my gaze over him, assessing how to take him out. I noted the outline of a gun shoved in his waistband, better make sure that's the first thing to go. "You thought stealing from The Brotherhood was a good idea?" I asked. Ice lacing my words.

"Fuck you," he spat. "Stupid bitch!"
Seriously, The balls on him!
I pursed my lips, "Excuse me?" I challenged.

"Fuck. You. Stupid. Bitch." He said slowly. His hand inching towards his waistband in a not-so-subtle move.

Before he could reach the gun, my fist swung into the side of his jaw, that was already no doubt broken. The unexpected impact causing him to stumble, my other hand gripped his t-shirt, lifting it, grabbing the gun and pulling it so that the kids temple was parallel with the barrel.

"Big mistake sweetheart." I sang. A dark smile crossing my lips as the sensation from punching him sent a satisfying thrill through me.

He stood frozen to the spot. But I was craving more action, more release. I slipped the gun into an empty holster at my hip and watched the kid relax a fraction. *Play time.* My fist thrusted into his stomach, taking him by surprise, and he tripped backwards a couple of steps, hesitating a brief second before throwing himself at me and knocking me to the floor. Speed has always been another strength of mine, as my back hit the ground I swung my body, throwing the kid beneath me before he could get anything else out of his little attack. With my legs grounded firmly on either side of him, I began throwing punches and easily blocking his attempts to fight back. Falling into a simple rhythm and allowing the pent-up anger inside me to take over, my punches getting sloppy, but far more vicious.

With a small, unexpected burst of energy the kid managed to throw me off of him and rise to his feet, wobbling and hunching in pain. Yet he still made a move to kick me, his boot aimed at my ribs, I rolled away before it connected, moving into a low crouch, ready to pounce and play a little more before pulling his gun back out on him and ending him.

Movement in the shadows behind him snagged my attention. He noticed that my focus was no longer completely on him, and turned to look at the spot where my eyes had shot to. I rose to stand, and my fingers quickly wrapped around the gun. A loud bang echoed, and blood splattered across my face. *Fuck.* The kid dropped to the floor. I lifted the gun, aiming towards the shooter and found myself staring down the barrel into a pair of intense dark eyes.

8

Meg

Anger ripped through me as my brain registered exactly who was stood before me and I stepped over the lifeless body between us. Keeping the gun in my hand trained between the arsehole's eyes.

"You!" I growled, "who the *fuck* are you?" He didn't speak, didn't move, didn't flinch at my tone, nothing. He stood anchored to the spot, a cruel smirk resting on his face as I drew closer. "Well!" I shouted, coming to halt a few steps in front him. My hand sat parallel with his, mine streaked with blood while his was covered in dark ink, both refusing to drop our weapons.

He cocked his head to one side and ran his tongue over his bottom lip, the motion distracting me and irritating me in equal measure. I stand by my assessment that this guy is an arsehole.

A low chuckle rumbled through his chest to his throat and his dark smile widened, "You're so easy to piss off, Megan." His voice was deeper than I'd expected and held a subtle accent, and I hated that a tiny part of me enjoyed the sound.

Wait. Megan? So I was right last time, he knew exactly who I was, but why is he here, on the same job as me, again. He must be working for Charon. The Wolves are the only gang in the area who are in the same league as us, our only real rivals. But the kid had stolen from The Brotherhood, and Charon had taken no interest in him, so why send some unknown new piece of shit here? Why did he want the kid dead?

"It's Miss Fields to you, arsehole." I said sweetly, while internally pulling my shit together. I could go into my thoughts about all of this later, talk through it all with Lorenzo, the man who may be able to make some sense out of it all. Right now, I needed to remember that the man in front of me also had a gun pulled on me, overthinking the reason that he was here wasn't smart right now.

Just as I was about to demand his name my phone buzzed. *Typical.* I pulled it from my pocket with my free hand and jabbed the answer button without breaking eye contact with the arsehole.

Lorenzo's voice met my ear, the disappointment in his tone causing me to swallow hard and let my other arm drop a fraction. *Fuck, please don't notice that.* Nope, I'm not going to get lucky there, the change of the arsehole's expression made it crystal clear that he had noticed. As my boss hung up, I felt the anger that was burning away inside of me rise to the surface. Anger towards this guy for fucking existing, to Lorenzo for speaking to me like that and exposing a weak spot, and to myself for allowing these two men to do this to me. I'm not sure who I was more angry with. Probably myself.

"You better run home, *Miss Fields,* Daddy's calling." I take it back. This guy wins. *This guy is the fucking worst.*

He lowers his gun, the first of us to let themself be defenceless, again. Except nothing about him in this moment made him seem as though he was genuinely vulnerable. This was a man who was always so sure of himself. Even with the obvious rage spilling out of me, he was certain he wouldn't die tonight. I hated him even more for it. Fuck him. Lorenzo better let me loose on him someday, and it better be someday soon. This arsehole is already playing with my ego, I won't be letting him destroy my reputation too.

I lower my own weapon and turn my back to him despite the burning desire to prove to him that I am far more capable and skilled than he is.

I decide to walk away with a confident sway to my hips, if Lorenzo won't allow me to do anything about this arsehole, then I can at least walk away with dignity.

"Until next time, Princess." He calls after me. I freeze on the spot and swing around to face him again, lifting the kids' gun and firing a well-aimed shot a couple of inches to the left of his beautiful, smug face. Lorenzo never said I couldn't send a warning. No one calls me princess. Never again.

He raises his brows at me, not even the tiniest flicker of fear crossing his face. "Tease" he mouths at me, then walks back into the shadows.

****

I arrive back at The Crown as instructed by Lorenzo, and storm through the bar, seating myself back in the same booth that we had met in earlier that evening. I'm the first to arrive. I grab a napkin from the table and wipe up some of the blood from my skin as the barman comes over and places another soda in front of me, completely ignoring how I look. I grab his arm before he makes his way back to the bar, "I'm going to be needing something stronger, add some vodka to that," I slide the glass towards him, "please." I add as an after-thought, it wasn't the barman's fault that I was in a horrible mood. He did as I had requested and as he arrived back at the table, he was holding a tray with two more drinks. Lorenzo and Grey strode up next to him a second later, Lorenzo sat himself opposite me, while Grey chose the seat next to me.

Lorenzo didn't look directly at me. He lifted his glass from the table and slowly began to drink, not putting it back down until it was empty, then stared past me at the wall behind my head. *Fucking hell.*

I glanced at Grey, hoping for some kind of indication as to whether I should speak or wait. He didn't give anything away, he just smiled with obvious satisfaction at my situation. Throwing fuel onto the blazing fire inside me. Silly me for thinking he might be helpful. I couldn't be higher on his shit list if I tried.

I sipped at my drink, giving myself something to do other than run my fingers through my hair in frustration. The vodka worked wonders to banish any nerves I had. Each sip slowly began to drown them, and in no time, I found myself halfway through the drink. Anger was pushing its way to the front to take the lead. *Looks like you guys are about to see how big my balls really are.*

"Twice in less than a week, that arsehole has showed up on my jobs twice. In less Than. A. Fucking. Week." I snapped, my voice raised, close to shouting, but not quite there. *Hi, I'm Meg and I have a death wish.* I lean into the table, pushing closer to Lorenzo, "why the fuck am I keeping him alive?" I made no attempt to control my rage.

Lorenzo's eyes snapped to mine, and the hardness of his expression should have scared me, but tonight I was too far into my own emotions to let myself feel fear.

"What the hell is going on boss, don't keep

me in the dark, this is going to fuck with *my* reputation too."

He clenched his jaw and let out a long, low breath. "Watch your tone." He whispered.

"Answer me, for once!" I snapped. A tiny trickle of regret sneaking in as I realised what I'd said. *Shit, here lays Megan. She pushed too far.* Silence hung over the three of us for a long moment. Grey was actually holding his breath. The satisfied look had left his face and was replaced with an uncomfortable grimace.

"Everybody out." Lorenzo bellowed, rising to his feet and staring around the bar, "Now." He raised his voice louder and every person in the room hurried to the door. The staff exchanged questioning glances with each other, "Yes, you too." he continued, and they all made their way to the door behind the last of the patrons.

Grey looked up from his position next to me to our boss and opened his mouth to speak.

"Don't say a word, Grey." Lorenzo roared at him, "Just leave."

Grey opened and closed his mouth repeatedly, shock slapping him hard in the face at the enraged dismissal he had just received.

Lorenzo raised a brow at his second. A fire was burning within his eyes. Grey pulled himself together and quickly moved from the booth and towards the door, he paused as he opened it, looking back at us with worry etched all over his face. Why was he worried? It's not like he gave a shit about what happened to *me*.

The door closed behind Grey and Lorenzo walked across the empty room to lock it. I threw back the remains of my drink, and walked towards the bar, ignoring the furious man approaching me. The tension filling the air around us grew thicker as I pushed up onto the bar and swung myself over to the other side, grabbing the nearest bottle from the wall and pouring myself a large measure. I raised my gaze up to meet my boss's face, and slowly raised the glass to my lips as I watched him slide his jacket off and neatly fold it over the back of a barstool.

I really should have been scared, and honestly, if he had looked at me this way a few days ago I might have been. But our moods were perfectly matched right now, adrenaline was coursing through my body, and I was certain I could handle whatever he threw at me. The slight glint in his eye made me think I might even enjoy it. I *have* been getting away with pushing more buttons recently. *This might be a little too far though hun.*

I sipped the liquid in my glass and tried not to scrunch my face up in disgust. *Tequila, what kind of dumbass doesn't check the bottle first.* Lorenzo pushed his tongue into his cheek in mild amusement as though he knew I'd poured myself something that I don't like. He reached over and grabbed the glass from my hand and swallowed the rest of it in one mouthful. As he placed the glass onto the bar top, he let out an exaggerated hum of enjoyment that sent a warm tingle straight between my thighs.

I leaned back against the wall of bottles in an attempt to keep some space between us until I was able to work out what he had in mind for me now.

"You're making a habit of pushing me amore mio" he finally said. His voice was low and even, but the fire was still blazing in his eyes.

"I wouldn't need to if you told me what was going on, *Boss*" I growled back. Not quite ready to let go of this anger. "Quite frankly I find it insulting how little you trust me." I continued, folding my arms over my chest.

"Insulting?" he raised his voice again, "what's insulting is how little *respect* you seem to have for me."

"I do respect you," I protested, "but I need to protect myself. *He* is a threat, we *always* eliminate threats. So what's different this time. Give me a reason to not go back out there and hunt him down." I stared deep into his eyes, willing answers to come from his lips.

"I will always protect you," he whispered. "Just leave it be."

"I don't need you to protect me, I need you to let me in." I threw my head back in exasperation, then stepped closer to the bar. I pulled myself back on top of the bar and dropped my legs over the side next to where he was stood. I still wasn't sure if he was going to hurt me. An inferno continued to blaze in his eyes, but he had made no threats, no moves to indicate that he intended to cause me pain.

He blew out a slow breath and rested his hand on my leg and begun to gently stroke his thumb back and forth. "No" he said simply.

"Please." I breathed, calming my temper to match the change in his, maybe a gentle approach would work.

"No" he said again and stepped back a fraction, tightening his grip on me to slide me in front of him. He pushed my legs apart and positioned himself between them. Resting both hands on my thighs and looking at me with a warning stamped clearly on his face.

I pushed my fingers through his dark hair and tangled them around his neck. Leaning in so that our lips were close enough to feel each other's breath, I whispered, "Please Boss."

A look of annoyance briefly crossed his expression, and I came to a sudden realisation. He hated that, the same way I hated him calling me M. I'd seen that look flash on his face so many times but I'd never considered his feelings may have been the same as mine. I hoped that I had read it right as I tried again.

"Lorenzo, Please," I kept our eyes locked together, praying that this was the right move.

A heartbeat later his lips crashed into mine and he slid his hands up to my waist, drawing my ass to the very edge of the bar. He groaned into the kiss and ground his arousal into me. The sound combined with the feel of his body sent a rush of need through me, watering down my rage just enough to lose myself in the moment.

He pulled away, leaving me panting and brought his hand up to my face. Stroking my cheek with his knuckle he smiled. *Fuck, he really is beautiful*, "Il mio tesoro, say it again." He murmured.

I almost do, I'm so entranced by this man that I almost forget why I'm alone with him in an empty bar. "Play fair, give me something first," I purred. Using the shift in the atmosphere to my advantage.

"I don't play fair, you know that." he said, then slowly swept his gaze over me. "You look like a warrior all painted in blood, I think this might be my favourite look on you." he changed the subject and slipped his fingers from my face and into my hair, twisting red curls around them and staring at me like I was the most enchanting woman to grace this earth.

"Clearly, but flattery won't make me drop this though." I removed my arms from around his neck and positioned them on the bar behind me to hold myself up as I reclined away from him.

"No?" he raised a brow at me and unbuttoned the sleeves of his shirt. I let out an appreciative groan as he rolled them up in perfect folds then dropped his hands and grasped my thighs again,

"What will?" His voice was pure temptation and his hands slid higher. *I wish I'd stayed in my work skirt.*

I let a seductive smile play on my lips and stayed silent, letting my thighs tighten around his waist. I supposed if he wasn't going to give me any answers tonight, the least he could do would be to fuck away my shitty mood.

"Well?" he pushed.

I glanced down at the place where his arousal was pressed up against me and gave him a meaningful look.

A chuckle rumbled deep from within his chest, and he shifted further forward so that his mouth brushed mine, our breath entwining with each shallow exhale. "Say it," he growled against my lips.

I took a sharp intake of breath before telling him what he needed to hear. "Fine, I'll drop it, *for now*, if you fuck me. Fuck me Lorenzo, make me scream."

His mouth pressed to mine, and he groaned against my lips. He ran his tongue over my lower lip, and I didn't hesitate, parting them for him and deepening our kiss. The taste of tequila was mingled with the addictively sweet flavour of this man, and this time I enjoyed how it tasted.

He pulled away and began to plant a painfully slow trail of kisses down my neck and over my collar bone. His hands gripped the hem of my shirt, and he tugged it up over my breasts. I didn't move though, stubbornly keeping my hands pressed firmly against the bar.

A sound of frustration filled the air, and he lifted his head to glare at me, "Ask me nicely and I'll cooperate." I said, just because I wanted him didn't mean I'd give it to him easily.

"Not a chance in hell." He pulled the fabric back into place. My brow creased, was he really going to give up this easily? A spark of anger rose back up through my body, my mouth opened as a torrent of insults made their way to the tip of my tongue.

Before I could utter a single word, he pulled a pocketknife from his trousers, and in one effortless motion, sliced straight down the middle of my shirt. The fabric fell open. His eyes locked on mine, and he smirked as he twirled the blade in his hand. I couldn't speak, the shock of what he had done silencing me. His gaze flicked to my chest, then back up to my face as I felt the cold press of the knife slide under the centre of my bra. My breath caught in my throat and a rush of excitement shot through me and soaked my panties. Lorenzo flicked his wrist, freeing my breasts from the satin and lace, then speared the knife into the wooden bar top and licked his lips appreciatively as he drank in his handiwork.

"Speechless," he whispered as he cupped my breast, "that's a first," he continued, rolling my nipple between his thumb and finger, tugging gently so that my breathy moans filled the space between us, "You've been awfully vocal this evening, annoyingly so, yet now you're at a loss for words, Amore, I expected more from that smart mouth." He tugged hard, pulling a cry of pleasure from me.

"Fuck you," my words came out on a shaky breath, "I'll show you just what this mouth can do."

A breath of a laugh escaped him, "Too easy, far too easy." Half a second later I realised what he had done, that bastard had goaded me into that, and he was right, it was far too easy. Damn my constant need to prove people wrong. I pursed my lips and glared at him.

"Unfortunately, I'm starving, so your mouth will have to wait its turn."

My jaw dropped and he smirked as he pushed his fingers into the waistband of my leggings and gave them a demanding tug. Still stunned, I willingly lifted my ass and felt my panties sliding down with them. It only took a couple of seconds for Lorenzo to strip me down, tossing my heels across the room and leaving a pile of black fabric at his feet.

He didn't pause, not for a single second. He spread my legs wide. His tongue met my aching core and he lapped up the evidence of his effect on me, groaning against me as he alternated between licking, nibbling, and sucking until I was writhing and grinding against his face. He devoured me like I was his last ever meal. He pressed the pad of his tongue hard against my clit and I threw my head back with a lust filled moan, my knuckles turning white as my grip on the bar tightened. He pulled back a little, letting the tip of his tongue flick in a rapid rhythm against me. Intense heat built inside me as his fingers joined the party and plunged into me, working a torturous symphony below my waist. I began to tighten around his fingers, the edge of the cliff in sight, and cried out his name as I went soaring over it.

    My legs shook at the intensity of the release. Lorenzo removed his fingers and sent an electrifying jolt through my body as he ran his tongue over me once more. Then he stood back up and pressed his wet lips to mine before pulling over a barstool and siting down.

    I watched hungrily as his fingers made fast work of his shirt buttons, letting it hang open to expose his perfectly toned torso. I reached over to undo his belt buckle and unzip his trousers. My fingers brushing over the hard line of his erection beneath his underwear. I slipped down from the bar to stand before him, discarding the torn scraps of clothing that hung from my shoulders. Placing my hands on his shoulders I kissed him gently. He caught my chin in his hand as I pulled away. "Face down on the bar." He commanded.

    I did as he said, shivering slightly as my breasts pushed against the cold wood of the bar and I rested my cheek down at the far edge. "You are the most infuriating woman I have ever met amore mio."

I breathed a laugh and braced myself as I felt him behind me. He freed his cock and teased the tip over my entrance. The anticipation making me squirm against him.

Lorenzo groaned with pleasure as he drove deep into me, filling me in one slow movement. "Fuck" we echoed together, and a wide smile spread over my face, rapidly followed by a gasp as he pulled out and slammed into me faster this time, quickly falling into a frantic, careless pace. Each punishing thrust making it clear that he needed this as much as I did.

His hand twisted into my hair, and he pulled my head towards him, arching my back and pushing deeper. He reached around and pinched my nipple, making me tighten around his solid shaft. "You're killing me." he murmured.

His anger filled me as he fucked me hard and fast, and he dragged my own rage from me as he stole a blissfully drawn-out orgasm from my body.

"Amore, end this for me." He demanded in a hoarse voice.

I felt a tsunami of pleasure build inside me, the desperation in his tone pulling one final, earth-shattering orgasm from me. "Lorenzo, fuck!" I screamed, giving him everything that I knew he desired, screaming out the word he was so desperate to hear. His name. I pulsated around him as he violently stuttered his release and pulled me close, wrapping his arms around my body as though the idea of letting me go was too much for him to handle.

I didn't resist the unusual show of affection and sank back into his body as he pulled us onto the barstool. I felt him plant gentle kisses along my shoulder while I slowly came back down to earth.

We stayed cuddled in a euphoric bubble for a short while until I let out a deeply satisfied sigh and removed myself from his lap.

"Where are you going?" he questioned as I hunted around the room for my heels.

"Home, Boss" I replied and leaned against a pool table on the far side of the bar and scowled at him, "Where the fuck are my shoes."

He stalked over to me with a playful glint in his eyes. When he reached me, he let his fingers brush a soft line from my navel to my throat. He eyed the pool table and chuckled darkly, "Fuck your shoes, I'm not done with you yet."

9

Meg

After a long night with very little sleep, and the frustrating news that the elevator at my office was undergoing maintenance the last thing my aching body desired was an intense session with my personal trainer. But annoyingly, I wasn't one to break routine. No matter how shitty I felt.

"Vixen! I'm sensing you forgot your A game today!" Toby teased as I sloped into the gym yawning.

"I could take you down in my sleep Tobias" I tossed back. Pretty weak fighting talk in all honesty but it would have to do. He wasn't wrong. *And you can only take him down because you play dirty!*

His contagious laugh boomed around the room, and I couldn't contain the giggle that came from my mouth. Toby had been my trainer for coming up to a year now, and he was the best I'd ever had. He pushed me to my very limit, challenged me, and taught me so much. It also wasn't a bad thing that he was nice to look at, all long hair and rippling pectorals. Rugged, manly, but with a smile that could light up the darkest room. *Maybe routine wasn't the only reason I never missed a session.*

I flopped onto a large, padded mat and stretched lazily. "So, we're doing some nice, calming yoga today, right?" I grinned up at him as he towered over me.

"Afraid not little one," he sat down in front of me, tossing a roll of fabric at me, then began to wrap his hands, "But don't slam yoga, it's good for the mind." He finished wrapping his hands and raised his brows at me as I reached for my toes. "You've already done that little Vixen, stop delaying."

I huffed dramatically and picked up the roll of fabric from the floor, "I'm not that little," I mumbled, just loud enough for him to hear me.

"You are." He grinned as he rose to his feet and hoisted himself into the training ring next to us.

On Tuesdays we do one on one combat. The rest of our sessions mostly consist of Toby shouting words of *encouragement* at me and guiding me while I swear at him and sweat over various pieces of equipment. It's my second favourite release.

I joined him in the ring and attempted to pull some fight into my body. We came together and fell into a simple back and forth of skilled attacks and blocks. After fifteen minutes Toby stepped away with a disappointed look on his face.

"You're tense as hell," he said, cocking his head. "and you're holding back. Why?" his brows pinched in a small frown. "And don't tell me it's just because you're tired."

"I'm not tense." I responded, a slight snap to my tone.

"Sure you're not," he rolled his eyes at me, "Whatever it is that you've pushed down, let it come back up, work out your emotions. Remember Vixen, you can either do this physically or verbally. You're choice."

My jaw tightened at his words. He was right. Last night I'd pushed my anger down, I'd let Lorenzo take some of it, but it wasn't enough, part of it had lingered. Some arsehole had taken my fucking shot, again, and my boss had tiptoed around it and been vague and dismissive, again. My life and my reputation were being threatened and all he said was that he would protect me. I didn't need that. I could protect myself. What I needed was answers.

As the thoughts rushed through my mind, I felt my fists clench and release over and over. 'I'm going to destroy you.' I breathed as my eyes connected with Toby's.

"Finally." He grinned and stepped forward, bracing himself for my attack.

I flew at him, catapulted by my emotions, and threw my fist into his rib. I swung perfectly planned punches into his solid body, feeling rapid release with each strike. He gave as good as he got, we decided a long time ago to never pull punches. I could take it just as well as he could. He moved back a fraction, far enough for me to lunge and slam into him with my shoulder, knocking him to the floor and diving on top of him, my hands entwining with his and pinning him down.

I felt him relax beneath me, and I loosened my grip on him. "There she is." He purred and I blew out a long breath as I threw myself off of his body and landed on my back beside him.

"Thank you, fuck that felt good." I said with a pleased groan.

Toby pushed himself up to sit and looked up at the clock on the wall. "Five minutes, and then we go again."

***

I dried off after my shower and threw on a baggy tee and some denim shorts. It was a warm evening, and I decided to let my hair hang lose and leave it to air dry.

I made my way out of the changing room and to the main doors. Toby was casually leaning against an empty reception desk and smiled when I approached him.

"You never fail to impress me, Vixen."

"I am pretty impressive aren't I." I declared and tossed my hair over my shoulder, flicking little droplets of water onto Toby's bare arm.

He looked down and wiped them away, still smiling. "I like it when you're cocky." He caught my gaze, his sparkling blue eyes enchanting me, then he looked away quickly, an air of vulnerability washing over him. He swallowed hard and then visibly shook it off. "Do you want to go for a drink with me?" He blurted.

The sheepish look on his face melted me, my cheeks ached from how wide I smiled. This beast of a man was nervous, I made him nervous.

My response sat on the tip of my tongue. How could I say no to him? He's funny, charming, and hot as hell. But. But I have so much baggage. It's one thing to be having causal sex with my boss, it's another to actually go on a *date* with a guy. I don't date.

"Toby, I..." I pulled my bottom lip between my teeth, searching for the gentlest words.

"Yeah, that was a dumb idea, forget I asked." He said before I could form a full sentence in my head,

I reached out to him, my hand coming to rest on his arm, completely unsure about what I was doing, "No, no, I have... stuff, it's not a no, just..." I sighed heavily. "Fuck, I don't know how to put it." I offered him a small smile and he returned it.

"Let's not make this weird little one, forget I asked, I'll see you on Thursday, get home safe." He patted my hand and turned and walked back towards the doors to the gym.

I lingered by the reception desk for a moment, wondering if I should have just said yes. I *wanted* to say yes, despite how I felt about relationships. He's not part of my world though, he has no idea what I do, to him I'm just an accountant who likes to keep fit and wants to be able to defend herself in the big, scary city. He has no idea about the danger that follows me. No, this is the right choice.

I nod to myself like an idiot and push through the door to leave, get into my car, and speed home. Pushing the tiny twinge of regret deep down until its buried away. Just like I always do, with every stupid, weak emotion.

10

Lorenzo

I rolled over in my bed to stare at the empty space next to me. The memory of waking up next to M the other morning filled my mind and a sad smile fell to my mouth. The refreshing scent of lemon still lightly clung to the vacant pillow, and I sighed with irritation at the longing I felt for her.

It had been two months since she first fell into my bed. Well, my guest bed. Two months of this secret *relationship*. I had hoped that inviting her into my private space, allowing her to sleep at my side, would have broken down that wall she was continuing to hold up. It became clear that it hadn't worked when she had called me 'boss' so quickly after waking, that clear sign we always used to keep business and pleasure separate.

My desire for her over time had become more

than just a physical thing. How could it not be? She was everything I could ever want, smart, funny, confident, sexy as sin, and feisty, so feisty. I wanted to make her mine. I could give her anything she could ever want. I could protect her, she thought she didn't need that, but one day she would, and she would always be safe with me.

    I threw back the covers and headed to take a shower, hoping that by the time I was dry and dressed I'd have at least three ideas that I could use to my advantage. I'd been letting her get away with far more than anyone else could ever have, and I was finding my feelings for her grow even more whenever she challenged me. I had thought that the special treatment may have pushed her to see that what we are doing meant more to me. If she could see it, she was choosing to ignore it. And if she was choosing to ignore it, then I'd have to stop letting her step that far out of line, I wasn't stupid enough to leave myself open to be ripped down and made a fool of, I was the leader of The Brotherhood, I had to draw a line somewhere.

    I found myself, for the first time ever, with no ideas. She wouldn't be won over with flowers and chocolate, nor with fancy trips or expensive jewellery. No matter how badly I wanted to spoil her. She craved simple gestures, that was clear, but aside from inviting her into the sanctuary of *my* bed I was out of ideas. I thought back to last night, the way I had held her after fucking her on top of the bar at The Crown, and she had let me, I had thought that she was going to cave with the way she had softened in my arms and had relaxed more than I'd seen her relax before. But she didn't, did she. She got up and she called me boss. That had hurt, but obviously I hadn't let on.

I'd never wanted a woman whose affection I couldn't buy, Selene had been so easy to win over. M is not. Anger was building inside of me at my inability to work this out. This was not a good start to my day.

***

A knock sounded on my office door, "Come in" I called and glanced at the time. "You're late." I scolded my second as he sat opposite me and slung his jacket over the empty chair next to him. Grey always wore denim and leather, just as I always wore suits. I was finding that his appearance irritated me more often these days. Did he have to *look* like such a thug?

"Sorry Boss, Deb's parents are in town," he rolled his eyes in tired frustration.

"If I tell you 8pm I expect you here at 8pm Grey, I don't give a fuck who's in town." I snapped. I had come no closer to a good idea yet and my mood had been a rollercoaster all day. Between business calls and check ins with the members of The Brotherhood I had spent my day thinking about M. Fantasising about our recent encounters, alternating between touching myself as I played the sound of her screaming my name on repeat in my mind, and coming up with over-the-top gestures that would probably just piss her off. My thumb had hovered over her number in my phone countless times too, but I couldn't even come up with an excuse to interrupt her day.

"Boss," Grey's tone was low, "what's going on?"

"The same as every other day Grey, I have some shit that I need you to handle." I ground out, annoyed at the question.

"Sorry boss, its just…" he hesitated for a second, "I feel like there is more on your mind."

"Of course there is, but its none of your fucking concern."

"It's her, isn't it?" he murmured. A look of frustration sitting on his heavily scarred face.

"You're getting dangerously close to forgetting your place." I warned, hoping he was smart enough to keep his mouth shut.

"And *you're* getting dangerously close to fucking everything up over some girl!" he countered.

"Watch your mouth." I snarled, rising from my seat. He mirrored my action and I leaned over the desk.

"Boss, I can't sit back and watch this happen, you're making bad choices, how the fuck do you think this will end if you carry on like this?" he pushed. "The lies are affecting all of us, your head has been all over the place recently and it's not going unnoticed. I will always keep your secrets, boss, but this one isn't benefiting anyone." He stepped away from the desk and scrubbed his hand over his face. "I don't give a shit about her, but you're only going to push her away the longer you hide this from her. I don't want to see how that affects you. How it affects us all."

I pushed away from the desk, straightening up and turning to face the wall behind me. "So I'm supposed to just tell her the truth?" I kept my voice low, not entirely sure what to do with my second's outburst.

"Maybe not the whole truth boss," he matched my tone, "maybe just the what, keep the why to yourself."

I hummed a thoughtful sound; he had a point. I didn't need to explain myself to her, not to anyone. Telling her the truth, even just a partial truth would most definitely set me back in my pursuit to make her mine, but he was right, if I let it go on much longer, she would walk away from me completely when it eventually came out. And it would have to come out.

"That was a very risky move Grey," I said, spinning back around to face him, finding him still stood opposite me, "Thank you for looking out for The Brotherhood, crossing lines to protect them all, even M, it's one of the reasons that I chose you as my second." He instantly relaxed, "I'll take your concerns on board." I sat back down in my chair, and he followed suit.

He stayed silent as I turned my attention to the computer screen and skimmed through my list of tasks that I needed him to complete. I added a couple more to the end of the list and emailed them across to him. His phone pinged, notifying me that he had the email and I reclined back in my chair as he opened it and read through.

His face contorted with confusion. "Don't you think some of these are a bit beneath me, boss?" he met my cold glare.

"No Grey, you are capable of completing everything on that list, and you *will* complete them all, you will remember your place." A subtle threat lacing my words, a clear punishment for being disrespectful written in the list.

He swallowed hard and nodded.

"You'll check in once each item has been handled." I said, turning my focus to my phone, dismissing him. He got up and went to leave my office. When his hand met the door handle, I spoke again, "If the truth pushes her too far away it will be on your head Grey."

He turned to face me, "But-."

"On, Your. Head." Death filled my glare as I met his worried eyes. He nodded quickly and made a hasty exit.

It wasn't his fault that I was keeping this from

her, not even a little, but I'd be damned if I was going to punish *myself* over it if she couldn't get over it.

I looked back down at the phone in my hand and pressed my thumb down then tapped another button on the screen.

"Boss," her velvety voice filled my office and I smiled.

"Come over il mio tesoro."

"On my way, see you in twenty." Her simple acceptance of my demand and the seductive purr to her words had my cock twitching already. Time to put in some groundwork to make sure that in a few days' time, when I'll allow her the truth, she won't completely hate me.

11

Meg

Heavy boots thud against the tile of the kitchen floor. Darkness surrounds me, I'm scared of the dark. Tears are streaming down my face, my scruffy stuffed bunny clutched between my shaking fingers, I want to scream, I don't want to be in here. Men want to hurt her, she's fighting back, I can hear it. A scream. Gunshot. Seven shots. Men leave me. Her body isn't moving. Blood is coating the tiles. Mum.

"You're safe, amore mio, shh, its ok." Whispered words find me, arms are wrapped tight around me, fingers stroke my hair, and my face presses against damp skin, a sweet scent wafts around me as I instinctively nuzzle closer.

The same words are repeated, and I open my eyes to a dimly lit room and realise that I'm clinging to Lorenzo. And that he is trying to soothe me. I'm shaking, tears flowing freely down my face and soaking his bare chest.

    I wriggle myself out of his hold, moving to sit cross legged on the bed, and focus on my breathing. My fingers automatically begin to caress the star shaped stud in my earlobe. *Stop M, no more signs of weakness, remember.* A few minutes silently pass as I try to compose myself. The last time I had that nightmare was almost 3 years ago.

    Lorenzo's fingers traced small shapes across my back, a kindness to his gesture that I'd never seen in him before. "You were screaming, can you tell me why?" he asked gently.

    I turn my face to him, the tears now held at bay. Concern is etched all over his face. "Nightmare, I'm fine." I tell him, offering him a small smile, hoping it will reassure him enough to not push me. I can't talk about Mum, not with him. I want to run away and hide right now, but for some reason I don't fight when he tugs me back down to lay back in his arms.

    "I want you to trust me." he sighs, pressing his lips to my shoulder as I make myself comfortable.

    "If I talk about it, I'll break." I confess into the darkness, feeling a wave of nausea at the vulnerability that my impulsive words show.

    "Then I'll put you back together." He says simply.

I hum appreciatively and snuggle closer to him. Unable to let myself open up but hoping that the movement shows him what his words meant to me. I let my eyes fall closed and feel him pull away from me. *Have I read him wrong again?* His switch of moods towards me are starting to give me whiplash, along with my own unsure feelings towards him.

I hear a faint click and then his arm is back around me again. *He was only turning off the lamp. Idiot.* I let out a long breath, frustrated at the way my mind had jumped to conclusions so fast. I really needed to work out what the hell was going on here, the boundary lines between us were blurring more and more each day.

His arm relaxed and his breathing feathered the back of my neck in an even rhythm, the occasional snore indicating that he had fallen back to sleep. Sometime later I followed, thankfully falling into a dreamless slumber.

***

"Lady love of my life! Please tell me you look *that* exhausted because you were getting some last night!" I lifted my head from where it had been resting on my desk and groaned at Eden as she stood in my doorway waggling her eyebrows at me.

"Partially." I smiled weakly at her, straightening up and pushing my messed up red curls away from my face as she closed the door behind herself.

"You don't seem too pleased about that?" her brows pinched together, clearly unable to understand why I wasn't jumping around screaming from the rooftops about the stupidly good sex I was having.

I slumped back in my chair and wrinkled my nose at her. "I am, you know it's amazing, but…" I trailed off, unsure if I wanted to share any of this with her. Nibbling on my lip I thought it over, she didn't need to know the full details, and getting an outside perspective on it all might help, especially a girl's perspective. I had debated calling Coop about it this morning, but he's not stupid, he would've worked out who I was talking about, and going over it all in my own head was just giving me a headache.

"My personal trainer asked me out for drinks last night." I began. Her eyes lit up and she leant forward, enticed by how open I was being.

"Sexy, muscly man-bun?" she asked excitedly. Of course she knew who I meant, she went to the same gym as me, but she preferred light exercise over a strict routine.

"Yep, that guy." I felt blood rush to my cheeks at the thought of how much I was willing to tell her. "And I think I kind of wanted to, but then I didn't really answer him, and he just brushed me off like it hadn't even happened."

"Kind of wanted to? Only kind of? Are you ok?" her brows raised so high that they disappeared under her dark fringe.

I laughed at her reaction, "I don't date, you know that." her face dropped, and I sighed heavily.

"Remind me why. Why won't you date when you're getting such amazing offers?" she asked.

"I have baggage, people can't handle baggage, so why set myself up for disappointment when I can just have some causal fun?"

"Ok, sure, so this whole thing with your mystery lover, that's completely physical then?" I wasn't ready for that question.

"Um, yes, no." I scrunched my face up in frustration, "I don't know." I practically whined. *Eugh, what am I turning in to?*

"Ah, so you like him?" she said with a small smile.

"Honestly, I have no idea how I feel about him. Or how he feels about me. He's hot and cold with me. I keep having moments with him where it seems like he sees me as *more*, but when I question it, he switches back. I don't know if he's just protecting himself from me, or if I'm seeing things that aren't there. Either way, I'm not sure about him." Talking about Lorenzo in such an emotional way feels strange to me, but I push myself to carry on, hoping that once it's all said I might be able to see it clearer. "He understands me, he knows me so well, accepts me, I have no secrets from him. But he keeps them from me. And sometimes he scares me, can I really open myself up to a guy who lies and scares me?" I search Eden's face for an answer, but I can't find one, all she offers me is a thoughtful nod. "This is another reason that I don't date."

"And Manbun?" she asks after an uncomfortable silence.

"Huh?" I frown at her.

"How do you feel about *him*?"

"Toby is sunshine in human form," I sigh, "He's kind, and fun, and easy. I can't imagine ever feeling sad around him. But he doesn't really *know* me."

"So? That's the point of dating." She laughs and I push my tongue into my cheek. "What I'm hearing here is that your lover isn't giving you what you need *emotionally*, and he might not ever. And you deserve someone who is honest and doesn't scare you. But Manbun could possibly make you happy, if you took a leap of faith and tried."

"But, I don't date," I protest weakly, and she raises her brows at me. "Eugh fine, maybe it wouldn't be the *worst* thing, and I suppose you're right, about my lover that is. But for some reason I don't want to give him up."

"Then don't, just be careful." She shrugs like it's the simplest thing in the world. "and go on a damn date with that hunky man who *clearly* wants you."

"But what if-."

"Meg, seriously girl, stop, you will never know until you actually do it, so go and do it. It might actually be great." She gives me a serious glare. "And you should see your face when you talk about Manbun, Lady you're all glowy. It's time to drop this dumb shit about not dating and go enjoy yourself."

"So you're saying I should carry on with my lover, *and* date Toby?" I frown, surely that isn't what she's saying.

"For now, yes. No commitment, just see what it's like. It's not like you're marrying either of them, it's quite simple." She rolls her eyes at me playfully.

I nod slowly, hesitantly, taking in her advice. Feeling a strange lightness in me combined with a buzz of excitement. I finally understood why girls needed other girls, no guy would've been able, or willing, to talk me into that.

"Sleep on it, but you know I'm right." She teased. "Now let's go out for lunch and I can fill you in on Lukas' latest disaster." She grinned and stood up, I followed her out, food was definitely needed after all of that.

12

Meg

I wake earlier than usual after a restless sleep, but my mind is finally made up. I lean over to grab my phone from beside my bed and stare at the time. It's far too early to message anyone. I throw it back down and wonder what I can do to waste some time.

I decide to indulge myself in a long bath, pampering myself as much as I know how to. I lay in the lemon scented bubbles with a blue mask on my face, and mentally try to compose the perfect message. It slowly becomes the opposite of relaxing. *Why am I so bad at this.*

An hour later I'm sat in a towel, finishing blow drying my hair as my toenails dry, I'm not sure when I last painted them, but it felt like a good way to use up a little more time. The fact that multitasking comes so naturally to me didn't help though. I tossed my hair dryer on the bed and huffed at my reflection, minimal makeup sat on my face, my eyebrows freshly plucked into the dramatic arch that I loved. My red hair sat in bouncy, smooth curls, carefully shaped the way a hairdresser had taught me six years ago. Shelly was so nice to me, a scruffy looking sixteen-year-old who had awkwardly shuffled into her salon without a single clue about girl stuff. I had spent every day since Mum died hanging out with boys, if I wasn't with my brother, I was mixing with the scrappiest young thugs Westeroak had to offer. Jase hadn't minded that we'd ended up in that crowd, he just saw them as more people to look out for and protect me, just as he always did.

  I had been ashamed of asking for help back then. For years I hadn't cared about being seen as feminine, I'd gone from a young girl who innocently clung to a battered stuffed bunny, to a moody teen who lived in jeans, but I'd finally reached a point where I craved a female's attention and guidance. We had no other family and mum hadn't had any friends to take us under her wing. So Shelly had spent seven evenings with me, and it had been enough to teach me everything I wanted to know. Shelly had given me a weapon I never knew I needed. It may be wrong to use my looks, but it's one thing I have that none of my Brothers do. Nowadays I drop in to see Shelly from time to time, but I never felt the need to ask for more from her.

I pulled on a satin blouse and pencil skirt and grabbed my phone again. It was finally a more appropriate time. I opened up the message thread and began to type, 'Hey', I paused, staring at the screen. *Just do it.* I took in a deep breath and continued to type.

Megan
Hey, how are you? I don't suppose that drink offer is still on the table?

I hovered over the send button, then released a long breath and tapped, quickly launching my phone onto my bed before I could think about what I'd done.

I paced my room impatiently, regret rising in me. What if he didn't reply? What if he said no? I'd have to see him for our session after work today, I can't exactly cancel, he will know why, and it'll just be awkward. *It'll be awkward if you go or not, dumbass.*

Making the decision to try dating, and to try it with Toby, had continued to be a battle in my mind through the night. Eden's words echoed in my head over and over, I knew she was right, but there had been one thing that she couldn't help with. Keeping him safe. But I remembered how simple she had made everything sound, and I realised that *maybe* it could be as simple as keeping him away from The Brotherhood just like Cooper does with Samantha. Also, I doubt one date would put him in any danger.

Lorenzo might get a bit mad at me if he caught wind of it, not that he would have any right, if he wanted more from me, he would have to make that crystal clear. But that would all be on me, if anyone would get hurt, it would be me.

I raked my fingers through my hair and resisted the urge to play with my earrings, no more signs of weakness, even in the privacy of my small apartment. A buzzing noise grabbed my attention, and I dove onto my bed to find my phone like an infatuated teenager.

Tobias
Hey you, I'm good, how are you? Hmm, maybe, what's in it for me?

I smirked as I read over the message and quickly replied.

Megan
I'm alright. You'd get the joy of my company, obviously.

I hoped that was a good response, I'm not bad at flirting usually, it's never been an issue, but this felt different. I *actually* felt nervous, and weirdly those nerves excited me. His reply came through as quick as I had sent mine.

Tobias
Erm, nah, I'm good. It's hard enough to put up with you for three hours a week. ;)

My heart began to sink as I started to read, then I realised that he was messing with me. A huge grin covered my mouth as I typed back.

Megan
Screw you, I'm a delight.
Oh well, your loss.

Tobias
You know what, I feel kind of sorry for you now. I'll let you take me out just this once. But no funny business.

Megan
Gee thanks. You're so sweet. And I'm sure I'll be able to change your mind on that last bit.

Tobias
We'll see about that. You free after our session later?

I sighed happily at our little exchange and agreed to go out after our session. *That wasn't so bad.* The nervous feeling in my stomach settled down, now replaced with hunger.

I grabbed my handbag and gym bag and headed down to the underground garage of my building. I hopped into my car and headed towards my office, deciding to grab breakfast on the way. It was only when I arrived at work that I realised that I hadn't bought a change of clothes with me, well, nothing *date* appropriate. Shit.

13

Meg

I make my way out of the changing room at the gym. My fingers fiddle with the hem of the satin top that I chose. I had run in to town on my lunch break and managed to find a cute, strappy, deep red top that I could pair with the dark blue jeans that I had recalled seeing in my car boot the other evening.

My usual black heels clattered on the tiles as I walked over to the reception desk where Toby had told me to meet him. He wasn't here yet, and nerves started to bubble away. Had he changed his mind? He hadn't mentioned it during our session, only a quick comment as I left to go and shower, telling me where he would be waiting for me. No, he wouldn't say that and then leave. Fuck, why has this whole dating thing suddenly made me so anxious?

Toby cleared his throat as he approached me

from behind. I span around to find his contagious smile beaming down at me. His hair was hanging loose around his shoulders in a dirty blonde mess. He was wearing jeans and a tight black t shirt that highlighted every strong, defined muscle. I'd never seen him in jeans. He looked delicious.

"You look beautiful, Vixen." He stated and offered me his arm. *Such a gentleman.* I took hold of it and let him guide me out of the building, feeling the tension in my body dropping almost instantly. "Have you been dreading this as much as I have?" he asked as we walked the short distance to the bar that I had picked out.

"Can't wait for it to be over." I teased back and he threw his head back laughing. The sound sent a tornado of butterflies to my stomach, fluttering excitedly. I think that might be my new favourite sound.

We sat in a dark booth at the back of the bar. I'd chosen this bar as it wasn't affiliated with any of the gangs of Westeroak, it was a nice quiet place, the perfect setting for a casual first date. *Holy shit, I'm on a first date.*

Toby got up to go to the bar and order our drinks, It wasn't likely that I'd be called into any jobs this evening, Lorenzo didn't usually call me this late, not for work purposes anyway. So I had decided on a Vodka, lime and lemonade. I pulled my phone from my handbag and saw that I had two messages. One from Eden wishing me luck, and one from Cooper asking if I wanted to go for brunch again this weekend. I quickly replied to both, thanking Eden, and telling Coop I would love to.

Toby arrived back at our table with two drinks and a menu in hand, "I'm feeling like a snack," he said handing me the menu. *You look like a snack.* "Want some chips and wings or something?"

"Sounds good, maybe some onion rings too?" I bit my lip, hoping he would agree.

"Onion rings too." he nodded his approval. "I'll be right back then." He smiled and headed away again. I sat smiling to myself. So far so good, even if we've barely spent ten minutes together.

Toby slid in next to me in our booth when he finally sat down. I had presumed he would sit opposite me, but I was happy that he hadn't. The warm skin of his arm brushed against mine and sent a spark of desire through me. Even though we'd been spending at least 3 hours each week up close to each other for the past year, this contact was intense, it felt completely different. I twisted my body toward him, and he mirrored my action, placing an arm on the table and staring down at me. His stare wasn't intimidating, he may have been a pretty scary guy with the stacks of muscles, tattoos and facial hair, but his eyes sparkled so brightly, like a stunningly clear ocean drenched in sunlight. I felt instantly safe and calm when he looked at me.

"You really do look beautiful." He said softly.

"You already told me that." I smiled.

"Well I meant it, enough to say it twice. I'm glad you asked me to do this, I felt so stupid asking you the other day. I've wanted to for a while now, but I didn't know if it was appropriate, and then I just blurted it out and your face, oh Vixen, I couldn't take the panic that I'd seen on your face." His expression turned sad for a moment, and I reached out, placing my hand on top of his where it was sat on the table.

"Toby," I whispered, he had let himself be vulnerable so quickly, so easily. My mind shot to Lorenzo, and how I couldn't picture him ever letting me see a side like this. "I wanted to say yes. But I've never dated before, not properly. I don't really know if I'm ready, but I want to see." I told him truthfully. He moved our hands so that he was now holding me, his thumb began to paint tiny circles on the back of my hand, and I let out a breath that I hadn't realised I'd been holding after my confession.

"Good, and I don't think you'll regret that choice by the end of tonight." He winked and dropped my hand to grab his drink, he swallowed a long mouthful and grinned at me as he placed the glass back down.

We ate, drank, and chatted with ease for some time. Every conversation was flowing effortlessly, and he was right, not a single drop of regret was felt. Toby told me stories about his Mum and Dad, they sounded like amazing people, even though he wasn't as close with both of them anymore. He didn't push me when I said that I didn't have many happy childhood memories. We discussed our favourite music, foods, and got into a heated debate over the correct order to watch Star Wars in. We had naturally gravitated closer to each other and he had draped his arm over my shoulder for a while as my hand had rested on his leg.

My phone buzzed as we finished eating and I pulled away to quickly check it, a text glowed on the screen from Lorenzo.

Boss
Come to The Crown ASAP.

I frowned at the message and glanced at the time. It was 9.30pm, at this time it was likely he was calling for pleasure and not business. I tucked my phone back away and apologised to Toby. Trying to bring my focus back to our date.

Fifteen minutes later I felt my phone vibrating where my bag was pushed against my leg. The buzz continued, indicating that I was receiving a call. I tried to ignore it. Inhaling deeply and nodding to whatever Toby had said. Less than a minute later it started up again, I tensed my jaw and internally cursed out whoever was calling me, most likely Lorenzo. I didn't hear a word Toby had said to me and searched his face for a clue. *Shit.* I made a humming noise in my throat and sipped my drink, hoping he'd not worked out that I'd been lost in my head and not listening. Silence hung between us, and the vibration of my phone started up again, this time he was aware of it too.

"Do you need to..." he gestured at my bag, and I gave him an apologetic look as I pulled my phone out. *Lorenzo.*

"Sorry, I do." I bit my lip, but he didn't seem to mind, he smiled and placed his hand on my leg with a shrug that said he was happy for me to handle whatever I needed to handle.

"I'm kind of in the middle of something," I quickly said upon pressing the green button.

"Well wrap it up M, this is important." *M, Oh. This is business. Shit.*

"Yep, will do." I hung up before he could comment on the fact I wasn't being as respectful as I should've been. I couldn't call him Boss in front of Toby, he knew I was my own boss, during office hours anyway. I couldn't call him Lorenzo either, not if he was calling for business. Boundaries and all that.

I lifted my head to meet Toby's gentle gaze. "I am *so* sorry," I started.

"It's fine, do you need me to walk you somewhere? Grab you a cab?" he knew already that I was leaving, his smile didn't drop though. Guilt hit me all the same, even if he wasn't showing any signs of disappointment. *This* is my life. This shit isn't fair to put him through. He'd need the truth if I wanted to do this for real, or I'd need to walk away.

"My car is down by the gym, I've only had

one drink, I'm fine to drive." I'll work out what to do about *us* when I'm not stressed about what I'm going to face at The Crown.

"I'll walk you there then, come on little one." He stood and offered me his arm the same way he had at the beginning of our date. Still playing the perfect gentleman.

We came to a stop next to my silver Mercedes, and I turned to face him. I reached up to trace a finger down one side of his face. "Thank you for a perfect date Tobias, I wish I didn't have to go." I whispered.

My hand dropped from his face, and he lent down, his face closing in on mine. The butterflies swooped back in, flapping manically in my stomach as the anticipation of his lips against mine sizzled between us.

His mouth landed on my forehead, his lips pressed gently for a brief moment, and then he pulled away. *What?* "Stay safe little vixen, call me when you're home?" It wasn't what I had expected, it was better, in a strange way. I didn't *need* to be treated as though I might break, but I didn't dislike it from him. It was who he was underneath the playful exterior, he was gentle, kind, and selfless.

I nodded in agreement and climbed into my car, he closed the door for me, and I sped away down the road. He stayed where he was, watching me go as I watched him through the mirror. I really didn't want to go.

***

I pulled up down the street from The Crown, knowing I wouldn't find anywhere to park any closer at this time. I walked down towards the bar, debating whether I had enough time to run back to the car and at least change my shoes in preparation for whatever I was being summoned for. I decided against it, I had already pissed off Lorenzo by taking so long to answer my phone, taking more time to arrive would only make it worse, and after the evening I'd been having, I didn't want his wrath. I wanted to enjoy this light, happy feeling that had stayed with me since leaving Toby.

I pushed my way through the main door of The Crown and spotted Cooper stood at the bar. "You've been summoned too then?" I asked as I bumped him with my elbow.

"Yep, me, you, and every other Brother." He turned to face Lorenzo's usual booth and I followed his gaze to see that he was right, All ten of us were here. "Why are you all dressed up?" he asked, but I ignored him. No way was I going to tell him where I'd been while we were stood in one of our bars, surrounded by our guys. I didn't need the teasing comments I'd no doubt receive over going on a date tonight. Coop knew how I felt about dating.

Lorenzo looked up from his place on one side of the booth, no one had sat beside him, the others sat opposite or chose to stand. Grey was stood at the side of the booth talking to Frank and looking like his usual pissed off self. Lorenzo's eyes locked on mine, and he cocked his head to one side before running his gaze over my body slowly. His brows lifted slightly, but his expression was annoyingly unreadable.

"What's this all about then?" I asked Cooper, pulling my attention away from our boss.

"No idea Sunshine, have you been up to no good? You little troublemaker. Has he gathered everyone to watch you get punished?" My jaw dropped a fraction at his words. Did he *know?* I frowned at him. "I'm joking M." he laughed. But that did nothing to ease my concern that he might know what has going on between me and our boss.

He handed me a cold glass of soda, "Shall we see what all the fuss is about then?" he grabbed my arm and yanked me to follow him over to the small crowd of Brothers.

They all greeted us warmly, apart from Grey, no surprise there. After we had all settled down, and conversations had politely come to a close, our boss rose from where he had been sat silently waiting.

"Buonasera i miei Fratelli," he swept his gaze over each of us with the familiar greeting that he always used when he gathered all of The Brotherhood at once. "I have some exciting news." I notice some of the men glancing at each other curiously. "The ten of you have been chosen carefully, only the best of the best have been selected to join our family. We have always kept our circle small, ten has always been our limit." The faces of many of my brothers twisted with confusion. I looked at Coop, but he simply shrugged at me and folded his arms over each other. "Until now." Our boss grinned, "Brothers, we have a new member joining our family tonight." Some of them started talking between themselves now, whispering to each other, but our boss raised his hands and they fell silent again. "Brothers, I'd like to welcome my stepson." He gestured to a spot behind where a few of us were stood, and we all turned to meet our new Brother.

 My grip on my drink loosened and it crashed to the floor, ice, soda and glass scattering under my heels. I heard Cooper curse under his breath beside me. My throat dried up and my eyes widened as shock fell on me like a tonne of bricks.

 Eye's darker than a starless sky, cruel smirk, tattooed hands.

 "Adonis."

14

Don

My eyes are instantly drawn to her, and I bathed in the anger that she was radiating. I didn't give a fuck about anyone else's reaction. Just hers. The sound of glass smashing had been priceless, it made me wish I'd recorded this moment. I wanted her current expression printed and framed.

I noticed from the corner of my eye that the pretty blonde guy stood next to her was staring at her too and wrapping his arm around her, I'd take a guess that this is Cooper. I'd not met him yet, but apart from dear old stepdaddy and Grey, he was the only one who knew who I was, and just how much I had managed to piss off our little lady.

Men began to crowd around me, welcoming me with handshakes and slaps on the back, all that typical man stuff. I politely greeted them back, but my attention fell back to her over and over. I wasn't overly interested in this whole meet and greet thing. I'd only agreed to Lorenzo's big welcome because I knew that she would be here. *Come on sweetheart, come say Hi.*

Coming here had never been part of my plan, Mum had moved to be with Lorenzo, and I had stayed in Italy with Uncle Sal, but when Mum died, no, when mum was *murdered,* I'd been called, but I didn't come back for the funeral. I was too angry, angry at myself for not being there to for her, angry at my stepfather for not protecting her, angry at the guy who killed her, for obvious fucking reasons. Sal helped me channel that rage, put it to good use, taught me how to make someone pay, how to take my revenge when the time was right. So here I am, ready to hunt down that bastard.

Grey approached me next, "Well done boy, you've really proven yourself, especially with the way you handle *that one.*" He sneered and shot a look at Megan, his dislike for the woman so transparent that I actually wondered what his reason for it was. I knew mine, she had been my competition, the thing standing between me and the prick who murdered mum, if I had failed, I'd have no way of finding him. Ok maybe that's not completely true, I'm very resourceful when I have to be, but this is the easiest way and I'd be an idiot not to take it.

She continued to stare at me like it might

cause me to drop dead on the spot if she focused hard enough and I couldn't stop the smirk falling on my lips.

"It wasn't hard, I'm better at all of this than she is, I suppose I'll have to play nice now that I'm one of you? No more pissing off the princess." I turn my gaze to the man in front of me with his scarred face and raise my brows as I notice a conspiratorial glint in his eye. He leans in close so that no one else can hear.

"The girl needs putting in her place, I won't stand in your way if you choose to be the one who does that. She's trouble and I wouldn't be upset to see her gone. The boss never needs to know."

"Good to know." I give him a tight smile and he responds with a wink, *Eiw*.

He disappeared into the small crowd of Brothers, leaving me standing alone. I found my attention drawn back to her. Megan and Cooper are the only two left to welcome me, and our *boss* is looking across from his throne – ok it's just a seat in a booth, but he's really perfected the evil ruler look – his jaw is tense and his eyes are burning into the backs of their heads, if neither of them move soon I have a feeling that they might get a little telling off from Daddy.

Cooper must sense this as he gives Megan a quick squeeze before releasing her and heading in my direction.

"Cooper Peterson, nice to finally meet you." I

stare from his outstretched hand to his million-dollar smile and can't stop myself feeling an instant dislike towards this guy.

"Yeah." I grunt dismissively, and make a move to pass him, but he steps in my way and leans in close to me.

"Play nicely new guy." He warns in an icy tone, pulling back and giving me a hard look followed by another dazzling smile, yeah, I really don't like this prick.

I don't respond, instead simply holding him in a deathly stare. A few seconds later he moves out of my way and heads over to the bar, tossing a quick glance in Megan's direction where she is now leaning against a table and furiously tapping at her phone. I look past her to Lorenzo and notice that he is pulling his phone from his pocket, a heavy sigh leaving his chest as his eyes scan over the screen. My guess is that is a message from her, no doubt a nice long rant, typical princess behaviour.

I head towards her and raise my brows at her as I catch her eye, a silent invitation to come and confront me, greet me, say anything, but she purses her lips in response and turns her gaze to look past me. *Fine.* I continue past her and approach our boss. "Lorenzo," I begin, flopping down on the chair opposite him and raising my voice loud enough for the girl to hear, "Your men are great. It really does feel like a family just like you said. I have a question though." I pause and his jaw stiffens as though he already knows where I'm heading with this.

"Yes son." He said, I hated him calling me that, and the look that flashed across his face told me that he was well aware of that fact. It wasn't worth starting an argument over though. Not right now.

"Is Megan always this rude?" I looked over at her after the words left my mouth and a warm feeling filled me as I found her rage visibly boiling over, storming towards us as she finally cracked.

Lorenzo opened his mouth to speak but her words came crashing down over us as she positioned herself between us at the end of the table.

"Me, rude? That's fucking rich coming from you!" she hissed, jabbing her finger at me, "You turn up everywhere like you think you're a gift from god, you mess with people's reputations, what did you expect from me? A big hug and a congratulatory speech about how I look forward to working with you?" she cocks her head and leans towards me, resting her hands on the table as she lets the next words come out with pure venom. "I'd rather eat my own shit than welcome you. Arsehole."

I can't stop it. A loud laugh bursts from my lips. I look to the ceiling to try to control myself. "I'm sorry," I splutter, "but you really are a dramatic little princess aren't you."

"Don't call me princess." She snarls.

Lorenzo's hand falls on top of hers, "That's enough, both of you. You're causing a scene." She looks down at where he touches her and lets out a long, slow breath. I watch them as their eyes meet, his stay firm, in charge, hers turn from rage to something I did not expect. She's hurt, emotionally, she's breaking. Her eyes have turned glassy, and she's swallowing thickly. My focus drops back to their hands, Lorenzo's thumb runs back and forth over her skin a few times before he pulls away.

Holy shit. The realisation churns my stomach, They're fucking.

15

Lorenzo

It hurts to look into her eyes and see how badly this news has hurt her. How badly I've hurt her. I knew I'd have to do this, Grey's little outburst the other day hadn't stopped replaying in my head. Adonis had completed his initiation tasks and I couldn't put this off any longer. But in her eyes, I had used her. I had allowed this guy, my stepson, to make a fool of her for his own gain, to prove that he deserved to be here.

"Why?" she asked quietly.

"I'm presuming you're asking me why I set those tasks for him?" I answered her with a question, keeping my tone even and tucking away the desire to apologise to her. We were in a bar, surrounded by Brothers, with our newest member sat opposite me taking in our exchange with a disgusted look plastered on his face. I had to keep face.

She nodded.

"It's a compliment M, if he can beat *you* to a kill, he's worth keeping around." I'd told him the same thing when I'd set him his tasks. Neither of them would get the truth from me about this. So I'd come up with this highly plausible excuse in preparation.

She seemed to think this over, then irritation flashed over her face. "Why didn't you just tell me that before?"

"I have my reasons M, don't push this." I replied in a low growl, maybe it was unnecessary to be so harsh towards her, but she couldn't question my motives here. Not when the entire Brotherhood was around.

She stepped back, pulling herself together and turned her attention on Adonis. "Your work is messy, *Adonis,* you need to work on a lot of things if you want to be taken seriously." she said flatly and spun away from the table towards the bar.

Adonis watched her go like she was a bad smell, then turned to me and opened his mouth to speak.

"You better not push me either, son" I warned. "I'm your boss now."

"You're fucking her." He said, ignoring my warning. He was clearly angry, the accent he had acquired from a lifetime in Italy came through so much stronger when he was angry. He should work on that.

"Adonis, if you want to discuss this, you will wait until we get home." I kept my voice quiet so only he could hear me and plastered a bored look onto my face for anyone who was watching our exchange.

"I've already told you I'm not moving into your house Lorenzo." He matched my tone, but the accent remained strong, and sat back comfortably in his chair.

"Boss, when we are here it is boss, I shouldn't have to remind you." I corrected him, frustrated by his inability to follow basic fucking rules. "And you *will* move in, a room has been made up for you, your mother would want you with family and that is where you will be Adonis, this isn't up for debate." I rose from my seat and straightened my suit jacket. Adonis ran his gaze over my attire approvingly.

"We'll talk about it at *home* then, *Boss*." He said, sarcasm oozing into every word, "the suit looks good on you, *molto bene*" he added after.

I smiled down at him and he returned it, quickly putting our disagreement on the back burner. It wouldn't be up for discussion later, but I wouldn't be repeating myself in front of the Brothers and making myself look as though I am unable to control my men.

"You were right son, that tailor was very good." Adonis and I had gone on a little father son bonding trip to get new suits, one of the few things we have in common is our eye for good quality clothes, not that you could always tell with him, he didn't have a very varied taste, mostly alternating between suits and fitted t-shirts, all black, but he always looked good.

He stood up and exited the booth with me, "I suppose I should *mingle*." He rolled his eyes.

"Try not to piss anyone off tonight." I joked, placing my hand on his shoulder in the closest thing to an affectionate gesture I could muster. I was quite fond of him; it had taken up until now for me to realise that though. His disinterest in joining my family when his mother had moved here to be with me had put a wedge between us. I had believed that her death would see the end of our connection, especially when he hadn't shown for her funeral. I hadn't been sad about it; I had felt nothing. But when he had turned up some time later with that bloodlust in his eyes, I knew that he belonged with me.

I made my way to the door. I didn't need to announce my exit, they would realise soon enough. The Brothers would enjoy their evening and I didn't plan on supervising it. Before I reached the door, I caught Grey's eye and lifted my head in an indication to come to me. He followed the order and was at my side with no hesitation, leaving Jen, the barmaid, holding a pint up and cursing after him, clearly annoyed that he had walked off before she had finished pouring it. I loved my staff here; they had no issues with calling out my men for their shitty behaviour.

"Keep an eye on everyone tonight Grey, I'd quite like a lay in tomorrow morning." He nodded, understanding my command.

"Will do boss, have a good night." He rushed back to the bar just as Jen's voice reached us, shouting an explicit threat to cut a certain appendage off if he was ever rude to her again. I smiled, the girl had balls.

I took in the room, briefly enjoying the moment as my Brothers were all gathered together, the beautifully dysfunctional family that I had created. My eyes fell on M, leaning against the bar, deep in conversation with Cooper. Filthy images flashed through my mind, a graphic reminder of how I had taken her on that bar top only a couple of nights ago. I felt my cock strain under the fabric of my trousers. She had got herself so far under my skin. I was finding myself willing to do anything to protect her. The look she had given me tonight was almost enough to make me drop the act that we put on for everyone else and hold her until she forgave me. If she'd let me.

I pulled my phone from my pocket, as I turned to the door and stepped out into the cool evening air.

Lorenzo

Come to mine. Now.

A simple request. One I prayed she would follow, no matter how angry she was with me. I needed her tonight, even if she pushed me, tested me and crossed every damn line. I'd take it and make my way back into her good graces.

16

Meg

My phone buzzed in my pocket, drawing my attention away from the irritated telling off that I was giving Cooper. I was angry with him too, but nowhere near as angry as I was with Lorenzo. Cooper had known all about that arsehole and he hadn't told me either, he had been working behind the scenes to ensure the jobs ran smoothly, and in turn, was allowing me to be made a fool out of. Not that I could really be too angry, he wouldn't have had much choice in his role, and he *had* apologised, profusely, which was a hell of a lot more than Lorenzo had done. But he could have told me.

"It's not like I'd have dropped you in it for telling me. I can play dumb if I have to. I'm quite the actress when it's necessary." I finished and looked at the screen of my phone. A message from our boss lit it up and I let out a low growl at the demand he had sent. Did he really think that he could just snap his fingers and I'd come running, after the way he had dismissed me? The fact that he clearly didn't think I could handle being in the know. He had said that it was a compliment that this new guy was put on my jobs, but it didn't feel like one. All I felt was betrayal, and that shit hurt.

I tapped out a single word and pocketed my phone.

Megan
No.

I leaned over the bar to grab Jen's attention and she quickly placed the pint that she had just pulled for Michael on the bar and headed my way.

"My favourite lady, how are you doing? I heard you caused quite the stir in here a couple of nights ago, had the boss kicking everyone out." She raised her brows at me in an impressed expression and grinned like a maniac, "Brave girl."

I let out a small laugh, "And I lived to tell the tale, shockingly. Can I get some shots please Jen, four? I'll let you decide what we have, just not tequila." I scrunched my face up, unless it was a lingering taste sitting on Lorenzo's lips I couldn't stand the stuff, and I didn't want to be thinking about Lorenzo's lips right now. Or the fact that I was leaning on the exact spot where he had bent me over and fucked me. I needed something to distract my thoughts.

"Sure thing." She turned to grab a bottle from the shelf and messily poured out four shots of vodka. *That would do it.* I placed a couple of notes on the bar, and she waved me away, "Boss has covered you guys' tonight girl, so you can just enjoy yourself." And sashayed away to deal with another Brother.

I slid two of the glasses in front of Cooper and lifted one of the remaining two to my lips, "To *Adonis.*" I said his name like it was painful to even form the letters and threw back the burning liquid.

Cooper just looked at me and sighed, "I *am* sorry sunshine." He said with a sad look resting on his face.

"Drink." I demanded and grabbed another glass as I felt my pocket begin to vibrate. I didn't bother to check my phone; I knew who it was. No-one said no to Lorenzo D'Angelo. Until now. There wasn't a chance in hell of me answering that call. The consequences for this could be future Meg's problem.

I emptied the small glass and frowned at Cooper as he ignored my demand.

"I'm gonna pass, someone will have to get you home." He smiled and slid his drinks back over to me. I shrugged and chased them one after the other.

"Thanks Coop, and I know you're sorry, *and* I know you'll make it up to me." I gave him a mock stern look and he wrapped his arm over my shoulder.

"You want to head home now? Or do you fancy sticking around for a while?" he asked.

I scanned the bar, noticing that the arsehole was watching me. My phone buzzed again, and I huffed out a long breath. "Take me home Coop, I want tonight to be over." He nodded and guided me towards the door.

"Leaving so soon *princess*?" a deep voice called loudly across the room. I didn't need to turn around to know that it was him. No one else would dare to call me that. Princess. They all knew why I hated it. The story of the last man who called me that was the main reason I was here.

Coopers grip around me tightened, he knew I wouldn't react well to that comment, hell he probably already knew that I'd fired a warning shot at the arsehole for calling me it once before. He continued to guide me from the bar, and I lifted my hand up and raised my middle finger, *Fuck you, arsehole*. As we walked through the door, I heard Adonis' laughter following after me, accompanied by someone else's, I had no doubt in my mind that it had come from Grey.

"My car is just down the road." Cooper said as he released me from his hold, and we walked silently side by side.

Once we were comfortably inside his car, I closed my eyes and rested my head back. "Wake me up when we get there." I said, exhausted from everything that had happened this evening. As I drifted in and out of light sleep, I thought of Toby and our date and let the happy feeling of those thoughts surround me.

***

"M, wake up." Cooper prodded my arm repeatedly until I cracked open an eye to look at him.

"Carry me up?" I said sleepily as I let my eye close again.

He poked me again, harder this time and I wriggled away from him and forced myself to open my eyes properly. I immediately noticed that it was dark outside, why had he not driven down into the garage, was he going to make me walk the long way to my apartment in the cold?

I squinted out of the window and pursed my lips as the realisation hit me.

This is not my home. Not even close. My so-called friend has brought me to our boss's house.

"Coop what the fuck!" I exploded.

"He text me, I'm sorry, he said it was important, and I can't be dealing with being on his bad side right now, I'll make it up to you. Promise." He said and gave me an angelic look. Batting his damn eyelashes and everything.

"I'm going to kill you." I ground out through clenched teeth.

"Nah, you're going to go have a big fight with

the boss and then have some mind-blowing sex. If anything, you'll be thanking me." he winked.

The accuracy of his comment took me off guard and my mouth fell open.

He chuckled and lifted my jaw with his finger, closing my mouth for me.

"How the-."

"Oh come on Sunshine, you're not always very quiet, and I work in that house a lot, I'm just very, very good at keeping secrets." He winked.

I chewed on my lower lip and felt my skin heat. "Shit, thank you Coop." I murmured. I had genuinely believed that we had kept our *thing* pretty damn quiet. I had a feeling that Grey knew, Grey seemed to know everything, but not Cooper. *Fuck I hope no one else knows.*

I stretched my back out and grabbed the door handle, taking a couple of moments to prepare myself for what would be waiting for me. It was starting to feel as though I had to prepare my head every time I entered this man's house.

"Wish me luck." I gave my friend a weak smile and stepped out of his car, he laughed and blew me a kiss. One day I'd actually manage to stay mad at him.

I walked to the front door and knocked hard, Clive would be waiting, the gate guard would've informed the staff that we were coming up.

"Good evening, M," Clive said as he ushered me inside, "In the lounge tonight."

"Hey Clive, thanks. Can I ask, how is his mood right now?" I leaned in close as if we were teenagers sharing secrets and he lowered his voice.

"Calm, he lost it when you ignored his calls, but he's been down in the gym since."

"Thanks." I headed across the foyer and through the lounge doors, I was starting to get to know the layout of this place quite well, but there were still parts that were a complete mystery to me.

"You're here." He breathed as he spun around to look at me, relief written all over his face.

"Yeah." I said bluntly, "You can thank Cooper later,' I went to sit down in a wing-backed armchair and kicked my heels off. It was clear I wouldn't be leaving this place tonight so I might as well make myself comfortable. "I really don't appreciate you going behind my back to get me here, you put my friend in a shit position."

"Your *friend,* your friend is one of *my* men, and how else was I supposed to get you here, you were ignoring my calls." He snapped. Looked like that work-out had only taken the edge off, his bad mood was still festering underneath.

"I was ignoring you for a reason." I spat back. My lady balls were in serious danger of exploding from how big they had become recently. Apparently the longer our little situation went on, the braver I became in his presence.

"Watch your tone, M." he said, starting to sound a little like a stuck record with how often he repeated that little phrase.

"Oh its *M* right now? So you've summoned me for business purposes?" I narrowed my eyes at him as he stepped closer and towered over me, apparently slightly drunk Megan didn't give a fuck about who he was, or what he was capable of doing. Slightly drunk Megan was an idiot.

"No, you're not here as a Brother,"

"Then don't speak to me like one," I crossed my arms under my breasts, "You're in my bad books Lorenzo." The look on his face was pure shock. I had even shocked myself with that declaration.

He quickly pulled himself together and placed his hands on the arm rests of my chair, caging me in and placing his mouth so close to mine that I could almost taste him. "And you're in mine."

"For not coming running? I don't have to Lorenzo," I brushed my lips against his, "I'm not your little bitch."

"No amore mio," he breathed, "you are so much more."

I pulled away and held his dark gaze, a whirlpool of emotions were swirling in his eyes. I had no idea what this man was feeling, and there wasn't a chance in hell that I'd be asking, I couldn't handle anything other than rage and lust right now. If he had something else to say to me, it could wait.

I shook off the weird feeling that had suddenly come over me. "Why am I here then? Are you going to fight me, or fuck me?" *Perfect, boundaries.*

He hesitated, seeming to be thinking. I wasn't aware that my question really took much thought to answer. I lifted a hand up to run my fingers down his still damp, bare chest, hinting at the direction that I would prefer this to take. I was mad, but fighting would result in me needing to get home somehow, and I didn't think it was very fair to call Cooper back here. He sucked in a sharp breath as my fingers met the waistband of his gym shorts and teased the flesh that sat just below the fabric.

"Well?" I purred and let my fingertips run back and forth slowly.

His lips found mine in a vicious kiss that answered my question as clearly as any words could have. We're going to do both. *That* I could work with. My hand slid lower into his shorts and easily found the smooth skin of his hard cock.

Since we had begun sleeping together, I'd found out some interesting things about Lorenzo, like the fact that he never wore underwear to work out, and I loved that.

He broke away from the kiss, groaning as I slid my hand up and down his shaft and pushed his shorts down with the other.

"Stand." He grunted. I followed his command, letting curiosity take over.

I kept pumping my hand up and down as I stared up at him and drank in the look of pleasure on his face. His chest was rising and falling in a slow, deep rhythm, and I couldn't stop a grin forming on my lips at the power I was currently holding.

He didn't let it last long though, abruptly grabbing my wrist and stilling my motion. *Had I just managed to get him close with my hand alone?* He freed himself from my grip and lifted my hand to press a gentle kiss to the back of it in a sweet gesture that confused me. He then swiftly grabbed me and threw me over his shoulder. Less confusing. A girlie shriek left my lips, and he swatted my ass playfully. *Fucker knew exactly what he was doing.* A giggle escaped me, and I cringed at the noise. But Lorenzo's hand came crashing down on my ass again, indicating that he might have enjoyed it.

"What are you-." I began, wriggling on his shoulder. A yelp cut through my words as his hand connected with my ass a third time and he carried me out of the lounge without uttering a single word.

He made his way up the stairs as I thrashed around in frustration, and he let out a low laugh in response. "Give up amore mio."

"Put me down!" I demanded but the words lost all bite as I realised that he was completely naked, and I couldn't stop myself from smiling at how ridiculous we must look.

He shoved through a door and the next thing I knew I was being thrown onto my back in a cloud of soft, white sheets. We were in his room, the room that I'd now slept in a couple of times, but had never done anything else in.

I tried not to think about what this meant, if it even meant anything. I pulled my focus back to Lorenzo, "Don't do that ever again!" I scowled and he stood before me with his mouth pulled into a cocky smile.

"Part of you enjoyed it."

"No, I hated it." I protested.

"Sure you did." The smug look on his face was equal parts gorgeous and infuriating.

I huffed in annoyance and moved to sit up. "Fight me, or fuck me Lorenzo, stop playing games."

"So demanding," He teased. "And a little overdressed." He looked me up and down.

"Are you going to strip willingly, or do I need to use force?" he questioned in a low growl.

"Force." I breathed. Excitement igniting between my thighs at the idea.

"Fine." He said simply. Placing his hands on the middle of my satin top and effortlessly ripping the fabric. A gasp fell from my lips, followed by a lusty moan. This man was slowly becoming an addiction, one that I had no desire to quit.

***

"Are you awake?" I rolled over to face Lorenzo and smiled at the warmth radiating on my back from the morning sun. He was sitting with his back against the headboard and a deep frown was sitting on his face. I can't have managed to do anything to annoy him yet could I? I'd only been awake for a few minutes. *I bet I was snoring or something.*

"What's wrong?" I asked gently, was he kicking me out already?

"You looked beautiful last night," he paused, then looked at me, "Why?"

I spluttered a short laugh. "*Why* did I look beautiful?" I threw the question back at him, unsure what response to give.

"Sorry, that came out wrong," he sighed. "You always look beautiful, but last night you'd put in extra effort. Was that for me? Or had you been somewhere else before coming to The Crown?"

It was not a question that I was expecting at all. He'd never taken any interest in what I do in my spare time before, unless it involved making me orgasm over and over again. I thought on it for a minute. I looked nice because I'd been on a date, I was dating, kinda. Would he be mad about that? Was there any point in lying though? This was Lorenzo D'Angelo; he could find out exactly where I'd been and with who without asking me if he wanted to. I suppose I should be pleased that he's asking me, like a normal person.

"Yeah, I had a date." I admitted, trying to put on a casual front about it. But the flush I felt in my cheeks clearly gave away how much I'd enjoyed my time with Toby. Lorenzo noticed and swallowed hard.

"Right." He said bluntly, returning his gaze to look out of the window.

I propped myself up on my elbow and reached out to rest my hand on his stomach. "Is that an issue?" I asked.

"We're not together M, why should it be." His words felt like a lie. I breathed slowly and removed my hand.

"Exactly." I said quietly, not sure if he could even hear me. He didn't move, and I wasn't going to push a man who clearly had no idea what he honestly wanted from me. Best to just ignore it.

I rolled onto my back and stretched, readying myself to get up and make an exit before things got more uncomfortable.

As I let out a soft groan at the ache that I felt over my entire body from the previous night, the door came flying open. I gasped and grabbed at the sheet that had pooled around our ankles, lifting it to cover myself and Lorenzo. I looked across at him and he rolled his eyes at the intruder.

"You don't know how to knock?" he said. His tone lacked the aggression that I would have expected and caused me turn to see who was there.

Adonis stood in the doorway, leaning against the frame with my stilettos dangling from a finger. Anger rose inside me instantly, and I shot him a deathly glare.

"Doesn't your *puttana* know how to tidy up

after herself?" he shot back, dropping my heels to the floor, and giving me a disgusted look.

"Don." Lorenzo warned and I felt his hand grasp mine under the sheets. *Weird.*

"Sorry." He said sarcastically and bent to straighten up my heels where he had dropped them.

"That's not what I meant, and you know it." Lorenzo snapped.

"I know." The arsehole smirked and casually leaned back against the doorframe again. The fabric of his black shirt tightening as he folded his arms. "So, what's this job then?"

"You couldn't have waited?"

"No, I wanted to make a good impression. First proper day on the job and all that." his eyes sparkled with mischief. But this guy was far from fun and playful.

"Try harder next time, throwing around stupid insults is not a good way to start." Lorenzo squeezed my hand.

Adonis shrugged and looked me up and down. I glanced at him with disinterest, attempting to hide how uncomfortable I was with being caught in bed with my boss. *Our* boss. *Fuck.*

"You and M will be working together tonight. Grey is sending over all of the information I need now, and I will have a solid plan formed within the hour."

I instantly stiffened. My grip on Lorenzo's hand tightening. *We're not done with this shit?*

"Absolutely not." Both me and Adonis spoke at the same time. Our eyes meeting, hatred electrifying the air between us.

"I wasn't asking." Lorenzo barked and removed himself from my grip to move off of the bed. He was partly dressed, wearing tight sweats, he looked mouth-wateringly hot. He rounded the bed and placed himself between the two of us.

"You will work together," he spoke with a level of authority that wasn't to be argued with and he pointed his finger between us, "You will not fail me," he stepped towards his arsehole stepson, "and you will not fucking complain."

Adonis broke our eye contact and looked at our boss, they stood at the same height, but it was clear who the smaller man was. He nodded sharply.

"Fine. Maybe *M* will learn something." He spun on his heel and walked off down the hallway.

Lorenzo turned to me and raised his brows, waiting for me to speak.

"Do I have to be nice to him?" I asked.

"It would be easier for everyone if you are, but no amore mio, you can be as mean as you desire."

A small smile played on the edges of my lips. "I guess it might be fun then." I slipped the sheets down, exposing the pale skin of my chest, "can I have some fun with you first though?" I held my breath, hoping I hadn't taken a stupid risk by trying to initiate something.

"Always." He growled, climbing on top of me and pinning me to the bed. I had no idea what was going on in this man's head and I probably should have walked away from him before it would get too messy. But for some messed up reason, I couldn't. I really was addicted to him.

He played my body like it was a delicate instrument and he was a world-class musician, moans and gasps rang out around us and as his hard shaft slammed into my soaking core a scream tore through my throat. I threw my head back as more screams escaped me. I came hard and fast, Lorenzo following a split second later, collapsing beside me and panting heavily.

The loud bang of a door being slammed pulled me from my post-fuck daze and I glanced over to see that the bedroom door was still open.

Lorenzo laughed darkly, "I don't think Adonis enjoyed the show."

17

Don

I sped down the long driveway away from Lorenzo's house. The place he expected me to treat as my home. The home he had made with my mother.

The sound of him fucking *her* was still echoing inside my head. Bile rose in my throat. I'd worked it out last night. I'd been disgusted then, but actually *hearing* it was so much worse. It made it real. He was over my mamma. He had claimed to be so in love with her, yet barely eight months after she was murdered, he has moved on. Probably sooner, I had no idea how long this had been going on for, but the fact that they were sharing a bed clued me in that it had probably been going on for some time.

Megan Fields. The girl with the deadly reputation. How much of that was really true? Had she just been sleeping her way to the top? I'll be putting a stop to that.

Once I've avenged mum, my plan is to take over The Brotherhood. It was a completely new direction for my life, but one that I now wanted so desperately. Seeing the power that my stepdad held, the respect, the opportunities, how could I not want to take it all on?

I'd never really looked at Megan as competition, I'd heard that she was good, great even. I'd not seen it. Sure I'd seen her beat down some kid, but that proved nothing. He was just some pathetic gangster wannabe, that had been child's play. Allegedly being able to outkill her meant a lot, but after what I now knew, I wasn't sure. There was no denying that girl had an amazing body, if I was in her shoes, I'd probably use it to my advantage and fuck the boss to get what I want too. But that meant she was an actual obstacle. I thought Grey would be the only one. I was naturally skilled, I never failed, but Grey already had Lorenzo's trust, and that was what I needed to gain to be considered as next in line. Megan had his cock though, and no matter how much he might protest, men always think with their cocks, at least just a little bit.

I drove aimlessly for an hour, still unsure about where I felt most comfortable in this city. I had an apartment above the shop that I'd bought, it was a small space where I'd been staying since arriving here. Lorenzo wanted me in the house though, and Lorenzo would always get his own way. I'd keep the apartment though, if I couldn't make him see sense when it came to *M,* id need a place to escape. No way was I going to listen to *that* again.

    I found myself pulling up in the carpark beside a café on the other side of the Lake from the house that I'd have to try to see as my home. Tates, it looked nice enough and I was starving. The sun was warm this morning, so I chose to sit outside, selecting a table at the edge of the seated area, looking onto the lake. Hopefully no one would bother me here.

    A short woman wearing a green apron came out as I was scanning the menu.

    "What can I get for you love?" she asked in a cheery voice. Her name tag read Gina, and I was sure that Gina must be a psychopath. Who was this happy to be at work in the morning?

    "Black coffee, and a sausage and bacon baguette." I replied and stared at the lake. I didn't want to make small talk with this woman. She didn't seem phased by my rudeness though, she just scribbled down my order and bustled away inside.

    Once my food and drink came to my table the seating area surrounding me began to fill. I huffed and took my plate and cup inside, hoping to find that it was quieter inside. I was wrong. There wasn't a single empty table.

    "Everything alright love?" the waitress asked. I shoved my plate and cup onto the counter in front of her.

"Can I get these to go?" I asked.

"Sure thing," she smiled brightly, "not a big fan of crowds?"

"No, or small talk." I gave her a pointed look, but she just laughed in response and handed me my breakfast and coffee.

"Hope your morning gets better." She called after me, but I didn't reply, I just walked out of the door and away from the café. I strolled around the side of the lake and soon found a quiet patch of grass with an empty bench. I doubted I'd see anyone else here, so I sat down on the bench. The view was stunning and tranquil, something I desperately needed in my life. I felt an instant calm wash over me as I sat and enjoyed my breakfast here. Maybe one good thing had come out of this morning, I'd found my perfect escape.

Once I'd finished eating, I stayed and gathered my thoughts. Re-focusing on my goals. I could be angry with Lorenzo for moving on and still earn my place. I'd begin by helping him. I made my way back to my car and headed *home*, hoping that the puttana had left, and I'd be able to speak to Lorenzo alone.

I pulled up to the huge house, leaving my car parked haphazardly in a shaded spot. M hadn't driven here last night, so I had no idea if she was still lurking or not. I pushed through the front door and nodded in greeting as my stepdad's, *no*, *My* head of household staff crossed the foyer, clearly busy with whatever tasks Lorenzo needed him to complete. I'd have to try to get used to that, I'd never had staff before, back in Italy we kept life simple, I could look after myself no trouble, but I now had people who were here to do those things. It felt strange.

"Enzo." I called out and paced the foyer a few times.

"You know I hate that name." he snarled as he emerged from his office dressed in a perfectly fitted royal blue suit that complimented his tanned olive skin.

"Yeah, but I like it," I smirked at him. "she gone?" I asked and gestured up the stairs.

"Yes, she had to get to the office," of course she had a day job, I don't know why it didn't occur to me before that she might, and I was suddenly strangely curious about it.

"What does she do?" I didn't mean to let the question slip out, but it had, and I couldn't take it back. Lorenzo raised a brow at me.

"She's an accountant, very useful woman to have around." I hadn't expected that, she was smart enough to sleep her way to the top, but I didn't realise she was legitimately smart. It didn't make me like her any more or any less, so I pushed past it.

"Hmm," I hummed, "I think we need to talk." I nodded at his office, and he pursed his lips.

"About?" he didn't budge.

"Business." I squeezed past where he stood still in the doorway and sat in a seat facing his desk. He reluctantly followed and sat on the opposite side and typed something on the computer in front of him. He turned his attention to me and rested his elbows on the desk, steepling his fingers under his chin and holding my gaze. I may be new, but I'm not stupid, I know what this gesture means.

"I'm worried about you, Boss." I began, ensuring to use boss rather than anything more familiar. "I think you're being manipulated, and I'd hate to see something bad happen because of it." He stiffened in his chair and his eyes burned into me, but he stayed silent.

"Megan might be a nice girl, but sleeping her way to the top is something that people won't take kindly to." I forced a look of concern to my face. It hurt a little. "I understand that you're a little bit hypnotised by her vagina, so you probably can't see what she's doing, but I can."

He sat back and pressed his forefinger and thumb to the bridge of his nose.

"You're fucking joking aren't you, Don?" he breathed. I slowly shook my head.

"She's bad news boss." All this arse licking and fake concern was not my thing, I didn't care about her, I was starting to care less about him, but I'd have to do it for now I suppose.

"I will tell you this one time Adonis, and if you dare to bring it up again you will be leaving this room in a body bag." He snarled. "M, and you *will* start calling her M, is not sleeping her way to the top, I don't fuck desperate whores, that girl has earned her place in The Brotherhood *and* in my bed. If she dared to try to manipulate me, she would not be breathing. It's insulting that you think that I wouldn't be able to see something like that *if* it was going on. Now get the fuck out of my office and go do something productive." He stared at me for another second. It was an intimidating look, but it didn't work on me, all I felt was anger. I guess I'll have to get her out of my way the hard way then. Knocking her down until she was nothing.

    Still, I rose to my feet and left the office to make my way upstairs and unpack properly. Tonight she would find out what it was like to play with me.

18

Meg

I pulled up around the back of Onyx and checked my reflection in my car mirror. My makeup had remained as perfect as it had looked when I'd left my apartment, all dark and moody, and my hair sat pin straight down my back in a glossy red curtain, I looked good. A dark shadow fell on my window, and I wound it down and jabbed the arsehole leaning against my car in the rib. He didn't move.

"Hey arsehole, move!" I jabbed him again. He turned and bent down to push his head through the open window.

"It's not a beauty pageant *M,* no one gives a shit what you look like." He stepped back, allowing me space to close the window and open the door.

"No *Adonis*, no one gives a shit what *you* look

like." I smirked and stepped out of the car, taking in his usual entirely black suit before heading to the boot.

"I'm presuming you're already armed?" I asked as I pulled a large bag from the boot of my car and hunted through the assortment of weapons inside. I'd chosen to wear a low-cut black dress with slits up both legs. Sexy enough to not look out of place, but practical enough to allow for easy access to the knives and gun that I was strapping to my thighs.

"Obviously." He opened his suit jacket to show off a beautiful smith and wesson sitting in a leather holster.

"Is that it?" I scoffed.

"It's enough," he said bluntly. *Oh well, his funeral.* I knew first-hand how bad nights like tonight could get.

We allowed all local gangs to attend our nightclubs, our bars we're off limits, but the clubs were fine. Except some of the smaller gangs liked to use this to their advantage and attempt to push their product in the venues. It was a known rule that Brotherhood members were the only ones permitted to sell in our clubs. Two simple rules. Don't sell your shit, and don't bring your fights inside our doors. Essentially, we gave everyone a neutral ground to have a good time, if they could behave. The Wolves had also implemented the same in their clubs. We had an even split over the city, Wolves rarely entered our venues and we never bothered with theirs. We were the two most feared gangs in Westeroak, but for the most part we kept out of each other's ways. Sure, we were rivals, but our fights were subtle and smart. Most of the time.

Word had reached Lorenzo this morning that The Vipers had a couple of new initiates, and their initiation tasks; sell out all of their product in the two biggest clubs in the city. Onyx, our place, and Underworld, The Wolves top venue. The arsehole and I had been tasked with the job of finding these idiots and removing them from Onyx if they broke our rules. Sounded simple enough, but more often than not they wouldn't go quietly, and if any other members of their gang were around a fight was bound to break out. I'd rather be prepared for the worst.

I closed my boot and turned to Adonis, finding him staring at me, an irritated look on his face. It made a nice change from the disgusted one he had greeted me with this morning.

"Shall we?" I asked as I adjusted the skirt of my dress and stepped closer to him to slide my phone and keys into the inside pocket of his jacket. He froze and frowned down at me. "I don't have any pockets." I shrugged and he ground his teeth and let out a slow breath.

"Let's go." he snapped, pulling his rage fuelled glare from my face and looking at the club in front of us. He walked a step ahead of me as we made our way around to the front of the club, the fact that he felt that he should be leading rubbed me the wrong way.

"M, you look lovely tonight." Reg said as I pushed past Adonis when we reached the main door.

"Thank you, Reg, this is Adonis, he's new. So I guess I'm on babysitting duty." I smiled and made my way past the man as he held open the door for us.

"Hey man, you're one lucky son of a bitch getting to hang with her tonight, M is the best." He slapped Adonis on the back and strode ahead, "Have a great night sweetheart." Reg called after me and I could almost feel the anger radiating against my back from the arsehole as he silently followed me inside.

"Cute." He said when we reached the bar and I frowned at him,

"What is?" I asked, grabbing a barmaid's attention, and gesturing to the small, seated area that we intended to spend the night in. She nodded and I walked away to select the quietest table for us. Adonis reluctantly followed.

"Your little attempt to make me look small. Darling you have no idea what I'm capable of. If anything, I'm the one who is babysitting you." He sat down next to me on the small sofa that I had selected. It was unexpected, I had presumed that he would pull over another chair and sit on the opposite side of the table. Being this close to him was irritating and distracting.

I shuffled away as far as I could and crossed my legs away from him. "I've seen what you're capable of, and don't call me darling, its M to you. Although, it was quite satisfying when you called me Miss Fields." I mused.

"I'll call you whatever I want, Little Nutmeg, oh that's very fitting, Nutmeg is, in my opinion, the worst spice to ever exist." He smirked and raised his brows at me, not needing to finish his thought out loud. The feeling was mutual though. So I really was not bothered. And it was far better than Darling, or Princess. *Thank god he'd stopped that.*

"Don't expect me to respond nicely if you ever call me that again, Don."

"Don't call me Don." His smirk dropped and a deadly expression replaced it. Apparently I'd touched a nerve. *Good.*

We sat in uncomfortable silence, and both scanned the room. As far as I could see, neither of the two possible guys that we needed to look out for had arrived.

I let myself relax a little and one of the barmaids came over to place our drinks on the table, I didn't recognise her, a new girl, but she obviously had been informed of who I was. She placed a tall, cold soda down first, they would all know that we were here on business, and I don't drink on the job. Next to it she hesitantly placed a pint of beer. I watched Adonis with a smug look on my face, pleased that they didn't know his drink preference, and more pleased that it was so clearly wrong. His face was twisted as though the idea of even taking one sip repulsed him.

"What the fuck is that?" he spat. "Do I look like I drink that piss water?" he turned his aggression towards the barmaid.

"Now now Donny, no one knows who you are, so how would they know what you drink." I spoke up before he could upset the new girl. "Sorry, I don't know your name." I said gently to the barmaid.

"Clara." She said in a quiet voice, a look of concern was etched all over her face. The poor girl wouldn't last long here, she seemed far too sweet.

"Clara, can you take that back," I gestured to the pint, "and get Donny here a," I pondered for a moment, "Whiskey, I'd guess. Probably something top shelf." I looked at the arsehole for confirmation and smiled inwardly as his jaw tensed and he agreed, placing a very specific order. Also completely forgetting his manners. "Thank you, Clara." I shouted to the girl as she scurried away. "Didn't your mother teach you any manners?" I asked Adonis.

"I don't want to talk about my mother." He snapped, "and stop calling me Donny, that's even worse than Don." He folded his arms over his chest like a moody teenager and I couldn't stop myself from laughing.

"Fuck, you're so easy to wind up." He didn't look at me, his expression was struggling to hide an emotion that I didn't expect to see, sadness. Realisation hit me, Selene, she would obviously be a sensitive subject. "Shit Adonis, I'm sorry." I bit my lip. I may not like the guy, but I'm not a monster, grief isn't a joke.

"Don't." he said in a voice so quiet that I almost didn't hear him. But I did, and I understood not to push him.

Clara returned with his corrected drink, and he made himself more comfortable. I found it interesting how quickly he got over the thoughts of his mum, did he not care very much or was he *that* broken. *Just like you, M.*

"So Nutmeg," I rolled my eyes, we were apparently both out to push buttons tonight, and he turned his body to face me, propping his ankle on his knee. There was not enough space on this small sofa for him to sit like that and when his leg pressed against mine the contact sent a jolt through my body that made me want to move away from him instantly, but I wasn't going to let him see that it bothered me. "Do you not think it's a little bit wrong to be fucking Daddy dearest."

I cringed at his words. "Why do you have to say it like that, he isn't your Dad, and no, not that it's any of your business but we have very clear boundaries."

"Yeah sure, looked like it this morning." He

snorted, looking completely disgusted again.

"Are you jealous Donny?" I pouted, "is that why you're being mean to me?" I batted my lashes at him teasingly.

"You repulse me Nutmeg." He said bluntly. But something about the way he looked at me made me question how much truth was in that statement.

"Shame," I smiled and turned to scan the room once again, but I could feel his gaze burning into the side of my face. *Wow it was fun to annoy him.*

A tall guy in a tight white tank top approached our table, and I felt Adonis' eyes leave my face. "What?" he snapped at the tall guy, but the guy ignored him.

"Hey cutie, wanna dance?" he held his hand out to me and I stared at it in amusement.

"No she doesn't want to fucking dance." Adonis snarled, rising from the sofa. I looked up at him in disbelief, did he not think I could turn down a guy by myself?

"I was asking *her*." The tall guy said, turning his attention to Adonis and puffing out his chest. Adonis mirrored him and I relaxed back, grabbing my drink, and preparing myself to enjoy a little show. *Damn, I wish I had some popcorn.*

"Leave. Now." Adonis warned. His muscles visibly straining under the layers of his suit. If I didn't want to kill him, I'd probably find him insanely hot. Ok, I totally found him hot. But being aesthetically pleasing wasn't enough to make him likable. *Just fuckable. Wait, what?*

"What 'cha gonna do arsehole, make me?" the tall guy said cockily. I could fight my own battles, I'd turned down enough persistent guys over the years, but sitting back and watching someone else start it was kinda fun.

"That's exactly what I'm going to do." Adonis said darkly, reaching inside his jacket. Jesus Christ, was he going to shoot the poor prick? Now would be a good time for me to speak up, I'm not willing to let some harmless random guy possibly die because he wanted to try his luck with me. Dammit, why couldn't Don have just punched him like a normal guy. *Why did he even step in in the first place though?*

"That's enough boys," I looked up at the tall guy, "I'm not interested, you should go." I said firmly.

"Oh come on baby, one dance." He said, and I almost vomited at his use of *baby*. It took a special kind of guy to pull that shit off, and he was not it.

"Seriously just go, he's going to shoot you if you don't." I sighed. The tall guy looked shocked. and his eyes flickered between me and Don just as Don moved his gun into the guy's view.

"Screw this, you two are fucking mental." He muttered and quickly walked away.

Adonis sat back down and sipped his drink. "Care to explain what the hell that was all about?" I asked.

"I didn't like the look of him." He shrugged. "Don't read into it, that wasn't some white knight shit. I'm just feeling a little shooty."

"Shooty." I laughed. "Fucking hell, he was right. You *are* mental."

"If you really think that, then I'm right in my assessment that you don't belong in The Brotherhood."

"Your assessment. Who do you think you are?" I choked.

"The person you'll be answering to someday, or not, I doubt you'll last much longer." He smirked, the expression sat on his face so often I wondered if he knew how to smile properly.

"You're underestimating me Donny, I don't know why, surely you're aware of my reputation?" I questioned him.

"Sure, I've heard, but you're not really living up to it."

The insult bothered me more than it should have. Of course I hadn't lived up to it, every time he had seen me close to the action he had come marching in and made a bloody mess. I'd have to be better tonight.

"Time to find out if all of those weapons are just for decoration Nutmeg," he said as his eyes locked on someone on the other side of the room. "The Viper's guy is here, and he's being a very naughty boy."

***

Staring at my reflection in the ladies' room in Onyx I took a couple of slow, steadying breaths. Blood coated my hands and speckles of it were painting my face and chest. I could feel bruises forming on my back, but other than that, I was mostly unharmed.

What the fuck though. Andrew, The Viper's initiate, had stupidly argued back when I had confronted him about his rule breaking, earning him a swift punch to the ribs from me, and a shot in the back of the head from Adonis. As expected, Andrew hadn't been alone, and the other Vipers weren't happy about losing him. My status meant shit to them tonight, if anything it was a challenge. If one of them took me out they'd become legends amongst their people. They'd also end up dead very shortly after, but silly boys like The Vipers don't think that far ahead.

They had descended upon us as a group, keeping a united front and working as a well-oiled team. Something that myself and Adonis definitely were not. Or so I thought. We fell into strange synchronicity with each other, when he used his fists, I used my blades. When I held any of the men immobile, he finished them off. The brief moment where one sneaky little fucker had thrown me onto the floor had ended with Adonis tearing him off of me, snatching up one of my knives from beneath my skirt, and slicing straight through the guy's throat.

Blood had sprayed over me, and he hadn't offered me a hand up after, he just moved on to the next guy. Not that I had expected him to help me, nothing had changed. But *holy shit* we worked well together. He was brutally chaotic, and I was ruthless and controlled. I should have hated how he worked, up until now I had. But up close, our differences complimented each other. *Dammit, I don't want to work well with him.*

    I washed my hands, trying to remove the stain of blood from my fingers before dabbing damp tissue on my face. It was pointless really, I needed to wash properly, but I needed to take a few moments to myself to calm the adrenaline high I was on, so I continued to 'clean' myself up.

    The bar was almost completely empty when I emerged, except for a couple of higher up members of staff and a handful of dead bodies, a few Vipers had escaped badly injured when our staff had calmly removed all bystanders from the club, they were very lucky. Adonis was leaning against the bar, sipping whiskey, his jacket slung over his shoulder and the top buttons of his shirt undone to reveal more of the dark ink that covered his skin. He was still covered in blood, apparently not bothered by it at all. I joined him and he pushed a fresh soda in front of me. I grabbed for a napkin from a pile near me and wiped off the red smudge that he had left on the glass.

    "Thanks, you called in yet?" I asked.

"Yep, done. Lorenzo want's us both back at the house as soon as possible." He drained his glass and headed behind the bar to retrieve a half empty bottle. "If you're going to be fucking the boss all night, I'll need something to knock myself out." He gave me the disgusted look again and I rolled my eyes.

"Really Don, do you have to keep bringing it up?"

"Yep. Just because you've proved you're not *completely* useless doesn't mean I think you're anything more than what I know you to be. You're still a piccola puttana. And don't call me Don." He walked to the door, "I'll be by the car when you're done here." I gave him a quizzical look. "I'm in no state to drive." He answered and took a long swig from the bottle before leaving the club.

I drank my drink slowly as I waited for the clean-up team to arrive. Adonis calling me a whore again had left an uncomfortable feeling in the pit of my stomach. Is that what people would think if they found out? I knew it wasn't true, I wasn't sleeping with Lorenzo to gain anything, except a hell of a lot of pleasure, but did it really look that way? I wasn't getting special treatment, I might have been getting braver with the way I spoke to him, and I pushed him a little further than before, but I didn't get away with shit. He just had different ways of punishing me. I wasn't getting anything out of it that any of the other brothers wanted. But maybe stepping away from Lorenzo's bed would be a safer option for now. Things were getting confusing anyway. Sometimes it's better to quit while you're ahead.

Adonis was sitting in the passenger seat of my car when I finally made it down to the car half an hour later. I grabbed my keys and phone from where he had tossed them into a cupholder and quickly scanned my messages.

"Are you fucking Cooper too?" he asked.

"What? No." I replied quickly, taken aback by the thought. *Fuck no.*

"Then why is he texting you asking what time you're free for lunch tomorrow?" he narrowed his eyes at me.

"You looked at my messages? What the fuck. Do you not understand the concept of privacy?"

"You *gave* me your phone. And I'm a curious by nature." He shrugged.

"I'll bring a bag next time." I put my key in the ignition and pulled out of the back road. "And normal people go out for lunch with their friends." I glared across at him. "But I don't suppose you have any of those."

He growled low in his throat but didn't speak. A tiny part of me felt sorry for him, living such a lonely life, but with the way he treated people it wasn't surprising. I might be a very dark, screwed up person, mixed up in some unthinkable things, but at least I was nice, to people who deserved it.

We arrived at Lorenzo's house in no time,

partially because the roads were so empty, partly because I was speeding the entire way to avoid being stuck in a confined space with the arsehole for too much longer.

Adonis climbed out of my car and slammed the door with unnecessary force. I was too tired of his attitude to react though. He pushed through the front door, and I followed in behind, noticing a startled Clive stood on the spot and pointing towards the boss's office.

"Thanks' Clive, sorry about him." I offered him a small smile and he nodded.

"He's going to take some getting used to." He muttered as he disappeared down a hallway.

Lorenzo was sitting in his usual chair behind his desk and was smiling like a madman.

"Beautiful work tonight you two, my little dream team, best friends in the making." We looked at each other, our faces mirroring each other with pure hatred.

"You're kidding right?"

19

Lorenzo

The looks on their faces were priceless, and I snorted a small laugh. "What a shame, you could use a friend Don."

"I have better taste than *that*." he said and side eyed M, who had slumped into one of the chairs and looked completely unphased by his insult.

"Hmm," I pushed the urge to defend her to one side. "Well I expect the rest of the Vipers will be enraged by how many men they lost tonight, 7 dead, 4 injured, honestly I'm surprised that they'd have that many men in one location, especially our venue, but then again, they are bottom of the food chain for a reason." I thought aloud. "Not really living up to their name. Anyway, nothing to worry about, you've shown them what happens if they cross us." I smiled between my stepson and the girl who had managed to captivate my every thought. Pride bubbled up inside me.

"If there's nothing else to discuss I'm going to go clean up and-." Adonis didn't bother to finish his sentence, just raised an almost empty whiskey bottle, and shook it before wandering out of my office. Well I suppose he deserved to celebrate however he wanted.

I turned my attention to M, "You look breathtaking in that dress il mio tesoro, and watching you tonight was mesmerising." She pushed her hair over her shoulder and sighed.

"Thank you, boss." *Boss. Ex-fucking-scuse me?!*

"Spit out whatever is on your mind then." I snapped, making no attempt to hide that I was not happy about her use of 'boss'.

Her mouth fell open in shock, I'd never given her a chance to voice her thoughts, sometimes she pushed it and told me anyway, but this was different. It was something that I'd been thinking about since my inability to work out how to break down her wall, it felt like it might work, but I'd been scared to use it, hence the poor wording. But I was giving her a level of power and it felt wrong.

"Maybe," she chewed her lower lip, "Maybe we should stop all of this." She dropped her gaze to her lap and twisted her fingers together. *No.*

"Is that what you want?" I asked, pushing all emotion out of my voice. This is what I didn't want,

I didn't want to give her a chance to hurt me. The idea of no longer being more than her 'boss' was something I didn't want to think about. But it was clearly something that had crossed her mind.

"I don't know, I don't know what I want." She kept her eyes down, she was telling the truth though, she wouldn't look that uncomfortable if she was completely certain of her choice.

"Is that why you've been out chasing other men?" I spat, instantly regretting the words leaving my mouth, I shouldn't be pushing her away with outbursts like that, but the revelation that I wasn't the only man who had her attention had been bothering me all day.

"I wouldn't put it quite like that," she looked up at me then, the feisty glint returning to her eyes. I loved that look. "But sure, I've kept my options open."

Her honesty was weirdly refreshing, even if her confession hurt. Only now I couldn't stop myself from wondering how many men she had taken a liking to.

"How many men amore, who else? Cooper? *Adonis?*" I snarled my stepsons name, despising the thought that maybe their hatred towards each other might be an act.

"You're insane if you think that," she snapped. "Cooper is my friend, and I'd rather fuck Grey than let Adonis anywhere near my vagina." She crossed her arms and shook her head in disbelief. "I'm not some whore, no matter what *some* people might think, and that is exactly why I think we need to stop."

"So one guy calls you a whore, a guy you don't even like, and you're suddenly willing to walk away?" I raised a brow at her.

"It's just sex." she sighed.

She was lying. She had to be lying. I'd show her, she would see that she was lying to herself. I couldn't lose her. Because if I lost her, it would be for good. I took a long breath as I quickly worked out the best phrasing to stop this stupid conversation from going any further south.

"You're unsure about this, you don't know what you want. So don't make any hasty decisions. Stay, for now." She shifted in the chair. "And I'll protect you. No one else will find out." I gave her a stern look, silently reassuring her that Adonis would not ruin this.

"I can't." she eventually said. I tensed. "I mean, I can't stay right now. I need space, I'll be back next week?" she gave me a small smile.

"Fine, until next week." We both rose from our chairs, and I rounded the desk towards her.

"I'm still confused though Lorenzo." She breathed as she ran her fingers down the centre of my shirt.

"For now." I tipped her chin up with a finger and lowered my lips to hers in a gentle kiss. I pulled away far too quickly, desperate for more, but aware that I'd leave her wanting too. I scanned over her blood splattered face and smiled. She was my dark soul's wet dream.

I dropped her chin and left my office, I needed a drink, and she needed to leave before I did something stupid, like beg her to stay. I could wait for her. I'd have to wait for her. But I would never beg.

Although something would have to be done about that little obstacle. The guy she went on that date with. I poured myself a large drink and pondered, who the fuck was he?

20

Meg

I spent the weekend trying to avoid thinking about Lorenzo and the conversation we'd had. One minute he was hot, the next he was damn near arctic. I couldn't keep up.

At first when he had given me the opportunity to voice my concerns it had felt like a tiny baby step towards some kind of real connection. But then he flipped the switch, accusing me of wanting multiple men, which I did not. Not exclusively anyway. And then he changed his tone again and had asked me to stay. I had no idea what to do. The man needed to learn how to set his intentions clearly. I supposed we were both as bad as each other though. I clearly had no idea what I wanted either.

On Sunday morning I realised that I hadn't heard from Toby at all since our date. I'd be seeing him that evening for our usual session, and an uncomfortable feeling sat with me. Had he not had a good time? Was it now going to be awkward this evening? This is why you don't try to date guys who you have to see again. I really liked that gym. I didn't want to have to find a new one.

I grabbed my phone and hovered my thumb over his number. I couldn't bring myself to call though. Damn I had the biggest balls in the world sometimes, I could take down guys twice my size, yet calling a guy that I kinda liked scared me. Fuck it, I'd see him later. That gave me the entire day to pull myself together and hype myself up to ask him what went wrong.

***

When it was finally time to go to the gym and see Toby, I had pulled myself into a better frame of mind.

"Why didn't you call?" I blurted as I walked up behind him in the gym. *Ok, maybe I was still a bit nervous.* He spun around to face me, startled by my outburst.

"Erm, Hi to you too." He frowned. "What do you mean?"

"You didn't call." I twisted my braided hair between my fingers, feeling stupid for the way I was acting. *Pull it together woman.*

"No, *you* didn't call." He walked away and began to stretch. I followed him and sat on a mat next to where he stood, grabbing my toes and feeling a small crack in my back as I stretched out my aching muscles. Fighting in inappropriate footwear was not good for my body.

"What? Since when do girls call first?" I asked. He had a point though, was my idea of dating that outdated? Why should he have called first? I'm awful at this dating stuff.

"You said you'd call later. At first, I was worried about you when I hadn't heard from you, but you're always telling me that you're a big strong girl who can handle herself, so I ended up presuming that you'd just not had a good time and that you were ghosting me." he shrugged. "Not the case?" he looked hopeful.

"Shit, no." I bit my lip as I remembered our parting conversation. "I'm so sorry, things got a bit -." I fumbled for an appropriate word. I'd found out that the guy who had been messing with my reputation was a new Brother, and then I had gone and angry fucked my 'boss', how do you put that into a word? "-stressful," *Sure, that would have to do.* "I had a good time, Toby." I smiled up at him. He sighed heavily and returned it.

"Maybe I'll let you make it up to me then," his gentle smile morphed into a wicked grin, "But for now, little vixen, I plan on torturing you for an hour, maybe two." The words made me swallow hard and he pushed his hair away from his face, securing it with an elastic. The way his loose tank-top lifted as he moved and teased me with a glimpse of his toned. tattooed stomach had me close to drooling. I was glad I hadn't completely fucked it up between us and I had a feeling that Toby could tolerate a lot of my less desirable traits, like disappearing without explanation. This guy was the full package. I just needed to find out if he could handle the dark parts of my life. Not yet though. Until the time felt right, I'd go back to having my cake and eating it too.

Toby's plan to torture me had not been a joke. Every muscle in my body was on fire after an hour.

"Ten more minutes?" he asked as I practically fell off of the bench I'd been laying on.

"How about ten more seconds?" I gave him my best puppy-dog eyes and he chuckled. It was a low, sexy sound that made my thighs clench.

"Ten minutes, and I'll sweeten the deal with the irresistible offer of dinner at my place. Cooked by yours truly." How could I say no to that, the man was offering up a second chance *and* a home cooked meal. I had no idea if he could cook very well, but the idea of him even trying made me want him even more. But I couldn't *just* agree.

"Seven, and I'll make dessert?" I pushed.

"Nine, and I'll *be* dessert." He gave me an exaggerated wink.

"Eight, and *I'll* be dessert." I tossed back.

"Deal." He grinned. I probably shouldn't have encouraged him to flirt with me while he was working, but fuck it, it was nice to have a little fun.

"Tobes, can you come and help me with something in the office real quick?" a guy approached us, he was huge, bigger than Toby, and wearing nothing but a pair of bright yellow shorts and matching trainers.

"Can it wait a few, Matt?" Toby asked, looking a little frustrated.

"Not really man, I've got a guy waiting and I can't do anything until it's sorted." He looked genuinely apologetic, but the way Toby huffed made me think that maybe this was a pretty common occurrence.

"Fine, you better pay attention this time though," he turned to me, "I'll be back, don't go thinking you're getting out of our deal." He ran his tongue over his lower lip, and I felt my face heat.

I watched him walk away, quietly admiring the way his muscles moved.

"Shall I get you a mop?" a voice came from behind me. Pulling me from my little trance. Every inch of my body prickled with irritation.

"What the fuck are *you* doing here." I snarled, turning to face him.

"My job, apparently." Adonis ran his eyes over my sweat coated body and narrowed them as they found their way back to my face.

"Which is?" I kept my voice low. People here didn't know who I was associated with.

"Firstly, retrieving you. And then a quick chat

with a man about a dog." I rolled my eyes at his stupid response.

"And that takes two of us?" I stepped back to ensure that I had enough space and began a gentle stretch, knowing full well my body would be screaming tomorrow if I didn't. It would probably be screaming regardless, but habits.

"Come on Nutmeg, don't make me carry you." he said, ignoring my question.

"You wouldn't dare." I growled.

"If it gets this over and done with then yes, I would." He gave me a hard stare and I bent forward to touch my toes. Moving slowly to ensure I was really annoying him,

"I need to go and change." I said as I straightened up, he shook his head sharply. "Fine, but I do need to go and get my bag."

He shook his head again and lifted my black duffle bag to my face. "Done." He said simply.

"Unbelievable." I breathed in annoyance. He threw my bag over his shoulder and walked off.

"Hurry up Nutmeg, we're already late." He called over his shoulder.

"Fucking arsehole." I hissed under my breath, noticing that every set of eyes in the gym were on the two of us. It was hardly surprising, seeing as he stood out like a sore thumb in his suit. I couldn't help but wonder how he would look in something more comfortable, he was clearly in good shape, and I doubted that he worked out in a suit. For some reason, I was now itching to see it.

I quickly caught up with him as he strolled past the reception desk and walked towards the front doors. I noticed a door marked private on the other side of the lobby swing open, and I turned to meet Toby's confused frown.

"Sorry," I mouthed. "I'll call you. Promise." I held my hand up to mimic a phone and then drew a cross over my heart. He squinted at the back of Adonis' head and then looked back at me and gave me a quick nod.

"You better." He mouthed back and lifted his brows. I bit my lip and smiled before rushing after Adonis, who was now stood outside and looking even more pissed off than usual.

"Is the boss not enough for you Nutmeg?" He asked as I made my way to his car.

"Why do you even care?" I tossed back.

"You're screwing with my family. Family means something to me." he said as he moved to the driver's side of the car. "and I'd quite like to see you removed from it."

"So you're going to go running back to Lorenzo and tell him that I was flirting with someone? He already knows, and I'm still here." I smirked and climbed into his car.

"For now." I heard him mutter as I closed the door. He got in his side and tossed my bag onto the back seat. I leaned over and rooted around for my phone. Once I'd found it, I got comfy and pulled open my messages. I found the thread I was looking for and typed out a message.

Megan
I'm really sorry. Raincheck on dinner? Maybe tomorrow? X

I pressed send and then opened my news app and scrolled through the top stories, I wasn't interested in reading them, but I didn't want to talk to the arsehole sat next to me. A few minutes later a message popped up.

Toby
Tomorrow. But it's your last chance Vixen. Don't break my heart ;) x

Megan
I'll call you later. X

 I sighed, happy that he wasn't mad. I tried not to think too deeply into that last part of his message. There was no way his heart was invested in this yet. But a tiny part of my hoped that it might be.
 "How old are you?" Adonis' voice cut through my happy bubble.
 "Twenty-two," I answered, "Why?" Why was he suddenly taking an interest in me?
 "Because you're sat there sighing at your phone like a little lovesick thirteen-year-old. Act your age." The last three words came out with so much authority that I froze. Staring at him with my

mouth open. I blinked and pushed my tongue into my cheek, having no idea how to respond.

I threw my phone back behind me towards my bag and looked out of the window. Men didn't usually render me speechless, but there had been something in his tone that had me shocked. If I didn't hate the idea of him telling me what to do, I'd say he would make a good leader. Luckily that wasn't likely to happen.

"Stay here." He commanded as he pulled up outside a bar that I recognised but had never been inside of. "I'll just be a minute."

21

Tobias

Who the hell was that guy? I'd only seen his back as he had walked out of the main doors. He had stood outside waiting for Megan, but the stupid frosted glass of the windows had only allowed me to see a vague silhouette and had stopped me from being able to see his face. But I knew that I needed to not make any presumptions, she said she would call, and I'd just have to trust that she'd remember this time.

When her text message came through shortly after she had left, I instantly relaxed. She was clearly trying to make up for her crappy communication. But I was still confused by her rapid departure. Why did she have to leave so fast and with no explanation. It all seemed a little strange. Was she wrapped up in something dodgy? There were enough gangs in Westeroak for her to have some kind of affiliation, I know she used to be close to The Brotherhood because her brother had been a member, maybe she now handled some of their accounts. Even if she did, what business would she have to handle at this time of night? And why did I find this mysterious side of her so hot?

    I shook myself off, putting a stop to my train of thought. If I kept trying to guess I'd start coming up with some insane stories and probably end up thinking she was an alien who had come to earth to kill us all or some shit. She said she would call, so I just had to wait. But not just wait, that would be dumb. I'd need a distraction.

    I pulled my phone back out of my shorts pocket and dialled the number of my favourite person in the whole world.

    "Tobias, sweetheart, are you alright?" my mum's voice came through laced with concern. She had no reason to worry about me, but I supposed that's what mothers did.

    "I'm fine Mum, is Dad around?" I asked.

    "Not tonight, business meeting, you know how late they can run." I could almost hear her eyes rolling.

    "Shall we have dinner then? My treat." I loved having dinner with my mum. Dad was rarely around, she didn't mind that, but I could tell she got lonely sometimes.

    "No no baby, no treats. I have pasta on

already, come over instead." I had secretly hoped that she would say that. Mum's cooking was the main thing that I missed since leaving home. I could cook reasonably well, she had taught me, and my closest friend, Emilia, was a chef, so I was always picking up new tricks, but nothing beat mums cooking.

"I'll be there once I've showered. Love you." I said out of habit, it didn't matter if I was seeing her in twenty minutes or twenty days, I'd never end a call with her without uttering those two simple words.

"Love you." she said back, and the line went dead.

Luckily Megan was always the last client of my day, we had hour sessions pencilled, but sometimes she wanted or needed more of my time, so I never booked anyone after. I just had to hope that the new guy, Matteo, wasn't having any more technical difficulties. The guy had only been here a week and had forgotten his staff login to access our computer system nine times. He was lucky he was a damn good trainer and had bought a lot of new business with him otherwise he would've been out on day one.

"I'm heading out." I called through the gym door after I'd showered. I pulled my damp hair up into a neat-*ish* bun. Mum would tell me I need a haircut, just like she did every time she saw me, and I'd tell her to tell Dad the same. She never would, she loved his hair, and I think she secretly loved mine too.

"Catch you later bro," Matteo called back.

"James is by the pool if you need him." I reminded him. "See you tomorrow."

I liked James, he was a great guy, a lifeguard, and I'd got into the habit of changing our schedules so that we were working at the same time. He didn't mind and it meant I always had someone to annoy when I got bored between clients, and that when we weren't here, we could always go grab a beer together.

I grabbed my bag from where I'd left it by the locker room door and left to go to my parents' house. It didn't take me long to arrive and Mum was dishing up an enormous bowl of pasta for me as I walked through the door.

"Worried that I'm going to waste away Mum?" I joked and nodded at the bowl before leaning down and planting a kiss on her cheek.

"You're a growing boy, you need it." she grinned up at me and lines creased around her eyes.

"I think I'd say I'm fully grown by now, wouldn't you?" I said and sat down at the small dining table.

"You seem bigger every time I see you sweetheart." She joined me and placed our food down on the table before pulling off the floral apron that she always wore when she was cooking and smoothed down her dress.

"And you seem smaller, are you shrinking in your old age?" her hand playfully tapped the back of my head.

"Less of the old, and get a haircut!" I rolled my eyes and smiled lovingly at my mum. I opened my mouth, but she beat me to it. "No, I will not tell your dad to get one too." We both laughed, never growing tired of the same conversation.

We ate and chatted for a long time, Mum refilled my bowl twice and I was sure I'd burst if I even attempted to eat one more thing. For once I turned down dessert and found myself smiling as I remembered my conversation with Megan. It may have been a joke, but I really did want to know what she tasted like. Especially her lips, they had been the first thing I'd noticed about her when she had approached me to ask about my services. I'd managed to hold a conversation with her, but I couldn't stop myself from staring at her perfect rose-coloured lips.

"Tobias, you have a dreamy look on your face, who is she?" mum asked, and I realised I'd been staring into space for a while.

"Just a girl from work, I'll tell you more when there is more to tell." I gave her a wink and she frowned.

"So you work with her? Or you train her?" she crossed her arms and gave me a stern look, and I sank into my chair like a child about to be told off.

"I train her." I winced, aware of where she

was going with this.

"Tobias, you cannot take advantage of some girl that you train!" she scolded.

"Mum," I quickly defended myself, "you bought me up better than to take advantage of anyone. And this girl can more than handle herself. Honestly, I don't even know why she comes to me, I guess for motivation on bad days, but overall, she doesn't need me."

"You shouldn't mix work and romance sweetheart." She softened a little, but kept her arms folded.

"If things go any further, I'll pass her on to Matteo, he can train her instead." I reassured her.

"Good, so what is she like?" she smiled now, a beautiful wide smile that could light up any room.

"Nope, I'm not getting either of us excited until there's anything to tell, but if it works out, oh Mum, you'll love her." I mirrored my mums smile, it was the only thing I'd inherited from her, and I loved it.

"I hope so." She reached for my hand, and I let her hold it for a while as we spoke about work, family, and food.

I checked my phone before I left and saw that I had another message from Megan.

Megan
Sorry it's so late, I'll call you soon. x

She was trying so hard to communicate better. It was beyond cute, and this girl claimed to not do cute. I'd seen it though, she had it in there, it just took a little work to lure it out of her.

I replied telling her that I'd be home in half an hour, so I'd be waiting for her call. I hoped she didn't take it too literally, but I would most likely end up waiting by my phone and bouncing around like an over excited puppy. The girl had that effect on me. She made me feel light and bouncy. Even if she wasn't that herself. I felt like I could be her sunshine. Her cool, hilarious, charming, ray of sunshine.

***

I parked my truck on a quiet road around the back of my apartment building and walked around to the main doors. An unfamiliar man was stood leaning against the wall where the intercom was. I didn't need to use it, obviously, I lived there, but I wasn't happy about some strange guy being there, he didn't look friendly. In the glow of the streetlights I could see that his face was heavily scarred. He was clothed in black leather and heavy looking boots. If Mrs Rowell from downstairs took her dog Terry out to do his business while this guy was here, she might have a heart attack. I couldn't have that, she was a nice old lady, and she made a mean apple pie.

"Hey, you waiting for someone? If not, I'm

going to have to ask you to move along." I said as I approached the scarred man.

"Yeah I am." He said in a deep grumbly voice, it sounded a little put on, but whatever. He was scary enough without the over-the-top voice stuff.

"Who?" I asked, not sure if I believed him or not. I knew every person in this building, if he lied, I'd know.

"You." he looked me dead in the eye. There was something familiar about him now that I had a better view of his face. I'd seen it before, but I couldn't place it.

"Me? Right." I said, trying to work out who he was. It shouldn't have been too hard. You don't see many people with a face like that. "So how do we know each other?"

"We don't. But you've pissed off my boss, so I'm here issuing you your first warning." he looked me up and down.

"Who's your boss?" I said, straightening up so that I stood tall. My size made me pretty intimidating, so pulling a subtle move like this should have been enough for him to think twice about starting anything. He pushed off of the wall though and did the same. He was smaller than me in every way, but I had a feeling that his size didn't matter.

"Lorenzo D'Angelo." He said with a dark smirk. *Fuck.*

It hit me; this man was Lorenzo D'Angelo's second in command. I'd seen him before. I didn't take too much interest in the gang stuff around here, but I'd seen him in action, being smaller than me *definitely* didn't matter to him. There was no doubt in my mind that he was armed. I'd have to be very careful here. Hold back on the sarcastic comments. This guy would not appreciate any jokes either.

"Uh huh, so what have I done to piss him off? I've never met the man." I held myself tall still, not showing any signs of fear. Careful, but not showing weakness.

"You're dating his girl, that needs to stop. Now." He took a step closer to me. "If it doesn't," he pulled a knife from inside his jacket and pressed the tip against my stomach. "I'll find very creative ways of hurting you." he smiled a sadistic smile and my brows pulled together.

"You sure you've got the right guy?" he pushed the blade harder against me, any more pressure and he'd probably rip my shirt and break skin.

"I never get the wrong guy. Stay the fuck away from Megan Fields." He pushed the blade, and a warm trickle of blood slid down towards the waistline of my shorts.

"Who?" I gritted out. It didn't hurt, he had only scratched me.

"Oh, of course, you'd know her as Megan Clarke." He said and stepped back and smirked as my face dropped at that name. "You won't get a second warning. So I wouldn't bother even thinking about pushing it, boy, she is not worth it." he shot me a look of repulsion and walked off down the road.

"I'm her trainer." I called after him, "he does know that right?"

"You better keep things professional then." He turned and said, "you can be easily replaced."

Shaking slightly, I took myself inside, climbing the stairs to my apartment floor and fumbling with my keys before letting myself inside. What the hell. Megan was with Lorenzo D'Angelo; she was trying to date us both? It wasn't a shock that she knew him, Jason, her brother who had died last year, was a member of The Brotherhood, the gang that Lorenzo was the head of. But dating him? How had that even happened? And *Fields*, who was she? Clarke or Fields, and why was she using more than one name?

I found my phone and saw two missed calls, Both from her. I had a million questions for her, but I couldn't risk calling her back. I valued my life. I wasn't going to make stupid choices. Ignoring that threat wouldn't just put me in danger. I had heard enough stories about Lorenzo to know that she wouldn't be safe if I came between them.

Oh Vixen, what the fuck have you gotten yourself in to.

22

Don

"Lorenzo D'Angelo sends his regards." I smirked as I let the lifeless body of *Skunk* fall to my feet and walked out of the bar. I wasn't covered in blood for once, choosing a clean method tonight. It was under Lorenzo's orders, go in, quick and clean, get out, send a clear message. It wasn't quite as satisfying as the brutal, bloody messes I usually made, but I had to stay in his good books after the number of lines that I had crossed recently.

I got back into the car and silently drove on. I fucking hated this stupid babysitting shit that Lorenzo had me doing. He didn't have to say that was what it was, but it clearly was. The only thing that bought me any joy was the knowledge that she hated it too, and anything that ruined her day made mine a little better.

I'd snapped Skunks neck, it was a new move for me, I'd only ever seen it done in films, thought it was a bit of a joke really. I'd had to use a lot of force to cause that fatal snap, and it had released a lot of pent-up feelings. When I'd first let Uncle Sal start training me, I'd learned that this kind of stuff worked as great stress relief, and tonight had been a pretty good release.

My little murder high didn't last for very long though, as little Nutmeg decided to speak to me, again.

"Are you going to tell me what we're doing then arsehole?" she asked irritably.

"Nope." I popped the 'p' and kept facing forward, focusing on the road ahead and hoping my lack of interest in her would shut her up.

"How am I supposed to get ready if I don't even know what we're doing? I'm calling Lorenzo." She moved to reach over into the backseat of my car, and I swung the steering wheel, making her jolt back into her seat, then straightened back up and continued down the road as if nothing had happened.

"What the fuck is your problem?" she shrieked. I didn't respond, so she attempted to go and find her phone, again. I swerved, again.

"Argh." The sound of her frustration was music to my ears. I couldn't wait to hear the noise she made when she realised where we were heading.

"You shouldn't need to *get ready*, you should be able to think on your toes." I said, knowing that my criticism would bother her.

She sat still in her seat, and I felt her gaze burning into the side of my head. I let a cruel smirk sit on my lips. She was going to lose her shit. I turned left, and she looked out of the window, another left and she snapped her head back to face me.

"Why are we here?" she said in a shockingly calm voice. I didn't answer, I just kept driving. "Adonis, why the fuck are we *here*." Oh, there it is, there's the rage. Her voice was icy cold. Little Nutmeg had finally realised what was going on.

"There isn't a job, is there?" she snarled.

"Oh, there *was* a job." I turned to her as I pulled up to the large gate and waited for it to open. "but you weren't on it." I quickly lifted my mouth to a sarcastic smile and then dropped it to a cold, stiff line.

The gate opened just as she let out a scream of anger. "So what, you're just some fucking courier service now? Picking me up and dropping me off to him whenever he sees fit!"

"It's more like a babysitting service," I said, "except I'd prefer an actual baby over your bratty ass."

"You're such an arsehole Adonis, fuck you!" she yelled in my face.

"Don't shout at me Nutmeg, I'm not the one calling the shots here." I raised my brows at her, and she sat back. Letting me drive up the long, twisting driveway in peace.

"Sorry Don." She whispered.

"Don't." I warned. I hated that. I didn't want her apology. And I didn't want her calling me Don. Mum used to call me Don, and now I could only tolerate hearing it come from a select few people's mouths. Megan was not one of those people. She never would be.

"Do you really hate me that much? You can't even let me apologise?" she asked, and I cut the engine. I had nothing to say. Yes, it was true that I couldn't stand her, but what was the point in saying it out loud.

"Fine, I take it back then," she leaned closer to me, pushing her lips towards my ear, "Fuck. You." she whispered.

"In your dreams darling." I looked at her from the corner of my eye, she was so close, I could smell the lemon body wash that she had used at some point today, it was subtle now, mixed with sweat. My jaw tensed as I breathed her in, how did someone that I found so repulsive smell so damn tempting. I blinked away whatever the hell had just come over me and opened my door. As I climbed out of the car I heard her exhale, a deep, ragged noise that sent a tingle through my entire body. I leaned back down to look inside my car with my brows pulled tightly together. She was sat with one hand on her chest, her fingers gently tapping, and the other slowly caressing her earlobe. *What was that?* She noticed me watching her and suddenly dropped both hands, straightening up and plastering a furious look on her face.

"Fuck off Adonis." She snapped.

"So aggressive, hurry up." I slammed my car door, instantly wincing at the noise, this was a nice car, I shouldn't let some pathetic *cagna* piss me off enough to potentially damage it.

She grabbed her bag and followed me into the house. "Clive." I nodded. That man was like a magician, always appearing out of nowhere and disappearing in the blink of an eye. The first few days here I didn't even know the guy's name, Lorenzo hadn't exactly given me some big house tour or introduced me to any of the staff, so I just worked shit out for myself, like I did with most things in my life. Listening to other people, watching them, working out what was what. It wasn't hard, but not many people seemed to be capable of it.

"Mr Knight, I have made up the guest room for you while the adjustments you requested are being taken care of. It shouldn't be for more than one night." I nodded and thanked him.

Lorenzo had selected a room for me, apparently Mum had set it up for me in hope that one day I'd come and visit. I hadn't. The room was fine, not to my taste though. The furniture was all glass and metal, it was harsh and cold, I could see why she had presumed I'd like it, it fitted my personality well. But I'd requested it all be removed and replaced with solid oak pieces. Something myself and my stepdad had in common was our appreciation of beautifully handcrafted wood. My room had floor to ceiling windows like the master bedroom and it was one of the only things I liked about the room as it was. I had laid in my bed the first night here and fantasised about fucking some girl against the glass, looking out onto the moonlit grounds. I'd have to make that fantasy a reality soon.

    The biggest change that I'd requested for my room had caused and argument between myself and Lorenzo. The room next to mine was a bathroom, I'd be the only one using it, but I didn't like the fact that I had to leave my room to access it. I wanted a door fitted from my room.

    Lorenzo had finally caved when I'd threatened to move back into my apartment. He had agreed to the changes so long as I sold the apartment. I said that I would do it, but it was a lie. No way was I giving up that place.

    "Good evening, M," I heard the man say as I made my way to Lorenzo's office. She greeted him with that overly polite way that she spoke to people, putting on the nice girl act that irritated me so much. "The boss has requested you wait for him in the dining room while he finishes up" he informed her. I glanced over my shoulder and was not disappointed when I caught the look on her face. Her tongue was pushed into her cheek and a small v shape had formed between her eyebrows. I tossed her a smug look, accompanied with a small finger wave, and continued into Lorenzo's office.

"Oh dear *boss*, you have royally pissed off your little puttana tonight." His eyes shot up to mine, a murderous shadow crossing them.

"Do you think it's wise to continue calling her a whore?" He asked, his tone sharp.

I clicked my tongue and flopped down into one of the chairs opposite him. I shrugged and smiled at him, "You're not going to kill me for it, so…"

"Don't presume Adonis, One day I might." His eyes darkened further, but the slight lift to the corner of his lips confirmed that I'd gotten away with it this time. "I presume everything went smoothly this evening." He adopted a comfortable position and glanced at his phone as a message notification pinged. An evil smirk spread over his face and curiosity sparked inside me.

"Smooth, clean, perfect. What's got you pulling out the evil villain smile?"

He laughed darkly, "Found someone I've been looking for."

"Should I head back out?" I asked, cracking my knuckles and praying this person needed to be taught a lesson.

"Not tonight son, Grey is dealing with this one." I scowled at his use of the word 'son', but I brushed it off quickly. "Do you need to discuss anything else with me? I'm late for a very important date." He said as he stood and unbuttoned his shirt sleeves and folded them neatly to expose his tanned forearms.

"No," I got up and walked to the door, "enjoy your *date*." I let disgust lace my voice and my face twisted to match it.

"I will, enjoy your right hand." He gave me a knowing look.

"Left, actually." I corrected him.

I wasn't going to be doing that though, it had been too long, and I needed the real thing. I'd managed to accumulate a few phone numbers since arriving here in Westeroak. I hadn't taken any of these girls up on their offers, I wasn't the type to sleep with random girls, but needs must. That barmaid from Onyx, the shy one, Clara, she would probably be my best option. She might be fun, she had already managed to surprise me by even giving me her number, and I didn't think she would be the type to show off about being with me. A lot of the girls I'd met seemed the type to brag about fucking a monster like me. I hated girls like that.

I made my way to the kitchen and sent a message to the shy girl inviting her over. She replied a few minutes later telling me she would be finishing work at 11pm and could be here by 11.30. It gave me enough time to grab something to eat, shower, and catch up on my own business. I'd not checked in for a week now and I was annoyed with myself for pushing it to the back of my mind for so long.

I started to hunt through a drawer, trying to find a takeout menu that looked appealing. Cooking wasn't my thing. I could do it, but I didn't enjoy it. Not when it was a meal for one, and I still wasn't completely comfortable with the staff here doing shit for me. Raised voices echoed from the room next door and I paused my hunt to listen to Nutmeg exploding at Lorenzo. She was furious with him for the stunt he had pulled tonight, and in all honesty, I was on her side. Not that I'd ever tell her that, but the way Lorenzo had planned to get her here was kinda messed up, if it had been anyone else, I might have attempted to talk him out of it. I smiled to myself as she went on a long rant. Had she forgotten who she was talking to? I waited for his response once she had finally stopped yelling. But it never came. He hadn't shouted back, there were no gunshots, nothing. Was he *tolerating* this? I had the sudden urge to be a fly on the wall in that room. How was she getting away with that?

I shook my head in disbelief and picked up the closest menu, I scanned it and called the number, ordering myself a large vegetarian pizza. Clive would get the door and bring it to me when it arrived, just like he had done the last time I'd decided that I didn't want to cook, or eat with Lorenzo.

Once I was in the guest bedroom I checked the wardrobe, finding a selection of my clothes hung carefully. Good, I wouldn't have to go to hunting for them. I kicked my shoes off and headed to the bathroom, feeling slightly annoyed that I'd had to argue for a door to be fitted in my room when the guest bedroom had an en suite. None of my own toiletries were in here, but a new toothbrush was sitting on the side and fresh towels were hanging on the heated rail.

I tossed my clothes into a hamper across the room and switched on the shower. The water warmed to a comfortable heat within seconds, and I stepped under the stream, closing my eyes and taking a few slow breaths.

I reached for the body wash bottle that sat half empty on a shelf and squeezed a generous amount into my hand. The scent hit my nose as I began to lather the soap over my skin. Lemons. I froze. She used this. This was hers. And now I smelled like the girl I despised. That tempting fucking scent. I rinsed it off as thoroughly as I could and hunted for something else, anything that didn't smell like her, But I came up short, all that was in here was lemon body wash and a honey shampoo and conditioner set, all hers. I coated my skin in the honey shampoo, scrubbing my skin until red marks were showing between my tattoos, sure that's not what it was for, but at least my brain didn't associate that scent with her as deeply as the lemon.

When I stepped out of the shower I was tense and filled with disgust and annoyance. In the bedroom, placed on a lap-tray on the edge of the bed, was a pizza box. It had come fast, but my appetite had completely gone. I flipped the top of the box open and hoped that the warm gooey food inside would bring it back. It didn't. I forced down a couple of slices as I sat in a loosely wrapped towel, the food now only serving the purpose of fuelling my body rather than being enjoyable. Fucking cagna had ruined my dinner without even being in the same room as me.

I pushed myself to ignore any thought that had anything to do with Megan and focused on the paperwork that Emilio had sent over from the shop. I'd bought the empty space when I'd been searching for somewhere to live, the huge space below the simple apartment looked like the perfect place to open my own tailors. Emilio had followed me across the sea when I'd told him my plan. We had worked together for four years back home in Italy, he was far more talented than I was, I had a great eye for style, but my business brain was what would make us an incredible team. It had only taken a couple of weeks for us to have the place ready to open. It helped that Lorenzo was supportive of this venture, and I had every single one of his contacts at my disposal. E D Tailors was doing well from what I could see, the launch had been successful, and the work had kept coming, I was proud of myself, of both of us.

"Mr Knight, you have a visitor." The head of staff announced from behind the bedroom door. I quickly checked myself in the tall mirror, I looked comfortable in black joggers and a fitted tee, but the look on my face accompanied by the dark ink that covered the majority of my skin was all danger, I wasn't sure if my features were even able to soften anymore. Not that I cared, I preferred it this way.

I opened the door to find him stood like a statue with his arms behind his back and his spine tall and straight, I wonder if this guy ever relaxes. "Thanks." I nodded sharply and he took it as the dismissal that I had intended it to be.

At the bottom of the stairs, standing in the wide, white foyer, was Clara, looking all sorts of adorable in a pale pink sundress and matching ballet pumps. My brows raised as I took her in, questioning why I had chosen a girl who was so far from my type. But she *had* agreed to come over with no hesitation, the bluntness of my message had made my intentions very clear, so maybe being my type didn't mean anything. I didn't need her to be that for what I wanted to do.

"Follow me," I said without properly greeting her, and headed into the main lounge. I grabbed two glasses and a decanter filled with Angels Nectar whiskey and placed them on the coffee table in the centre of the room, Clara had followed me in and was perched nervously on the edge of a large red sofa, "Drink?" I offered, and she nodded and thanked me in a quiet voice as I handed her a glass. I threw myself down in the high-backed armchair and sipped my whiskey. Lorenzo's whiskey. I could see what mum saw in him; the man has excellent taste. In *most* things.

After a few minutes of silence I spoke, "How was erm, work." Her lips curved into a small smile before she replied.

"We don't have to do that, you don't care about my day, and I don't care about yours," she said softly, "I know why I'm here," she placed her glass on the table and stared at me with her big blue eyes, "and you kinda suck at small talk." There was a nervous giggle in her tone. I was rendered speechless for a moment, and then I sighed in relief, thank fuck I didn't have to pretend this was something it wasn't to spare her feelings. This girl was bold in her words and cute in her delivery. She was the kind of girl you'd want to take home to meet your parents, she'd probably put on a little apron and bake cookies with your mum and then get on her knees and blow you in your childhood bedroom. Shame that wasn't what I was looking for, but she would make some guy seriously fucking happy someday.

"Do you know what I do to girls who insult me?" I asked darkly, it was a test to see how she would respond, her answer would tell me how far I could push her.

"Punish them?" she answered and pulled her plump lower lip between her teeth. She opened her legs slowly, revealing white lace panties beneath her dress. I leaned on one elbow as I held my gaze on the fabric, not bothering to look back up at her face.

"Yes," I confirmed, pleased by her response. She seemed to be willing to do what I wanted, but I'd give her a choice. "You have five seconds to decide if you're going to stay and be punished, or leave and forget that I ever invited you here." I kept my eyes on her panties and begun to count down. "four," she stood up, "three," she lifted the skirt of her dress a little, "two," she slipped her panties down her tanned legs, "one." She stepped out of them and sat back down. A smirk crept along my lips, "Stand." I commanded, pointing to the floor before me, she did as she was told, I shot a look up to her face and saw that her lip was trembling slightly, was she scared? I'd given her the opportunity to leave, this was the choice she had made. "Turn, bend over, and place your hands on the table." I instructed. Once she was in position I stood. Her dress hung just low enough to cover her bare ass. I trailed my fingers up from the back of her knee, lifting the pale pink fabric of her dress to expose soft skin. Without warning I struck her ass, forcing a yelp of pain from her lips. Her skin instantly reddened, and I removed my hand to repeat the motion again, ensuring to hit the same spot. The same noise left her, but the third time my palm made contact with her stinging skin the sound turned into a long moan. Good, I needed her to enjoy it a little.

    I stripped off fully before sitting back down in the armchair, the same armchair that I'd found little Nutmeg's shoes beside the other morning. I wonder if the puttana had been doing something similar to this when she was in here with my stepfather. Anger rose inside me at the thought, but I didn't want to think into the reason for my reaction.

    "On your fucking knees." I snapped at the girl whose ass was still glowing in front of me. I had the perfect view of her already soaked pussy, but I didn't want it. Not yet. Instead I gripped my cock, and once she was kneeling before me, I gave her a pointed look. She obediently wrapped her lips around the tip of my hard cock and teased it. I was in no mood for teasing though. Instead of letting her 'show off' I twisted her hair around my hand until my fist was tight against the back of her head. I closed my eyes and pushed into her mouth hard and fast, giving her very little time to adjust to the brutal movement of my hips and hands, she choked around my shaft and saliva dripped down to my balls. It didn't take long for her to start to moan around me, this sweet girl was enjoying the way I fucked her pretty mouth. The sound of moaning filled the room and I groaned, feeling my release coming closer and closer, until something hit me like a slap to the face. I could hear someone else moaning. My eyes snapped open, and I looked around, ignoring the woman bobbing up and down on my cock and noticed the two bodies just outside the lounge doors. I'd stupidly left them open, and now had a clear view of Megan sitting on the console table in the foyer, moaning in delight while Lorenzo's face was buried between her legs. Her eyes opened and met mine and she moaned louder. I wrenched Clara's head back and let go of her hair. Megan was deliberately trying to piss me off.

    I looked down at the girl on her knees and took in the confusion on her face. *Fuck it.* I wouldn't let Megan bother me again. "Get on." I patted my lap, "and show me how well a good girl can ride." I growled. Clara straddled me in the chair and lowered herself onto me, her mouth found my ear and she let out a breathy moan as I filled her, but I was distracted. Out in the foyer I could see that Megan was trying to leave, "Surely that has convinced you to stay?" I heard Lorenzo say. I couldn't hear her response due to the moans from the girl riding me that were getting theatrically loud, and I couldn't stop my eyes from rolling in frustration. I looked at Clara with her head thrown back and realised that this was doing nothing for me. A squeal drew my attention back to Megan and I caught a glimpse of her ass in the air and legs kicking as Lorenzo carried her away over his shoulder. My jaw tensed. A soft hand caressed it and I growled deep in my throat. I realised that all of the moaning had stopped, and the girl on my lap was sitting still.

"What do you need?" she asked between heavy breaths. *At least someone had been having a good time.*

"This." I gave in to my anger and frustration now and tugged her dress off, ripped her bra from the centre and dug my fingers into her full breasts, groping the sun-kissed skin and tugging on her perfect nipples. The noise that left her lips was honest, pure delight, and she finally had me where I needed to be.

I threw her from my lap and rose to my feet. Her eyes sparkled as I wrapped my hand around her throat and directed her towards a wall, and she cried out when I hoisted her leg up and slammed my cock deep into her. My hand dropped from her throat to lift her other leg, my fingers digging into her plump flesh, and she moulded herself to me, wrapping her legs around me and allowing me the perfect angle to make her scream. I clawed at the skin on her thighs as I drew closer to my release, marking her body and feeling every fragment of stress inside me push to the edge. I claimed her pussy, fucking her like I doubted any man ever had before, I didn't care who she was, what she liked, anything, I didn't want to know anything about this girl, I just wanted to destroy her. She clung to me and shattered around me repeatedly, barely recovering between each orgasm. I felt my cock swell, and I dropped her legs to pull out of her. She wobbled and sank to the floor, her back against the wall, and looked up at me with a plea in her eyes. I pumped my dick, and she opened her mouth and stuck her tongue out. I squeezed my eyes closed and let myself spill over her.

    Eventually looking down, I saw the mess that I'd made on her face, my cum was coating her lips and dripping from her chin down to her chest. She smiled up at me and licked her lips, I let a satisfied expression sit on my face as I felt how much I'd needed that release. I crouched down in front of her and smeared my cum over her nipple, and heard five words echo in my mind. *"Your work is messy, Adonis."* Oh little Nutmeg, you have no idea.

23

Meg

I woke to the sound of running water and stretched out in the huge bed. Lorenzo had left the bathroom door open, and from where I was laying, I could just about make out his perfect bum surrounded by the light shower steam. *Yum.*

I ached, last night had been a rollercoaster and had ended with me collapsing on my boss's bed and falling asleep naked and moaning gently as he massaged kinks out of my back after drawing multiple orgasms from my body.

I reached for my phone and felt my stomach sink. My night had ended on a happy note, I was beyond satisfied, but it had taken a lot to get there, to push away the sad confusion that had washed over me after dinner.

Lorenzo had ordered us a huge feast from the

best Chinese in town, and after allowing me to thoroughly tell him off for sending Adonis to collect me for no apparent reason, he had convinced me to stay and eat. *Damn my traitorous stomach!* The telling off I'd given him did not go unpunished, I had the bruises to remind me of that, and would apparently be making up for it for some time, *Hello shit jobs that no one else wanted to do,* but the meal had been amazing. Swings and roundabouts.

After we had eaten, Lorenzo had excused himself to check in with Grey on a job, so I took the opportunity to call Toby and explain, somehow. I didn't have any idea what I'd say to him, and he hadn't answered. I'd called a couple of times, and each call ended up going to his voicemail. I sent him messages, and hoped he'd just been caught up at work or something.

Now though, the next morning, I still hadn't heard from him. I looked back towards the bathroom and saw that Lorenzo was still washing. So I grabbed my phone and bought up Toby's number and pressed the green button to call him.

After three rings he picked up and relief flooded over me. "Toby, Hi, how are you?" the words rushed out.

"I'm fine are you ok?" he said bluntly. *What the fuck.*

"Yeah, yeah I'm ok. I'm so sorry about last night, I -." I began, but he cut me off.

"It's fine. It's for the best anyway. I shouldn't

have led you on like that. I'll see you tomorrow for our session as usual." He ground out the words like they were painful to say, and quickly cut the call.

    I blinked in shock. What the hell was that. How had we gone from fun, flirty and about to have dinner together, to this. *'Led you on.'* I was calling bullshit, there was no way he was faking last night. Not a chance in hell. Unless was it payback for the way I'd stupidly behaved after our first date? Had he actually convinced me that I'd get a second chance with him just to make me feel like crap?

    My stomach twisted in a tight knot and my eye's stung with tears that I refused to let fall. Fuck, I *liked* him. One date, and I was upset. How had I let that happen? I knew how. He was the picture of the life I'd always wanted, the little fantasy that I never thought I'd have, a happy, simple, carefree life where I wouldn't be watching my back. Being with Toby would've been as easy as breathing. Now that fantasy had been crushed before I'd even had the chance to live one single day of it.

    I took a few moments to pull myself from this sadness, knowing that if I settled in it for too long, I'd begin thinking about the other future that I'd lost. I couldn't cope with thoughts of the family that I'd had taken from me right now. They would tip me over the edge, and I was all too aware of where I was currently sitting. No, all of these feelings needed to be placed in a little folder and shoved to the bottom of my mental pile, I'd cry about it all later. *Eugh, no.* No I wouldn't, I'm not the girl who cries over a guy she had one date with. *Snap the fuck out of it M.*

Looking back over to the open bathroom door I realised there was a very simple way to shift my mood right in front of me. Lorenzo was rinsing his hair, most likely now finished with his shower, so I'd have to move fast. Climbing out of the bed I padded across the heated floorboards, my legs ached already, but I could ignore that. Physical pain never really bothered me much anymore, and aches, they were just a mild annoyance.

"Need a hand?" I offered as I posed naked in the doorway, putting on a sensual voice that didn't match my mood, yet. Yep, I was going to use sex to get over this shitty feeling.

Lorenzo turned to face me, the stream of water crashing over him having the exact effect I had hoped it would. "I'm done amore, do *you* need a hand?" he held his hand out to me, inviting me to step into the shower with him.

The warm water cascaded over me, and I understood why Lorenzo had spent so long in here, the pressure felt amazing. I groaned in delight as I tipped my head back to soak my hair and Lorenzo chuckled, a low, hungry sound that sent a whole new ache through my body.

The smell of his soap hit me as his hands began to caress my body, he pulled me close to him as he lathered the soap over my back, and a small gasp left me when his hard length pushed against my stomach. His hands slipped between our bodies as he continued to work the soap into my skin, lingering on my breasts and gently toying with my nipples. I let my fingers trail featherlight circles up and down his biceps as he teased me. Lorenzo's hands wrapped back around to my back and up into my hair, he tugged firmly to tip my head back, forcing our eyes to meet.

"You are a goddess amore mio," he breathed and dipped his lips to mine in a soft kiss that left me desperate for more. "Did you have an enjoyable evening?" he asked.

"Of course." I had. Once I had calmed down, he had treated me to my idea of a perfect meal and had then fucked me senseless. Although, I had attempted to leave after dinner, wanting to go home and speak to Toby. In hindsight I'm glad that he convinced me to stay now that I knew Toby wasn't interested.

Memories of Lorenzo ripping my yoga pants off and shredding my panties in the foyer flashed through my mind, the way he had sat me on top of a table so that he could 'enjoy his favourite treat' as he had put it, had my core clenching. Adding the knowledge that it had annoyed Adonis was the perfect little cherry on the cake. Noticing that he couldn't focus on that sweet barmaid because of us only made me enjoy our unintentional performance even more. Anything to ruin his day.

"Do you see how happy we could be?" he murmured and nipped my earlobe. I hummed at the sensation, then realised what he had said.

"Lorenzo, what are you aski-." I stumbled on my words as his fingers left my hair and landed between my legs, he gave me a devilish smile and plunged two fingers inside me. He pumped them lazily, making me swallow hard and attempt to get back to my train of thought. "What are you asking exactly?" I panted.

"I'm asking you to imagine a life where you come home to me." he said, his fingers working away slowly inside me, "A life where I'm the one who makes you happier than you have ever been." I searched his eyes for the joke, but all I could see was lust.

I trailed my gaze over him, taking in the man stood bare before me, he was perfection, why was I so hesitant? I let my eyes settle on his chest where three light scars marked his otherwise perfectly smooth skin, three healed wounds to remind him of how he got to where he is. Only three, to remind everyone else just how hard it would be to kill him. Lorenzo D'Angelo was not easily hurt, there had only been one man to ever leave a lasting mark on him, Charon. They were enemies for a reason that was far deeper than just gang rivalry.

Lorenzo D'Angelo was my boss. My deadly, secretive, untrustworthy boss. My boss who I had started fucking on a stupid murder high, a murder I had failed to complete. My mind blurred, anger and grief battling with temptation and the fire burning in my core.

My pussy began to tighten around his fingers, but he stilled, waiting for my response. "I," I swallowed and steadied my breathing a little, "I'm not sure if I can." I admitted refusing to look at him.

He pulled away from me, sliding his fingers out of me and leaving me wanting. I couldn't blame him though, the words that had left my mouth hadn't even come close to what he apparently now wanted to hear from me. Last night had been a date in his eyes, and he was throwing his cards on the table, declaring his desire for more. He stepped out of the shower and grabbed a towel. When he reached the doorway, he turned to face me.

"I opened up il mio tesoro," his expression was stern, "You know what I want now, but I will not wait for long. I'd like you to try. Once you've showered, I'd like you to leave. Come back when you've thought this over."

He turned and left me standing speechless in his shower. What am I going to do?

24

Meg

I had to stop by my apartment before heading into the office. Adonis' surprise ambush last night had left me with only my gym clothes and a sundress that was a little too casual for work. So when I finally arrived, an hour later than usual, I found myself being dragged by my arm into an office that was not mine, and having a cold coffee shoved under my nose.

Eden was lucky I didn't use violence in the workplace, well, I didn't use it in *this* workplace. I don't appreciate being manhandled, most of the time.

"It would've been hot if you were on time." She glared at me, then her lips curved up and she burst out laughing. "What have you been doing this morning Miss!"

I took a sip of the cold coffee, not particularly bothered that it wasn't warm, I liked my coffee black, but that was about as fussy as I got.

"I wish I had something great to tell you, but I don't, girl it's all such a mess." I sighed. Eden knew the majority of my man drama already, minus a few details that I didn't think would be a good idea to share, like the fact I'm actually a member of one of the gangs that practically rules this town and my *lover* – as she likes to put it. – is my terrifying boss. As far as she knows, he's just some mysterious guy whose identity I've kept secret because its complicated. So kinda true.

Eden gave me a pitying look and I scowled back. "If you're going to look at me like that," I waved a hand at her, "I won't talk about it." I warned, rising to my feet.

"Oh sit down Meg, fuck it's obvious you've not really had any girl friends before." She laughed. I sat back down and shrugged. She wasn't wrong. "Start from the beginning." She prompted.

After I'd filled her in as best I could without giving any details that could give away who my *lover* was, I went back to my own office and busied myself with work. Eden had told me to not give up on Toby, she thinks there's more to it, and a small part of me was hoping that she would think that too. She wasn't much help with the Lorenzo situation, but I didn't expect her to be, her advice was to just walk away, but I wasn't sure if it would be that simple.

I let three hours pass before I shut down my computer, I couldn't focus on anything with all of these pent-up emotions. Luckily my workload was light, nothing that couldn't wait another day, so I grabbed my handbag and fished out my keys and made my way out of the office and down to my car.

I drove aimlessly for a short while, then finally decided where I was going to go. I pulled up in the small carpark by the lake and headed into Tate's. Gina was working, as usual, and waved from behind the counter as I walked through the door. There was a pretty long queue, so I found an empty table and waited for it to die down, it was lunch time, so it wasn't surprising that the café was busy.

I people watched while I waited, playing a game with myself that me and Jase used to play when we were younger, making random guesses about the people we saw. Creating lives for them. The old couple who met when they were just teenagers and had been inseparable ever since, or the sharply dressed man who was tapping his foot impatiently had just received his big promotion, but was now constantly exhausted, making him agitated and snappy, It was a pointless game, but it kept me distracted from real life.

I was just sat piecing together a life for a mother with her toddler when Gina approached me with a takeaway coffee and my usual baguette. I hadn't even noticed that the queue had gone. "Oh, Thanks Gina," I smiled at her and dug around for my purse and handing over a little more than the cost of my meal. "Don't worry about the change."

"You don't have to do that every time." She chastised, "but it's lovely that you do. How are you, my love? How's work?" she raised a brow at me. Gina knew about The Brotherhood, she knew who I was, what with her being Grey's sister. You'd never guess that they were related, they had a couple of similar facial features, if you looked past Greys scars, but their personalities were polar opposites. Gina was sweet, bubbly and saw the good in everyone. Grey was hard, cynical, and cruel. And for some reason, Gina loved him for it. Teased him even.

"You know how it is, the boss always keeps us busy, you have to work hard to stay at the top." I gave her a modified version of my usual response, it wasn't that Gina was a threat, it was just part of our ways, we don't share information unless it has been deemed appropriate by Lorenzo.

"Ha, you and that grumpy brother of mine are so alike, always so aloof!" she chuckled, the sound making it hard to be mad at her for the insult. I'd hate to turn out like Grey. I could live this life and still be a decent person, on some level.

"That's me," I shrugged with a smile, "aloof."

"Well, I won't keep you, but you better bring the hot blonde chap down here soon, really brightens my day he does." She tossed me a cheeky wink and bustled off towards the kitchen. I swear there wasn't a single woman alive who wasn't attracted to Cooper, even I could appreciate that he was quite nice to look at.

I took my lunch and headed to the bench in the quiet little spot that I'd found the other week. The peace and calm that I'd felt there was exactly what I needed today. A place to escape.

Except when I made my way through the trees to the secluded area, I found that it was already occupied. I huffed in frustration and turned back on myself to find somewhere else, but wait, there was something familiar about the man sat on the bench eating a baguette and reading a newspaper. *Who reads those nowadays?* I turned back to face him as I tried to place him, Short dark hair, black suit, tattoos creeping from the collar of his shirt up the back and sides of his neck. I recognised them, but I still couldn't place him. It was only when I realised that the way he sat was irritating me that all the pieces fell into place. Fucking Adonis.

I cleared my throat. "Hey arsehole, find somewhere else to sit." I said as he turned his head enough to glance over his shoulder. He huffed a laugh and turned back to his paper.

"No." he said bluntly.

"No?" I questioned and walked around the bench to stand in front of him.

He looked up from the paper, his features were set in a cold, harsh expression that made my body tense. It took a lot to unnerve me, but that look did it.

"No."

I held his gaze, even though I wanted to look away, he was so broken, so full of hatred, but so was I, and I needed this space. "I'm in no mood to argue with you Adonis, just find somewhere else to have your lunch." I stood my ground. Sure, it was only a bench, but it was the only place where I've felt any real calmness in such a long time.

"Megan, If you don't fuck off, I will shoot you and throw you in this lake." His use of my name bothered me more than it should, I don't know what I'd have preferred him to call me, his little nickname for me irritated me, I suppose M would be fine, he is a Brother after all. And Brothers don't shoot each other, not to kill anyway. Otherwise he wouldn't be sat there. But something about the way he reached for his gun so casually and the warning in his eyes told me that he would do it, strategically, nothing lethal, just something to hurt. The last thing I need today is to nurse a bullet wound. And I'm not a big fan of swimming, especially in lakes. *Make a smart choice M.*

I held his gaze for a moment longer, then

silently walked away. I probably could have shot him; I never went anywhere completely unarmed. But I wasn't sure if I trusted myself to make a smart shot. I was finding my dislike for Adonis growing with each day, and I hated myself a little for how much I let him get to me.

I decided to just go back to my car. Once inside I dug around in my handbag for my phone and made a call that would hopefully cheer me up.

"You busy?" I asked when they answered.

"Not overly, nothing I can't cancel, what's up sunshine?" Cooper's answer instantly boosted my mood, just like I'd hoped it would.

"I need to shoot something." I sighed; Cooper would understand. I could happily go to the shooting range alone, but having decent competition would be way better.

"One of those days? I'm having one too, but I have a better idea." I wondered what had affected Cooper enough to dampen his mood, nothing seemed to get to him.

"What's your idea?" I questioned.

"How do you feel about archery?" I frowned at this idea, my brother had been really into archery and had pushed me for years to try it out, he eventually passed that love on to me, and it had become our thing, *our* escape when things got too much. I hadn't been to the range since before he had died. I was still a club member, but I had no idea that Cooper was one too. At least, I presumed he was.

"Archery, I dunno." I chewed on my bottom lip, was I ready to do this with someone else?

"Let me re-phrase that, are you ready to go and do something that I *know* you love, but have been avoiding because it's hard to think about doing it without Jason? You know it'll be fun." Dammit, of course Cooper knew. There was no point hiding it from him. And I *had* been looking for an escape today. Fuck it, if there was anyone in this world that I could potentially lose it and break down in front of it was Coop, if it bought back too many memories he would understand.

"I hate it when you're right, fine, let's do it." I agreed, then planned out our afternoon.

I arrived ten minutes early. I was always early; it was a habit that I'd picked up from my mother. She was always early to everything, it was an anxious habit for her, she took a lot of risks in life and was on edge a lot of the time. She was right to be though, as one of the risks that she took ended up being the reason she was killed. Blackmailing a gang leader was never going to end well for mum. It also didn't end well for Carl either. Seeing your mum's lifeless body in a pool of blood on your kitchen floor at the age of nine can send you one of two ways. You either end up traumatised, or you end up seeking vengeance. I don't think it's hard to work out which way I went. Carl never saw me coming.

Cooper pulled up next to me exactly on time. "Sunshine," he beamed as we both stepped out of our cars, "ready to show me up?"

"Always." I strode ahead confidently, but Cooper caught up quickly and threw his arm around my shoulder playfully and nuzzled into my hair.

"I've never done this before." He confessed.

"Really? Then why did you suggest it?" I frowned.

"Because you need a release, and I knew that Grey was up at the shooting range today, that wouldn't have helped, would it? So it was either this or taking you over to Lorenzo's place." He waggled his eyebrows at me, and I shoved his arm off of me.

"Eugh, I can't believe you knew about that." I groaned. He was right though, Grey would piss me off, and I couldn't even go to Lorenzo's if I wanted to.

"*I* can't believe you thought you were subtle." He threw me a cheeky grin and I rolled my eyes.

"Touché." I smiled back at him, "Oh, Gina was asking after you, she wants me to drag you down to the café soon, you've got yourself a little admirer Coop." I said and nudged him.

"Well I am pretty irresistible, you'd have to be mad not to want a piece of this." he winked, and I shook my head at him.

"Cocky prick."

Cooper led the way inside, and I found my membership card and presented it to the woman behind the desk. Cooper got himself signed up, I had presumed that he would just come along as my guest and we would pay the fee, but apparently he thought he might have a hidden talent and wanted to ensure that he could keep on top of his undiscovered skill.

He was wrong. Cooper may be a good shot with any gun you could put in front of him but put a bow in his hand and he's a disaster. I had to stand behind him and help his positioning, he used the opportunity to wiggle his bum against me and declare that I was *'so hard'* for him. Even with my guidance, he sucked.

"Come on then Cupid, show me how it's done." He teased as I pulled my hair into a messy bun and kicked off my heels. It only took me a few slightly off shots to get comfortable again. Then each arrow sunk into its target smoothly, and my tension began to ease away. I'd had a crappy morning, a frustrating lunch, and now, I had the best company *and* the growing calmness that I had needed.

It didn't take long for Cooper to give up, declaring that archery was 'for losers anyway'. He had left me outside to continue alone while he packed away and grabbed us coffees. When he came back, I put my bow down and rolled my shoulders, enjoying the movement and letting out a little groan.

"Eiw, don't tell me that *this* is what gets you going," Cooper wrinkled his nose, "Does the boss dress up like Robin Hood and poke you with his lucky arrow?"

I sighed heavily and glared at him. "Don't be a dick Coop, and please don't bring up Lorenzo, I'm trying to *not* think about him."

"Oh, trouble in paradise, fill me in." he sipped his drink and placed a cup of black coffee in my hand.

"I really shouldn't." I began. But I did.

"Oh, my, god." Cooper laughed, "you're going to be Mrs Boss! Will I have to answer to you too? Will I start getting special treatment because you love me? Can I be your maid of honour when you guys get married? I'd look super-hot in a little pink number, or maybe blue to really bring out my eyes." he teased.

"That isn't helpful Coop." I whined, "I had no plans of it becoming a *thing*, and if I walk away from it, what's going to happen to me? Can you see him just letting it go?"

Cooper composed himself and gave me a gentle smile, "He knows your worth M, you could walk away and not a damn thing would change. He isn't stupid." Coopers reassuring words felt like being wrapped in a comforter, I hadn't considered how Lorenzo's mind worked, that he was a business first kind of man.

It wasn't much help though; I still didn't trust him. Could I be with a man that I didn't trust just because when he wanted to, he could treat me like a queen? Then again, it's a little hypocritical of me, when I was expecting Toby to accept me without knowing the truth. Toby. I was still hurt by that. That incredible man had got himself under my skin, and he didn't want me, and I had to see him in a few short hours. Fuck. My. Life.

25

Tobias

Tonight I have to see Meg, and I have to pretend that I don't want her. Luckily, I'm a professional so it's not like I could, *should*, make a move on her while I'm working. No matter how badly I want to. It's not worth the consequences, from my employer, or her boyfriend, if that's what he was.

I'm not dumb, I know not to mess in gang shit. But I was still struggling to wrap my head around the fact that she's dating the leader of The Brotherhood. *The fucking Brotherhood.* I had known Jason had been a member and the pair of them used to be joined at the hip. I'd presumed Meg might have had a thing for bad boys, but Lorenzo D'Angelo was whatever comes after bad boys.

I sat by the pool with James. I had some time

between clients, and I wasn't in the mood to write up the meal plan that I had promised to do for Mrs Adams. She wasn't back in for a couple of days though, so I didn't feel much guilt over not rushing to do it. Plus, meal plans bored me.

"Dude, are you even listening?" James snapped his fingers in front of my face.

"Yeah yeah, some girl, really hot, perfect ass, I was listening." I lied; I'd only been vaguely listening to him.

"I was telling you about her ten minutes ago, what's going on? You've been acting weird for days now." He raised his brows at me, and I pulled an apologetic face.

"Sorry man. Its nothing, just girl drama, I'll get over it." I shrugged as though it was no big deal. It absolutely was though, for months now I'd been trying to grow the balls to ask her on a date. She had captured my attention the minute she walked into the gym last year, but I didn't do anything about it. Her brother scared the shit out of me. He hadn't been a big guy, but he had a presence about him that screamed danger, and he was protective as hell over his little sister. At one point I almost found the balls to ask him if he'd be ok with me asking her out, but then he went and got himself murdered. He had left a broken girl behind; you don't make a move on a girl who's grieving. Over the months I watched her pull herself back together piece by piece and every minute that I was around her I found myself more into her. More desperate to shoot my shot.

"I hope so, this mood doesn't suit you." I knew James wouldn't push, not like Emilia had the other night. After my little confrontation with Grey I had called Emilia. I couldn't relax so I headed around to her place to cheer myself up, but no matter what she did, like baking the best brownies I'd ever tasted, I was stuck being a tense, miserable bastard. Her advice was to ignore the threat and just date her if it makes me happy. It *would* make me happy, but I don't think Emilia really understood just how badly that could end for me. Naïve little sausage.

I flashed James a wide, mocking smile, "I'll be back to shitting rainbows in no time," I glanced up at the clock, five minutes until she arrived. "Drink after work?" I asked.

"Delightful mental image, thanks dude. Sure thing, but seriously, perk up, I need a decent wingman tonight." He winked and got up, slid his trainers back on and climbed back up the ladder to his chair. There was no one in the pool, I think he just enjoyed feeling like some water king on his worryingly unstable looking throne, dude was way too big for that flimsy thing. Maybe it would cheer me up if it collapsed.

I waited hopefully for a few minutes, but I knew it wouldn't happen. I lifted my feet from the water and quickly dried them off before pulling on my trainers and heading away from the pool. By the time I'd walked from the pool to the gym she would be ready. I knew she was already here, she was always ten minutes early, but she wouldn't emerge from the changing room until 8pm on the dot.

"Toby," her voice hit me first, followed by the fresh fragrance that always coated her skin. I spun around in the corridor and found Meg stood in the doorway of the ladies' locker room. "Are we, erm, ok?" her fingers were tugging on the star shaped stud in her earlobe, I'd never seen her do that before, it wasn't hard to tell that it was a comfort move. My stomach sank at the realisation that she had never needed to comfort or calm herself around me before.

I cleared my throat and plastered what I hoped was a pretty convincing smile on to my face, "Of course little Vixen, now hurry your ass up, otherwise I'll put push-ups back into your warm-up." There, normal conversation for us. That wasn't so hard.

She groaned at my threat and pushed past me, a small smile sat on her lips, but it seemed about as fake as my own. She held the door open for me to follow her inside, then went to sit on a mat, twisting her hair into a quick, messy braid and began wrapping her hands in pale pink fabric. I did the same and ran through what today's warm-up would actually be and left her to start while I went to fill my water bottle and give myself a little talking to. *You are a professional Toby, remember that when she's on top of you. You are a professional and you value your life.*

Once she was ready, we began our combat session and went through the usual motions, but we were both holding back. I wanted to be close to her, but I didn't trust myself and kept tapping out whenever she managed to pin me down.

"Stop holding back." She panted after half an hour.

"I could say the same to you." I shot back, walking away from her to take a long swig of water. "If there's something on your mind you know the options. Let it out verbally, or physically." I turned to walk back towards her, unsure which option I'd prefer her to pick. I wanted to know every single one of her problems, but I knew that I needed to avoid that emotional connection. I also wanted to have her body wrapped around mine, but could I continue to stop myself from making a move? "What do you want to do little one?"

She tensed and seemed to think on it for a moment, then her body suddenly collided with mine, throwing me to the floor, her fist connected with my ribs and my breath rushed from my lungs with a pained exhale. She didn't stop, her technique becoming sloppier with every punch. I let my own fists mirror hers, I had to keep it aggressive, I could not let myself become distracted by the warmth of her thighs as they held me down, or the way her breath was coming in short, heavy pants that were all kinds of sexual. I threw her off of me far enough to have time to stand again and waited for her next move. She didn't make one though, she just stared at me with fire burning in her eyes. I had to stay focused. I made a move to kick her, but she caught my leg in such a swift movement that I lost all control of my balance, crashing down onto my back again and groaning at the impact. She came and stood above me, her feet planted either side of my hips, she opened her mouth to speak but before the words came out I grabbed her ankle and laughed as she fell backwards.

"Dick." She muttered under her breath, and I sat up to check on her. She was fine, if anything she looked happier than she had all session. She narrowed her eyes at me, "I'm taking that as a win, that was a dirty move, Toby."

I swallowed hard at her choice of words and closed my eyes. I felt her shifting beside me and when I opened them again, she was on her knees, her face inches from mine.

"Vixen," I warned in a low growl.

"Did you really mean what you said?" she questioned quietly.

"I..." I wet my lips, it was one thing lying to her on the phone, but having her knelt in front of me, her eyes searching mine so intently, the words got stuck.

She leaned in closer, her lips gently brushing against mine and I froze. "Take it back Toby, please." She whispered and closed the gap between us. My hands lifted to cup her face as hers tangled around my neck and drew me even closer. My tongue swept across her lip, and she moaned softly as I deepened our kiss and I swear I stopped breathing.

We reluctantly broke away and she sighed in relief. Just as a feeling of dread washed over me. I forced my hands to drop from her face and turned my head away. *Fuck, what had we just done? Did I have a deathwish?*

"Meg, I can't." I choked the words out. "I'm so sorry."

I stood up and walked away, I didn't turn to look at her until I reached the door. Her jaw was tense, her eyes on me and a mixture of anger and disappointment filled them.

"Why?" she demanded.

"We just can't."

"But you *want* to?" she pushed and rose to her feet.

"Meg, please just drop this." I tried to get a hold of myself, to put some force behind my words.

"You don't get to kiss me like that and then walk away without any explanation, I'm a big girl Toby, I can handle whatever truth you throw at me. Tell. Me. Why." She said firmly, grounding out those last three words with such power, but I couldn't tell her. I needed to be harsh to keep her safe.

"I just don't want you." The words burned my throat, but there it was, if I wasn't inside my own head, I'd have believed me. Inside I was screaming. On the outside I hid it with a blank face.

Meg shook her head, but I didn't wait around to hear what else she had to say. I couldn't give her the chance to tell me something that would pull the truth from me. She didn't need to know the real reason. I may not be some scary motherfucker, but I could at least keep my mouth shut and protect us both from one.

26

Meg

I collapsed back down onto the mat in the gym, disappointment and embarrassment filled every inch of my body. Thankfully we'd had the room to ourselves this evening so there was no one around to witness my desperate attempt to get the guy that I wanted so fucking badly.

Toby's rejection stung so much more now that he had done it to my face. I shouldn't have pushed him, kissing him was a stupid move. I lifted my fingers up to my swollen lips and let out a shuddering breath. I didn't want to give him up, even if he wasn't really mine anyway. But I knew I'd have to. He didn't want me.

I steadied my breathing as I unwrapped my hands, letting the damp fabric fall to the floor around me in a messy pile, usually I'd have neatly folded them as I unwound them, and the fact that I hadn't only added to my annoyance. I needed to get out of here, now.

I composed my face and grabbed the pile from the floor and marched out of the gym and down to the locker room. I wasn't concerned about bumping into Toby, he wouldn't be lingering, he wouldn't make this any more uncomfortable for me than it already was. Unfortunately, underneath how he was acting towards me, he was a nice person. It might have been easier if he wasn't.

I quickly showered and tossed my sweat covered clothes into my bag. I didn't bother to dry my hair, instead I twisted it back into a braid and threw on my clothes. I'd been home between leaving Cooper and coming here and had changed into a baggy band t-shirt and little denim shorts. Comfort won today and I was glad of that.

My car wasn't parked far but the walk in the warm evening air helped calm me, I had to just be thankful that the only thing that was hurt was my pride. I was embarrassed and annoyed, but my heart was still intact. Now I knew how Lorenzo must have felt when I had all but rejected him. I got into my car and turned on the engine, my body deciding what I was going to do before my mind caught up.

***

"He isn't expecting me, but can you please let me through." I asked through my rolled down window.

I'd reached my destination faster than I thought I would, and my thoughts still hadn't settled themselves. Who kisses someone like that if they feel nothing? Toby, apparently.

The man ducked back inside the small brick building and a few moments later the gate began to open. I raced through them and sped up the winding driveway. As I approached the building, I saw that the front door was open, and a silhouette of a man stood on the threshold.

Toby didn't want me, and that stung. But someone else did. My bruised ego needed a boost, and I knew where to get it. But was I ready to give him what he had asked for? Was an ego boost really worth making a rushed decision?

I grabbed my bag from the passenger seat and quickly came up with an ultimatum as I stepped out of the car. I'd get what I needed.

"I have a proposition for you." I said as I made my way to the front door.

"Whatever it is, the answer is no." an unexpected voice replied. The wrong man was stood in front of me. Adonis smirked down at me, and I shoved past him.

"Arsehole, where's Lorenzo?"

He didn't reply, he just closed the door and stayed standing where I'd left him with his arms folded and an amused look on his face.

"Fine, I'll just call him then." I huffed and rifled through my bag for my phone before chucking the black duffle down on the console table next to me. I pulled up Lorenzo's number. It only rang out twice before he answered.

"M, Is this important?" he asked in a quiet voice.

"Shit, are you working?" I nibbled my bottom lip and avoided looking at Adonis.

"Yeah, but I can drop it if you need me." his words shocked me, I hadn't expected him to be so… nice.

"Erm, no, no its not important, I'm at your place though, shall I go home? Or wait?" I continued to chew on my lip and kept my gaze on my feet, feeling all sorts of uncomfortable. A cold hand touched my face and tugged my chin slightly, releasing my lip from my teeth. I bought my gaze up and found Adonis frowning at me. He quickly removed his hand as if I had electrocuted him. I shook my head at him, and my brows pulled together in confusion. *What the hell was that?*

"Wait there for me, I won't be long." Lorenzo's voice caught my attention just before the line went dead.

"Don't touch me again." I scolded Adonis as he remained stood in front of me.

"Stop biting your lip like that then, you are so fucking transparent, at least *try* to hide your emotions a little." What was it with these men and telling me to try today?

"I am not transparent," I protested and

stormed into the lounge. Adonis followed me in and laid down on the long red sofa as I slumped into the armchair that I desperately wanted to take home with me. It was so comfortable, and I felt like a boss bitch sitting in it.

"You are," he glanced at me, "when you're happy you literally bounce up and down, when you're turned on your eyes get all hooded and turn a darker green than usual, when you're angry you grind your teeth, which is really bad for you by the way," like he was one to talk, his jaw was almost permanently ticking away, "when you're sad or scared you play with your earlobes and when you're nervous you chew your lip. You do this thing where you tap your chest sometimes, I've not completely worked that one out yet, but I will." He shot me a sarcastic smile and then threw his head back against the cushion as if he was about to have a nap.

"Fuck me Donny, don't be too subtle about your obsession with me." I shook my head.

"Ha," he barked a humourless laugh but didn't raise his head to look at me, "being observant is hardly the same as being obsessed. I'm sure anyone who's ever met you could tell you the same things."

Irritation flooded me, it was a nice distraction from the rejection pain that was still lingering, but it wasn't exactly what I'd wanted coming here. "Whatever, Why are you here Don?" I asked in an attempt to move away from talking about me and the emotions that I thought I hid quite well.

"Because I live here. And don't call me Don." He opened one eye and narrowed it at me.

"Yes, I know that, but why are you in *here*. In this room, annoying me." I crossed my arms.

"Because I live here." He repeated and a noticed his usual smirk had fallen on his lips again. He was enjoying himself.

I stood up and went to pour myself a large drink, throwing it back in one long mouthful and refilling the glass. I now had to hope that Lorenzo would accept my proposition and not throw me out, because if he did throw me out, I'd be walking home.

"So what's this proposition that you have for Daddy?" Adonis asked as I went to sit back down, his eyes were barely open, but he was tracking me across the room.

"Call him that again and I will make myself your new Mummy." I shot back, aware that it didn't really make sense, but it was enough to make him sit up and sneer at me in disgust.

"You're not *that* special Megan. You really think he'll keep you around much longer?" I ground my teeth at my name on his lips. "Oh dear, you're angry." His expression changed to one of smug cockiness and I slammed my glass down onto the coffee table, splashing the dark liquid onto the wood.

"Fuck you." I stood up and walked towards

him, "Fuck you Adonis, I've had a crappy day and I really don't need your shit right now."

He stood up as I reached the sofa and pushed his body hard against mine. He towered over me, but in that moment I was too irritated to find him intimidating.

"You know where the door is then." He growled.

"So do you, and *you* don't get to dismiss me. Ever." I shoved him and walked away, deciding that he wasn't worth the energy. I could find somewhere else to wait.

"Cagna." I heard him mutter under his breath as I walked through the doorway into the foyer. I spun around and marched back in, for some reason unable to ignore him.

"Excuse me?" I stood in the doorway with my hands planted on my hips. He didn't repeat himself, just looked me up and down and smirked.

Before I had the chance to say anything else a broad hand gently landed on my shoulder and I turned to find Lorenzo stood behind me. "Down girl." He whispered in my ear, and I sucked in a sharp breath as the tone of his voice instantly flooded my panties. I looked back over at Adonis and found that he had sat down in my favourite chair and was ignoring us.

Lorenzo's hand fell to the small of my back and he guided me into the foyer, "Bedroom or office?" he asked, knowing that my answer to this would be enough of an indication of what I wanted to discuss.

My stomach rumbled and I realised that I had skipped dinner. "Kitchen?" I countered and he narrowed his eyes at me in suspicion.

"Ok," he said after a beat, "Kitchen."

He kept his hand in place on my back as we headed down the corridor to the kitchen. A couple of women were in the room, and they jumped in shock as we entered.

"What do we want to eat?" Lorenzo asked me and the two women approached us to listen to my request.

I looked at Lorenzo and tilted my head. "Can you cook?" I asked.

"Yes." He said simply.

"Will you cook me something?" I pushed gently, if he said yes this could lead nicely to my proposition.

"Can *you* cook?" he asked me.

"Kind of, a little." I admitted, my cooking skills were basic, like cheese on toast basic.

He looked thoughtful for a moment, and I drank in the way he pondered my request. He always looked so serious when I'd seen him in thought before, this was different, he looked happy.

"Ladies," he addressed the two women, "we shall be cooking for ourselves this evening, take a break." The women both looked shocked but quickly left us alone in the large kitchen.

"I know you're probably expecting something Italian, but do you mind if we do something else?" he asked and I smiled at his genuine question, I had presumed I'd get no say in what he made for me.

"What do you have in mind?"

"Burritos." He looked hopeful and my smile turned into a wide grin.

"Absolutely, I love Mexican food."

He directed me to a stool next to a counter and quickly gathered up the ingredients that we needed. "Watch carefully and you might learn something." He rolled up the sleeves of his deep blue shirt and wrapped an apron around himself. I stifled a giggle at how seriously he was taking this.

"Talk while I cook?" it was more of a demand than a question, but I think he was trying. "I'm guessing you are here because you have thought about my request."

"I have." I began, and resisted the urge to play with my earring. Now that Adonis had pointed it out, I had realised I'd not been making enough of an effort to stop doing it. "and I would like you to hear me out before you get mad at me for making demands."

He glanced at me from where he stood slicing raw chicken. "Go on."

"I will try, but," he tensed, and I second guessed my decision to do this. It was a hastily made choice anyway, but one that I hoped would work out for the best. I couldn't lose this man, even if I didn't love him, I couldn't do it. I'd already lost one man today. "but I need you to try something too."

He tossed the chicken into a hot pan and washed his hands as the meat sizzled. He threw in an assortment of spices and poured rice into a pot of water. "Are you going to tell me what that is?" he asked with his back to me as he continued to prepare the rest of our food.

"Yes," I said quickly, "Lorenzo, I don't trust you, and you scare me." I declared and winced as he turned to face me.

"Understandable." He nodded, "and you have a solution for that?" his brows lifted as he waited.

"Sort of, It's quite simple really, I will try to come around to the idea of something more between us, if you can try to be honest with me and control how often your mood switches on me." my lip made its way between my teeth and I released it quickly and mentally cursed Adonis for making me so fucking aware of what I was doing.

"Deal." He said and I frowned at how easy that had been. He came over to where I was sat and swept his thumb over my forehead, smoothing over the worried lines that had no doubt formed there. "Now tell your other men that you're done with them." He demanded, but there was a playfulness to his tone that I'd not heard before.

"There are no other men." I admitted, attempting to keep the sadness out of my voice. I didn't want him to think I was settling, even if it did feel a little like I was. But I had a man stood before me, willing to try, and he understood the darkest parts of me, in fact he worshipped them. We lived the same lifestyle, I wouldn't have to keep him safe, and one day lust could grow into love. Couldn't it?

His lips met mine in a passionate kiss that dragged the air from my lungs, and replaced it with hope. "Good." He smiled and turned back to finish making our dinner. I watched him and sighed. I doubted I'd see him cook for us again, so I rested my head on my hands and enjoyed the moment as the view and the smells filling the kitchen made my mouth water.

He plated up our steaming hot wraps and placed them on the counter. "Bon appetite." He gestured to the food, and I stood up and tentatively wrapped my arms around his neck. He hesitated then placed his hands on my hips.

"Thank you, Lorenzo." I whispered and pushed up onto my tiptoes to kiss him softly.

He looked down at me, "No, Thank you amore mio."

"It only works if we both try though. I'm not good at this stuff, casual is all I know, so I need you to be patient with me, and I'll be patient with you." I said, sliding my fingers down his arms.

"I know, I will, and I *will* make you mine." he promised.

"I look forward to seeing you try." I smirked, feeling a buzz of confidence enter my body.

"I'll show you right now." He breathed and dipped his head to my ear, "I'll make you mine right here," he pushed me against the counter, "over and over again."

My fingers roamed around to his back, and I tugged on the cord of his apron and smiled. "Only if you keep this on."

He pulled back and raised a brow at me, then stepped away. He held eye contact as he slowly, slightly awkwardly, stripped, and I felt my cheeks flush. I didn't think he would do it, but it wasn't long before he was stood proudly before me in nothing but an apron.

"Happy?" he asked.

I licked my lips and let my eyes travel over him appreciatively, lingering on the clear bulge that lifted the fabric. "Yes."

He cleared his throat and I looked up to meet his stern expression.

"Yes, *Chef.*"

27

Lorenzo

As tired as I felt, sleep was evading me. I sat up in my bed and stared down at the beautiful, naked woman next to me. The risk had paid off. Opening up to her just enough to not leave myself vulnerable and making my intentions known had been the perfect way to chip at her wall, she may not have given me a full commitment, but that would come soon enough, I was sure of that. So long as I could hold up my end of our deal.

I twisted a strand of her fiery hair absentmindedly around my fingers. Now that she was here, and offering me some level of certainty, I was able to focus on other important things.

Adonis was fitting into The Brotherhood perfectly, but I knew what his goals were, avenge Selene, and then take over from me when the time was right. He would need to focus his attention on more than just the violent side of things if he had a chance of me allowing that. I'd have to nudge him in the right direction.

The Brotherhood functioned differently from other gangs around here. Charon would lead The Wolves until his last breath, there was no way out but death. I would lead my Brothers until I was ready to hand the reins to someone else. I had presumed that my successor would be Grey, typically our seconds would take over, just like I had taken over from Sal. But now, I wasn't so sure that he was the right choice.

My brother-in-law, Adonis' uncle, had taken an early 'retirement', not only leaving The Brotherhood, but leaving the country, choosing to put this life behind him and start fresh with his childhood sweetheart. I visited him in Italy often, my mentor was like family to me, even before he officially became it. During my visits I had caught his sister's attention. Then during one long summer weekend she had made her move on me. In that moment I knew I had to make her mine; I'd never met a woman with such confidence in all my life. Until M.

I sighed and gently dropped her hair, careful not to wake her, and slid out of my bed. I'd be able to think better in the office. I pulled on a pair of loose shorts and quietly left the room.

Once I had sat down in the leather chair at my

desk with a freshly made coffee, I felt focused. I fired up the computer and scanned through all of the updates I had received in the past week. I'd been giving the little things less attention recently, and that needed to stop. Everything needed to be controlled to avoid our status being taken down. I had kept The Brotherhood at the top for the past six years, we would stay there too.

    I reclined back in my chair once I'd got myself back on top of things and checked the time. It was just past midnight and Don was out. He had decided to go to Onyx for our big summer event, I rarely attended the nightclubs events, I kept myself in the loop, and showed my face if I needed to, but I never went for the pleasure of being there. Getting hit on by young scantily clad girls didn't interest me, especially when I had my own beautiful creature already in my bed. I had been shocked that Don had decided to go, he wasn't exactly a social butterfly, but it was also no secret that he hated my woman, so going out was likely the lesser of two evils in his eyes. Michael was at the club tonight and he had sent me a message an hour ago to inform me that the event was going well. I trusted Michael to be my eyes, and to make the right decisions. Don had yet to prove to me that I could trust him with the same. Tonight *could* be a good test though.

    I sent a message to Michael telling him to relax and that Adonis would be taking over so he could enjoy himself. Michael would have Rebecca with him, and she had most likely been pestering him all evening to have some fun. She would be very happy now.

The phone rang on and on when I dialled Don's number and I tensed as it went to voicemail. I tried him again, my jaw clenching as the seconds ticked past. He eventually answered just before I gave myself a toothache, and the sound of a girl panting came through the speaker.

"What the fuck are you doing Adonis." I snapped, and heard the girl ask if they should stop.

"Don't you dare," he told her and the sound of skin slapping made my lip curl. "What's up *Boss*." He said, sounding casual as fuck, like he wasn't blatantly fucking some girl while on the phone to me.

"Finish up now Adonis, you have a job to do." I demanded.

"*Fuck, Clara,*" he said under his breath and the loud sound of his phone hitting a surface made me jolt and pull my phone away from my ear. "You're on speaker," he informed me, "What's the job?" *This fucking kid.*

I ran my hand through my hair in frustration, "Don't be an idiot son, you have three minutes to finish and call back. When I next speak to you, I expect you to be focused." The sound's coming through the phone didn't stop and I paused before I hung up, "Oh, and Clara, you can go home when he's done with you, you're fired." I ended the call and opened a file on my computer that held all of my staff records and found Clara's information, I'd transfer her an extra months' worth of wages and then remove her from the system. She was a sweet girl, but it was no real loss, she would be easily replaced by the morning.

Two minutes and sixteen seconds passed before Don called me back.

"Good, you can follow time sensitive instructions." I said bluntly and was met with a low chuckle.

"I was practically done anyway. Could you not have waited until later to fire her though? She got all emotional and wanted a cuddle." he sounded exasperated, and I guessed that he hadn't given her what she wanted.

"That'll teach you to fuck my staff."

He scoffed but I carried on before he could say something he'd regret. "You're my eyes for the rest of the night Adonis, I need you to be me, make the right decisions, prove to me that you can handle something other than violence."

"Is that all?" he asked, sounding bored and I closed my eyes and inhaled slowly to calm my rising temper.

"If you can't handle this then you'll never be able to run things, son." I said.

I snapped my eyes open at the sound of my office door creaking and saw that M was standing on the threshold, wearing nothing but one of my white shirts. The fabric stopped at the very tops of her thighs, and she had lazily only done up the bottom three buttons.

"I can handle it." he replied. I was still listening to him, but I couldn't keep my eyes off of her, I was entranced by the way her hips swayed as she slowly moved across the room towards my desk.

"Don't let me down." I told him just as the goddess climbed on top of my desk and knelt with her knees spread apart, offering me the most tempting view. "Check in within the hour." I said and promptly ended the call.

"What are you doing amore mio?" I asked in a husky voice.

"Seeing if you want any company, why are you up?" she asked, and I smiled at how comfortable she was already appearing to be.

"Work amore, it never ends. Although if you stay down here, I doubt I'll get much done." I said and sucked in a sharp breath as she proved my point by sliding to the edge of my desk and climbing off to straddle me.

"I'm sure the great leader of The Brotherhood is capable of multitasking." She whispered and ran her fingertips up and down my bare chest.

"You are insatiable." I murmured, but I didn't stop her, too curious about what she would do.

She hummed in agreement then pressed her lips to mine in a passionate kiss, before reaching down between us and slipping her hand inside my shorts. Her fingers wrapped around my already solid length, and I groaned as she didn't hesitate, instantly working her hand up and down in a smooth rhythm.

"Carry on with your work *Boss.*" She purred.

"I would, but you're in the way." I looked her up and down. She laughed softly and the noise had me twitching in her palm. She removed herself from my lap and wriggled her way under the desk, flashing me a sly grin.

"Better?" she asked as her hands gripped my legs and pulled my chair closer.

"Much." I said and pushed my shorts down just enough to free my cock for her. It only took a breath for her tongue to run from the base to my tip and she began running it over me in teasing licks. I turned my attention to my computer screen and pulled up a log of previous applicants for our bar roles. The goddess under my desk continued to tease me as I scrolled through the names. I found the one I was looking for, an older woman with a hell of a lot of experience. I opened the file and mio amore pushed my cock deep into her mouth, taking the entire length down and holding me in her throat, I threw my head back and let out a long, deep moan, she slowly moved back, gliding her lips along my shaft, and repeated the motion over and over. I moved my hand under the desk and grabbed her head, encouraging her to keep the pace.

She released me from her mouth and growled, "Get back to work." She instructed and I laughed, only allowing her to get away with it because she was so fucking close to making me come.

I did as she said, bringing my hand back above the desk and cursing quietly as she took me back into her mouth. I turned my attention to the application for the woman, Anita, and checked that I had remembered her correctly.

M bobbed her head up and down and I dug my fingers into the arm rests of my chair, all concentration lost, "Oh mio dio, fuck, sto venendo." Words came falling out of my mouth and my cock swelled. She moved me deeper, and moaned around me as I exploded into the back of her throat.

I rested my head back and levelled my breathing. M tucked me back into my shorts, but she didn't come back up next to me. I lifted my head to search for her, and found her sat in one of the chairs on the opposite side of my desk, looking like the cat who'd got the cream. Licking her lips and grinning.

"What are you doing over there?" I asked and lifted my brows.

"Letting you work." She replied and threw me an innocent look.

"Nope," I shook my head at her, "come back here." I commanded. She smirked back at me and mouthed the two words that she *knew* would push me. 'Make me.'

I pushed my tongue into my cheek and stood up. Fear and excitement flashed in her eyes as I made my way around the desk and continued until I was stood behind her chair. My hands landed on her shoulders, and she craned her neck back to look up at me.

"You get one chance mio amore." She bit her lip and looked back ahead, crossing her arms over her chest in defiance.

I sighed and rounded the chair. Then bent over and effortlessly threw her body over my shoulder. She squealed in protest, but we had played this game enough times for me to know she was enjoying herself. I walked back to my own chair with her over my shoulder and with my free hand I pushed my shorts down before sitting back down and placing her on her feet in front of me. I turned her around and pulled her on to my lap, positioning her so that her back was pressed to my chest and her legs were draped wide open on either side of my own. The soft, warm skin between her thighs was slick with her arousal and she ground it against my already half erect cock.

"Stay still, and silent." I whispered in her ear as I pushed us both forward and reached for my phone. I unlocked it and handed it to her, then let my hands slowly trail up the insides of her thighs. "Call Cooper and put it on speaker."

She tensed, but did as she was told and placed my phone on the desk in front of us. As it began to ring, I dragged a finger through her wetness and circled her clit. She let out a gentle moan, "Shh," I reminded her and continued to work my finger on her sensitive flesh.

"It's late," she panted, "maybe he's asleep." She inhaled sharply as I rubbed harder, then Cooper's voice came down the line.

"Boss." He said, "sorry, I had to fight my way outside, Onyx is packed tonight."

M writhed in my lap and her mouth fell open as I pushed two fingers inside her, my thumb taking over on her clit as I pumped my fingers mercilessly.

"I need you to hire a new barmaid." I told him.

M clamped a hand over her mouth as I pushed her quickly to the edge. My woman was so easy to please. I yanked her hand away and replaced it with my own, holding her face close to mine. "Hold on mio amore." I murmured into her ear and felt her clench around my fingers.

"For Onyx?" he asked. Cooper was a smart guy, not a lot got past him, he'd already know what had happened with Clara.

"Anita Belfast," I said, "that older woman who interviewed last month. Call her first thing and offer her the basic contract." M began to wriggle on my lap desperately and I pulled my fingers out of her and spread her legs wider with my own. My cock was hard and ready to go again, and she reached between her legs to grab it. I tutted and batted her hand away before torturing her clit some more. "Greedy girl." I breathed and she ground her ass down on me in agreement.

"And if she's already found another job, how badly do you want her?" he asked, Cooper could easily turn on his charm if he knew I wanted something badly enough.

"Don't go overboard Coop, but yes, I want this one. I need at least one girl in that place that I can trust to not fuck my guys." I lowered my hand from M's mouth to wrap around her neck and she thrashed around on top of me, "Not yet." I warned her.

"Gotcha." He said with a small laugh.

"I'll send over her details in a minute." I released my grip on her throat and she gasped, then clamped her mouth shut. She was trying so hard to keep quiet and I realised I'd found my new favourite game. She wriggled against me again, grinding as if she was searching for my cock and I pushed up so that she could feel it against her entrance.

"Great, anything else Boss?" Cooper asked.

"No, that's all Coop." I said and M took the hint, reaching forward to hang up the phone. *That's how it's done.* The line went dead, and she let out a loud moan. "Such a good girl." I praised her, and pulled her tight against my chest, my fingers working relentlessly on her clit, and my erection pressing against her, "Do you want to come?" I asked.

"Yes," she cried, "please."

"Then come." I growled and thrust my cock deep inside her. She screamed and fell apart, soaking me and pulsing around me. Her pussy contracted in frantic ripples, and I groaned at the incredible sensation.

"Fuck." She breathed as she came back down to earth and I held her close. I slipped out of her, satisfied enough with her display to just sit with her, and she twisted in my lap. She nuzzled her head into the crook of my neck and stifled a yawn.

"I think you need to go back to bed." I whispered as I rested my cheek on her head.

She hummed in response but made no move to get up. I scooted the chair closer to the desk so that I could quickly forward Anita's details to Cooper in an email and closed the computer down. I grabbed my phone and stood up, then realised my shorts were pooled around my ankles. I could either put down the sleepy angel in my arms, or kick them off completely.

I made my way up the stairs with my ass on show for the second time and smiled at the madness of it. This woman had me doing all sorts of stupid things and that wasn't like me at all. And if I was being honest, I didn't hate it.

I tucked M into my bed and sat next to her. She shuffled around until she was comfortable and drifted off to sleep in no time. I unlocked my phone and found two messages waiting. One from Don telling me everything was fine. And one from Cooper. 'Thanks Boss, enjoy your night. ;)" Cheeky Bastardo knew exactly what had been going on during that call. I ignored Don and replied to Cooper. 'Don't push it C.'

28

Don

Sitting alone at a small table in a dark corner of the club I sipped my drink. I'd switched to water when Lorenzo had called and asked me to step up for the night.

I'd come here looking for a fight, but so far all I'd done was let out some of that built up rage by fucking Clara again, and subsequently getting her fired. I wish I cared, but I really didn't. She'd probably be better off away from this shit anyway. I'd probably done her a favour.

I was still looking for a fight. Lorenzo had told me to make good decisions or something, so I guessed if someone acted up that just meant I had to talk to them first, and hope that they didn't want to listen. I could prove myself by *trying* to be the bigger man, and then do what I do best.

Michael came over and hovered next to the chair opposite me, "You good bro?" he asked.

"Yep." I replied and scanned the room for the hundredth time. Why the fuck was everyone being so well behaved?

He waited a moment and when I met his gaze, he gave me a sharp nod. "Well, if anything happens, I'm only over there." He gestured to the table that his extremely drunk wife was attempting to dance on top of and cringed. "I'll send her home." He assured me.

"Good." I said in response, hiding all emotion from my voice, but inside I felt a swell of self-confidence. He was treating me like I was really running shit tonight. That felt good. A little taste of what was to come.

He rushed away and hauled Rebecca from the table and dragged her over to the bar, presumably to call her a taxi. She shoved him away and ran to the dancefloor, wobbling like a baby deer in her heels but managing to move faster than expected. She wriggled herself into the middle of a group of young girls and I watched in amusement as Michael fought his way after her, but was halted by a pretty blonde who proceeded to assault him with a red feather boa.

Rebecca collapsed on the floor giggling and the group of girls quickly helped her back up. Michael looked furious, but the blonde continued to wrap him up and bopped him on the nose. Apparently being a terrifying gangster didn't faze this little group.

He eventually wrangled his wife and removed her from the building, and I turned my attention to the bar, taking in the faces of each person stood waiting for a drink. A couple of boys were stood looking a little shifty, but when I looked closer it was clear that it was because they were underage. I managed to catch Michael's eye from his new spot at the bar and shot a meaningful look at the boys, he clocked them and nodded in understanding. Words were exchanged between him and a barmaid and a few minutes later a security guard quietly removed them from the bar.

I briefly checked in with Lorenzo, shooting him a message to let him know everything was fine. Then went back to watching the room.

The pretty blonde with the feather boa approached me, and her little group cheered her on as she glanced back at them. She blushed a little as she got closer then pouted in a way that I guess she thought made her look attractive. It wasn't necessary. For one, she was already attractive, and two, she was barking up the wrong tree, I really wasn't in the mood.

"Hey handsome, you're really working that whole dark and mysterious thing." She purred and perched on the edge of my table, her short red dress rode higher on her thighs to expose the frilly edge of her pink lace underwear. She looked down and bit her lip, but made no attempt to cover herself back up. I gave her a disinterested nod and turned my face away to look elsewhere.

A tickle brushing my cheek drew my attention back to her and she wrapped the boa around my neck. I scowled at her, but she didn't stop, pushing further and sliding herself off of the table and on to my lap. "I bet you're really dangerous." She said seductively and I gently nudged her in a hint to get the fuck off of me.

"You have no idea." I murmured and she shivered but made no attempt to get up.

"Danger gets me so hot." She breathed and pulled on the boa that was still wound around my neck. I glared at her and reached behind my head. In one sharp tug I ripped the boa in half and her mouth fell open.

"I'm not interested." I said flatly, but she just flashed me a playful smile.

"Come on big boy, of course you are."

"I will only tell you this once," I began, pushing my face closer to hers, "If you don't get the fuck off of my lap in the next five seconds, I will ensure that it's not just me who isn't interested in you, no one will want to fuck you if you're bleeding out all over the floor." My tone dripped with ice and her eyes widened. She quickly jumped up and went to head back to her friends with a terrified look on her now ghostly pale face.

"Don't forget this." I called after her and lifted the ripped pile of feathers from the floor at my feet. She hurried back over, refusing to look me in the eye, and retrieved her accessory, then disappeared in the direction of the lady's restroom, flanked by her little girl gang.

I sipped my drink again and took note of the Brothers in the club. Including myself there were only three of us still here. Michael and Cooper had taken up position by the bar, both leaning with their backs to it while holding a casual looking conversation. But they were focused. The three of us clearly able to sense that something was going to happen.

Only a couple of seconds passed before a girl came running from the ladies room screaming, shortly followed by another girl who was holding the blonde that I had just rejected tightly to her chest with a gun pressed into her temple.

The blonde locked eyes with me as I stood and approached them. "Help me." she shrieked.

The girl holding her pushed the gun harder against her head, "Shut up, you dumb whore." I looked at the girl and racked my brain, seeing if I knew who she was. I drew a blank though.

"Put the gun down." I said to her, keeping my voice calm but firm. She didn't look like the violent type, in fact she looked completely normal, cute even with her dark bangs and polka-dot dress. This wasn't a threat on The Brotherhood, so I had to try to de-escalate it first, I couldn't just go in and shoot the stupid girl for pulling a gun in our venue without trying to talk her down. Mild irritation crossed me; I'd really hoped that another gang member would start something. Not this.

Michael and Cooper emerged on either side of me, both with their broad arms folded and looking threatening as all hell.

"No, she's been making her way around this bar hitting on men who are spoken for." She snarled and her eyes flickered between my Brothers.

"That's a shit reason to shoot someone." I said and Cooper flinched, probably expecting her to pull the trigger in reaction to my criticism, but she just hardened her stare as she continued to flick her eyes between the three of us.

"Put the gun down Sam." Cooper snapped, and I froze. Fuck. Sam, as in Samantha, Coopers fucking girlfriend. Where did we stand on shooting each other's girlfriends? I looked across at Michael and he slightly shrugged one shoulder, apparently as unsure as I was. I turned to Cooper and jerked my head at Samantha, encouraging him to take over. Sure, I had wanted to get my hands dirty tonight, but this was his girl, so it was his mess to handle. If he couldn't, I guess I'd finally have an excuse to break that perfect nose of his.

A small crowd had gathered around all of us, but the majority of the club goers were drunkenly oblivious to the scene taking place where we stood. Cooper stepped forward and Samantha's gaze finally settled on him. "Sam, you're not going to shoot some girl for flirting with me. That isn't you." he said softly. The way he spoke to her made me glad I didn't have a girl to worry about, I couldn't do that soft, gentle crap.

"Isn't it Coop? Like you'd even know anymore." She said, her voice wobbling slightly and her grip on the blonde loosening a fraction. The terrified girl noticed and attempted to wriggle out of Samantha's hold, but she didn't get far as Samantha quickly tightened around her and cursed under her breath. Tears began to fall down the blonde girl's cheeks and I glared at Cooper, silently telling him to hurry this shit up.

"If this is about me then take it out on me, not some girl who, honestly Sam, is pretty harmless, aren't you darlin'" he smiled at the blonde and I rolled my eyes, fucking moron.

Samantha screeched and turned the gun on her boyfriend and tossed the girl to the floor. The blonde girl's eyes darted around as she realised that she was safe for now, and she scrambled to her feet. She threw herself towards me like I was her hero, or some shit, and I hadn't just threatened her a few minutes ago, but I sharply shook my head at her. She stopped dead in her tracks, "but, you'll protect me, right? You didn't let her shoot me, so you're going to protect me?" she whispered, her voice hoarse.

"Leave." I commanded, but she hesitated. I had to agree with Sam, this girl really was a dumb puttana. My eyes flicked to Michael, and he nodded, anticipating my request and moving forward, lifting the girl over his shoulder and marching her towards the exit.

My attention was drawn back to Samantha as she closed in on Cooper. "Looking for *another* girl to rub in my face Coop? Like it's not enough that you constantly blow me off for that fucking slut *Megan*." My stomach clenched at her words. Insulting Nutmeg was *my* thing, and apparently, I didn't like hearing it coming from anyone else.

"Careful Samantha," I growled, and Cooper's brows lifted slightly. "I'd think twice before you insult our girl again."

"Whatever, new guy," she narrowed her eyes at me, "this is about *him* anyway, I'm sure he has a whole harem of women hidden from me. That's where he is late at night when he claims to be with you lot."

"Sam, you know that isn't true." Cooper said, still keeping up the soft approach. "you know I keep things separate to protect you, there is nothing else going on." He stepped closer so that the gun was pressed to his chest. Seeing him step up to a girl who was clearly a little unhinged marginally changed my opinion of him. He wasn't quite as shit as I thought. "give me my gun baby, you can shout at me at home." He whispered.

She stared deeply into his eyes, and it was like watching snow melt, her whole body sagged, and she placed the gun in Coopers hand. "You're going to take me home?" she asked quietly.

"Yes, I'm taking you home." He confirmed. Apparently this was all that she needed to help her calm down, and she sighed heavily.

"Ok, I'll go and get my bag."

I stared at Cooper in confusion. "What the hell was that?" I asked.

"That, my friend, was me taking a massive risk, she is not okay, her protection isn't the only reason I keep things separate. Fuck I'm in for a long night." He scrubbed his hand over his clean-shaven chin and blew out a long breath, then gave me a thoughtful look. "*Our* girl?" he asked.

"Don't read too much into it, pretty boy." I grunted, "Gotta defend her, for appearances sake."

He gave me a slow nod, his expression sceptical, like he definitely thought I was lying. "For appearances." He repeated, then went to find Samantha.

I rolled my shoulders, easing the tension that had been building in them, and frowned to myself. Why the hell *had* I called her that? Like fuck was I going to dwell on it though. I didn't need to dedicate another second to thinking about little Nutmeg. Instead I pulled out my phone and sent a message to Lorenzo, filling him in on what had just happened, then looked at the time. One hour until this place closed. One more boring hour until I could call it a night, head *home*, and spend a couple of hours in the gym. A punching bag would have to satisfy me tonight.

29

Meg

Sitting with my feet up in Lorenzo's lap while I ate flaky, buttery croissants and sipped black coffee, much to his disgust, while he read the newspaper out loud to me had become an almost daily occurrence. The past couple of weeks I had barely been back to my apartment, only spending a few nights there and popping in to change my clothes. I felt comfortable in this huge house strangely quickly and fell into little routines with Lorenzo that made me more comfortable with my choice. He was trying, and I was starting to feel… something.

He was keeping me doing the jobs that no one else wanted, as I had expected he would, but I was fine with that. No one new knew about our situation and I didn't want anyone growing suspicious of it until we both knew where we really stood with each other. He was controlling his moods with me far better than before, keeping things professional in public, but behind closed doors I had stopped questioning how he felt.

Every evening that I spent with him was filled with delicious meals, late night trips to amazing places, and him telling me about his day, just like a normal couple would.

"I really appreciate all of this." I murmured to him as he paused to turn a page in his paper.

"The news?" he questioned and dropped the paper enough to look over it at me with an amused look on his face. I was starting to enjoy those special expressions that he rarely showed to anyone else.

"No, you holding up your end of our agreement." I smiled at him.

He closed the newspaper and folded it before placing it on the table. "I'm a man of my word mio amore, if you try, I try." His hands fell to my feet, and he began to rub deep circles into them, "Are you happy?" he said carefully.

I groaned as he kneaded my aching feet and tossed him a seductive smile, "What do you think Lorenzo, do I *look* happy?"

He ran his gaze over me hungrily, I was sitting in a dark blue silk nightgown that skimmed my thighs. Lorenzo had bought it for me after the second time that I came down to breakfast wearing one of his shirts, telling me I should wear nightwear made for a goddess. He presented me with a box that evening filled with various silk nightgowns and camisole sets. I had tried to refuse them at first, I could bring over some pjs if he wanted to give me a drawer or something, I couldn't accept such extortionate gifts, but he had put his foot down, well, he had a raging tantrum and threatened to burn them if I refused them. God forbid Lorenzo not get what he wants. Drama king.

"You look many things amore mio," he said in a rough, lust filled voice that sent a rush of heat to my core, "I think," he searched my face, "I think I can see a hint of happiness," he gently placed my feet on the floor and leaned closer, "right there." He said and placed the pad of his finger on the corner of my mouth.

I smiled into his touch, and he returned it before swiping his finger softly over my lower lip. "I have a request." He didn't move away and ran his finger back and forth over my mouth.

"Mm." I hummed, waiting for him to continue.

"I have been invited to tomorrow's charity gala, and I would like you to attend with me." he said and dragged his finger down from the centre of my lip to my chin to meet his thumb in a gentle hold.

"With you? or *with* you?" I asked quietly.

"I want to show the world how lucky I am to have you il mio tesoro, I want you on my arm for everyone to see." he said and pulled me in to place a chaste kiss on my lips.

He released me and sat back, retrieving my feet from the floor where he had placed them and placed them back on his lap as he waited for me to respond.

"So everyone will know, everything will change?" I asked.

"Yes, everything will change." He agreed, "you don't have to decide now, but I will need your answer by tomorrow morning amore."

I nodded slowly and forced a smile to my face, "I'll think about it, thank you Lorenzo."

"You couldn't have covered up a bit Nutmeg?" Adonis said from the doorway where he was leaning and scowling at me. How long had he been there?

"Bite me, Donny." I narrowed my eyes at him, and he barked a hollow laugh, but didn't respond. He walked over to where we were sat and leaned over my legs to grab the newspaper from the table.

"You done with this?" he asked Lorenzo who nodded and began to rub my feet again.

Adonis tucked the paper under his arm and reached over me again, grabbing my coffee from the table and sipping from the half empty cup.

"Are you fucking kidding me Adonis." I snapped and pulled my feet away from Lorenzo's lap to stand up, face to chest with the arsehole. He smirked down at me and wiped the corner of his mouth with his thumb.

"Delicious." He said with a low laugh.

"Go and get her a fresh cup Adonis." Lorenzo said in a voice that was sounding like he was growing more tired of our shit each day. Adonis hadn't been around as much as I thought he would be, often staying out for the whole night. I had no idea where he went, I didn't really care, so long as he wasn't around me all the time pushing my buttons.

"She has legs; she can get her own." He said, continuing to stare me down.

"*That* was mine." I snarled and shoved his chest. A growl rumbled in his throat and before I could blink a hand was on my chest. But it wasn't his, it was Lorenzo's. I had been so consumed by my anger towards Adonis that I hadn't noticed him stand up, he had now placed himself between the two of us.

"Can you two please try to get along." He said and stared between us.

I didn't speak, choosing to sit back down and try to keep a hold on my temper, while Adonis swatted Lorenzo's hand away from him and turned to leave the room. A few minutes later he returned with two full cups of coffee and wordlessly placed one on the table where mine had been sitting before he had stolen it. He gave Lorenzo a sarcastic smile and sauntered back out of the dining room.

"You will have to drive yourself into work today amore, I have a job for you later" Lorenzo said, a simple change of subject that worked perfectly to take my mind off of the coffee stealing arsehole.

"What is it?" I asked with mild curiosity, recently I'd spent a lot of early evenings running around on drug drops, something I hadn't done for years, but being in Lorenzo's bad books at 'work' had shitty consequences.

"I need a message sent to Charon." He said and his eyes glittered as he watched me quickly perk up. *Finally something big.*

"Okay," I said slowly and attempted to wipe the wide grin from my face.

"Do not go overboard though. I don't want any retaliation from him." He warned, "I have a few things to handle, but Cooper is around, go and see him before you leave for work." He stood up and bent to place a kiss to my forehead. I reached up and looped my arms around his neck before he could pull away and dragged him back in for a deep kiss that perfectly conveyed how happy I was to be back in his good graces.

After I was washed and dressed in the clean

outfit that I had picked up before hitting the gym last night, I went in search of Cooper. He would either be in the little office that our boss had set up for him and filled with computers and all sorts of gadgets that I had no idea about, or he was taking full advantage of working here and enjoying a morning workout in the gym.

 I checked the gym first, but it was empty, so I moved on to the door at the end of the hall. Loud music was thumping through the door, and I winced a little at the sound, not my cup of tea at all. "Coop" I hollered over the music as I opened the door and he paused the song.

 "Good morning sunshine!" he exclaimed and grinned up to me from his swivel chair in the centre of the room.

 "Good morning, Boss says I need to come and speak to you about the Charon job today?" I tilted my head and leaned on the door frame.

 "Oh, and here I was thinking you'd come to see me because you missed me." he pulled a dramatically sad face.

 "Seriously Coop, we had lunch together on Sunday."

 "And now its Wednesday, it's not good enough M, I'm starting to feel abandoned." he teased. "Take the day off and hang here with me?" he widened his eyes at me in a plea. "I'm already bored and its only 8am."

"I have work to do, important work." I folded my arms, "and so do you, I'm guessing."

"Who's?" he raised a challenging brow at me.

"The boss's," I said, "you know, the client who might actually kill me if it doesn't get done."

Cooper spread his arms with a triumphant smile, "Then what better place to be than his own damn house with the man himself just down the hall, easily accessible if you have any questions," I frowned at him, "Come on M, play with me!" he pouted.

I rolled my eyes at his theatrics, I thought *I* was bad. "Let me go and speak to him." I sighed, knowing already that Lorenzo would most likely agree to me staying here for the day, but not wanting to give Cooper that satisfaction just yet.

I strolled back down the hallway and turned to head towards Lorenzo's office. The door was open a crack, so I peered through it before entering, making sure he wasn't in the middle of a call.

"Amore mio, is everything alright?" he said as he looked up from a stack of paperwork.

"Everything is fine, I have a request, can I work here today?" I asked.

He looked a little taken aback then gave me a small smile, "Of course, but don't let any of us distract you too much, do you need anything?" he stood up and crossed the room to me.

"Just a computer, a printer, and unlimited

coffee."

He chuckled low in his throat, "Done, and we can have lunch together?"

I nodded in response, "I'd like that."

He walked with me back to the room where Cooper had turned his music back on. "C," he bellowed, "turn this shit off, M will be working here today, make sure she has everything that she needs, and go make some fresh coffee." He commanded and Cooper nodded like a mad man, then wiggled his eyebrows at me behind Lorenzo's back as he shot out of the room.

"Thank you, *Boss.*" I turned to him and ran my hand up his chest, toying with the two buttons at the top of his shirt that he had left open.

"I love how you look when you're about to go to work, wear your hair like this for me this evening?" He murmured and I smiled as he brushed the loose hair that framed my face behind my ear. I wore it in a chignon for work and usually unpinned it the second I left the office. His fingers lingered on my earlobe and his brows creased slightly. "You deserve diamonds amore," he stroked my lobe, "We can shop for some tonight." He released my ear and pressed his mouth to my cheek. I half nodded, then realised that he meant earrings. No, I couldn't.

My fingers shot up to my earlobes and I swallowed thickly. "These are important to me," I whispered, my voice wobbling slightly, "I don't want anything else." I bit my lower lip, "Thank you though." I added.

Lorenzo's face twisted with confusion, but he didn't push, "Maybe a necklace then?"

I considered it for a moment, "Maybe." I agreed.

Cooper cleared his throat as he moved past us and placed drinks on one of the many surfaces in the room. My shoulders relaxed at the interruption; I hadn't been aware that I had tensed up so much. Lorenzo straightened up, adopting his big scary boss mask, and turned to Coop, "Let her work, otherwise you can kiss goodbye the special treat that I have coming for you from Andreas." he threatened, and Cooper's face lit even brighter than usual.

"You didn't?" he bounced in the chair he had sat back down in.

"I did, do your research before you use them though." Lorenzo glared at him, and he agreed, still bouncing.

I went to sit in the only other chair in the room and wriggled to get comfy. Lorenzo gave me a sharp nod and I returned it; we were in work mode from now until lunch.

When he closed the door Cooper grabbed a cup of coffee and spun in his chair to hand it to me. I took it and thanked him. "What's this special treat then?" I asked, hella curious about what had him so excited.

"Explosives." He grinned and his blue eyes twinkled. I nodded, completely understanding his excitement now, and knowing that they had come from Andreas meant we absolutely were not supposed to have them.

"Explosives that I can play with later?" I asked, full of hope.

"No chance, and the boss doesn't want to make a statement *that* big, randomly blowing up one of Charon's guys is not sending the right message, that's starting a war." He gave me a stern look.

"Fine," I slumped in the chair and pouted, "What's the deal with this *message* anyway, boss said to come and talk to you about it." he twirled his chair from side to side, and steepled his fingers, looking like a hyperactive bond villain.

"Take your pick, a group of his guys will be at the shooting range this evening, rumour has it that the big dope is planning something unpleasant for the boss tomorrow evening at the gala." I nodded along, "Boss wants you to make sure he understands that if he does anything stupid, his men will pay. Get creative sunshine, but don't go too far. And for god's sake keep me in the loop, boss will kill me if anything happens to you."

I scoffed at the idea of anything bad happening to me and thought for a moment. "Couldn't I just kidnap and hold one of his guys hostage? I've always wanted to do that." Cooper spluttered a laugh.

"Sure, you crazy bitch, you going to rock up in a balaclava and throw him in the back of a van?"

I laughed with him, "Maybe not."

"Just stick to what you know, select one, get him alone, make a threat, spill a little blood, but leave him able to *actually* send the message."

I sighed in satisfaction, "It's nice to be out of the boss's bad books."

Cooper raised his brows at me, "Did he spank you?" he winked.

I pretended to zip my lips closed and he groaned, "You're no fun." He spun back to one of the many computers that he was working on. "Stop distracting me and get to work."

I laughed and turned away from him to face the only screen that he hadn't fired up and sipped my coffee as I waited for it to wake up, then opened my emails and found the documents that I'd need today. I liked it here in this room with my friend far more than I liked my quiet office. If it wasn't for the fact that I needed my own space and separate friends, like Eden, I'd probably ask Lorenzo if I could work here permanently.

***

"Be careful sunshine." Coop's voice came through the headphone I had in my ear.

"I always am, call you in a bit, enjoy the show." I hung up and waved up at the cctv camera on the side of the building before slinking into the shadow of the trees that bordered the mountainside shooting range to wait for the three wolves to come outside.

I had gone over my plan with Cooper, and we had agreed that a simple approach was the best idea. The three men always arrived in separate vehicles, so I could mess with one car, the other two will drive off, and I'll be left with my poor victim stuck and alone. Then I could pounce. Coop had advised me to use a gun as the chances of anyone noticing the shot outside of a shooting range would be pretty slim. I took his advice and had my favourite Beretta 92 in a shoulder holster, but I'd also equipped myself with other items, which I'd not told him about.

From my hiding place I had a clear view of the main entrance to the range and the vehicles parked out front. I'd selected the car furthest from the entrance, but in clear view of the camera. Coop had already confirmed that he had intercepted the feed and would do whatever Coop does when the time was right, I wasn't listening, It only really mattered that *he* knew what he was doing, so if anyone in the security office was watching the screen during my little attack, they'd be none the wiser.

The heavy front door swung open, and two men in black denim jackets stepped out laughing, followed by another matching man who was checking his phone and not paying them any attention. *Hello little pups.*

The two cheerful guys made their way to their cars, "Drinks back at The Hound?" one called out over the roof of his pickup to the other two. The man he had been laughing with agreed enthusiastically and slid into his blue Maserati and the man who continued to type away on his phone nodded his head distractedly.

The man put his phone into his pocket and strode over to his silver Audi, the car I'd taken great joy in messing with. I'd not done a lot to it, nothing that couldn't be easily fixed, but his car was not going to start when the spark plugs were missing. He climbed into the driver's seat and his friends pulled away and sped off towards the winding mountain road that led back to town.

The Audi made a painful choking noise a couple of times before the man got back out with a frustrated scowl on his face. I cracked my neck and trained my eye on my target, lifting my weapon and waiting for the perfect moment.

The wolf walked around to the front of his car and popped the hood, as he leaned in to take a closer look at what I'd done, I released, watching with satisfaction as an arrow shot through the air and sunk into the front tyre, emitting a pop and a soft hiss. The wolf jolted upright and moved to the side of the car and crouched down to investigate. He flicked the arrow and groaned, clearly aware that once he ripped it out, he would have to replace the tyre.

I dropped my bow to my side and stepped out of the shadows just enough to be visible as the guy searched the area for me. After my afternoon out with Cooper, I'd fallen back in to practicing the sport that I'd fallen in love with all that time ago and couldn't help myself when I had been told I could get creative. When the guy's eyes finally fell on me his face twisted in disgust.

"Lady Brother." He hissed. I had no idea that I had a little nickname. Cute.

I gave him a devilish smile and strode slowly over to him, tossing my bow behind me and pulling a small knife from the selection that I had strapped to my thigh and twirled it around in my hand. I was pretty much winging it from this point.

"I'd heard you were dramatic, but this," he gestured to his tyre, "is unexpected." He said in an amused tone as he yanked my arrow out and straightened up. "I take it you are also the reason my car wont start." He folded his arms and raised his brows, he knew who he was facing, but he wasn't scared. The fact just made me smile wider.

"Maybe," I shrugged as I came to a stop a couple of feet away from him and reached into my jacket pocket and pulled out the missing car parts. I held my hand out to him, but he made no move to take them.

"Smart." I laughed and tossed the parts on the floor at his feet.

He bent slowly to pick them up as I leaned a hip against his car and tossed my knife in the air a few times. He kept his eyes on me from his crouched position and pulled a knife from his boot. So predictable. He lunged towards me, but I was ready, grabbing his outstretched arm before the sharp blade in his hand could connect with any part of my body, and twisting him into a secure hold, pressing the tip of my own knife to the side of his throat.

"You won't kill me." he panted and writhed in my hold.

"Won't I?" I said casually as I ran the tip of my blade in gentle teasing circles over his throat, putting an instant stop to his attempt to escape my hold.

"Of course not, you're not *that* dumb." My jaw tensed but I refused to bite. I simply shoved him to the floor and slammed my heavy boot onto the centre of his back. He grunted in pain as my foot connected with the side of his ribs next, and he rolled to his side as he cursed me out.

I crouched in front of him, and grasped his face, turning his head so that his eyes met mine. "I *was* planning on just shooting you in the leg and being done with it, but I think I've changed my mind." I gave him a feral smile as I ran my knife down one side of his face and he sucked in a pained breath as the skin broke and blood began to trickle across his cheek. I pushed him onto his back with my knee and held him in place on the gravel. Turning his head the other way I ran an identical line down his other cheek. He cried out as I pushed deeper this time, and I sighed.

"Oh shh you big baby, chicks dig scars, if anything, I'm doing you a favour." I knew this wasn't necessarily true, Grey was covered in scars and the only woman who wanted him was Deb, but it worked for *some* guys. This guy might be able to pull it off, although If I were him, I wouldn't be telling any girls how actually I got them. No, if I were him, I'd come up with some epic story where I come out on top.

"Are you done?" he growled as I admired my work, having added a couple of short slashes to his left eyebrow.

I held my knife over his eye and hummed a thoughtful sound. "Yeah, I suppose I am." then pushed his head hard against the ground.

He winced, "Good." He said as I stood up and I frowned down at him. The rumble of a car engine drew closer, and I shook my head at him.

"The cavalry?" I asked. Then pulled out my gun and swiftly shot him in the leg. He screamed and rolled around at my feet, and I felt my eyes roll in frustration as the blue Maserati approached. I squared my shoulders and aimed my gun at the windshield as I moved around the Audi and walked closer to where it had stopped. The driver's door opened, and a tall man stepped out, but it wasn't the wolf who had driven away from here ten minutes ago.

"What did I miss?" the heavily tattooed, well-dressed arsehole asked as I lowered my gun.

"What the fuck are you doing here?" I snarled. "and where's the wolf?" Please don't have killed him. Please don't be that stupid.

"In the trunk." Adonis smirked, "Where's your guy?"

I pointed to the Audi, "Behind there," I frowned back at Adonis, "why are you here?" I asked again.

"Because you needed me." he said cockily and closed the Maserati door and stepped closer to where I was stood, still in my power pose, but with my gun pointed to the floor now.

"I didn't *need* you. I'm guessing the guy in the trunk was coming back to help his friend out?" he nodded, "I could've handled him." I said firmly and he kept making his way closer until his Italian leather loafers were toe to toe with my scuffed black boots.

"Sure you could Nutmeg." He looked down at

me and I pursed my lips.

"Does the boss know you're here?" I asked.

His deep laugh irritated me, "Who do you think sent me? Clearly he doesn't think you can handle things by yourself anymore."

I blinked at him in an attempt to hide how that had made me feel, it hurt, that Lorenzo didn't trust me to do this. But he trusted Adonis? *What the fuck.*

I slid my gun back into my holster and turned, "Whatever, don't be stupid Donny, return the nice wolf to his owner unharmed."

We both walked away, him back to the stolen car and me heading back past the Audi to where I'd parked my own car. The guy I'd been handling hadn't made any more noise and I presumed that he'd passed out from the pain. I'd check on him before I left, make sure he hadn't bled out and was able to go home.

I heard the engine of the Maserati start and felt a fragment of tension leave my body. As I rounded the Audi I was knocked to the floor, a solid mass colliding with me, and it took me a moment to realise that the wolf was now on top of me as I laid awkwardly beside the back of the car. "Fuck." I shouted and held my arms over my face as his fist came hurtling towards me. It connected with my arm, and I locked them in a hard barrier as I anticipated the next blow.   It didn't come.

Instead a rush of air washed over my body as

the man's heavy weight lifted from its place on top of me. I dropped my arms and searched for him.

Adonis had him by the scruff of his shirt and was dragging him towards the front of the Audi. I scrambled to my feet and quickly checked myself over for any serious injury, but nothing felt too bad.

I stumbled around the car and sped up as I heard a loud thud and a sickening scream. I got as far as the wing mirror then stopped, taking in the scene in front of me.

Adonis was stood with his hands pressed down on the hood of the car, the hood that was not fully closed. His black shirtsleeves were rolled part way up his forearms, and the exposed skin was smeared with blood. Had that been there before? The wolf was bent over, half of his body inside the car. Adonis lifted the hood and peered inside, a disgusted look on his face. "Don't you ever touch her again." He growled and straightened up.

My eyes widened at his words, and met his dark, dangerous gaze. He looked me up and down where I was stood clinging to the side of the car and then rushed towards me. He moved me so that my back was against the side of the car, and he began checking me over, "Are you hurt?" he asked in a low, quiet voice.

"I thought you'd left." I murmured.

"I didn't, are you hurt?" he repeated.

"I'm fine Don, is he?" I bit my lip, "Is he still

alive?"

Adonis' hands continued to search my body for any injuries, "He's fine, they'll get the message." He reassured me. "You *are* hurt." He said with a slight growl as his he removed his hand from where it had been carefully examining my head. There was blood on his fingertips, but I didn't feel any pain in my head.

"I'm fine," I repeated, "It's probably not my blood."

"What if it is?" he asked, sounding annoyed, and pushed his hand back through my hair, gently searching for any cuts.

"It isn't." I said with more bite this time, "get off of me." I lifted my hand and tugged his wrist.

"Just wait Nutmeg." He said sounding more irritated.

"No Don," I tugged again, and he snarled at me.

"For god's sake Megan, just let me check." He snapped and my mouth fell open. I looked up at him and found him looking back at me, his eyes burning with intense anger.

I dropped my hand from his wrist, and he slid his hand from my hair down the side of my face, slowly, softly. My breath caught in my throat as I was dragged deeper into the depths of his midnight eyes. I let out a shaky breath as his fingers reached my chin and he held me and tilted my head back.

His head dipped lower, and his lips hovered over mine. I froze. His breath was warm, his scent was intoxicating, a combination of cinnamon and gunpowder, and I couldn't stop myself from being drawn in by him. My lips brushed his and a spark of electricity flashed through me. *Did he feel that too?*

Suddenly I pulled away, startled by the realisation of what had almost happened. His hand dropped from my chin, and he blinked rapidly then scrubbed his hand over his face.

"What," I breathed, "What the fuck was that?"

He stared down at me with a fire burning in his eyes now, but he didn't speak.

"What was *that*?" I shouted, and shoved his solid chest.

He stepped backwards, a few paces and his jaw tightened. He glared at me for a moment then turned and wordlessly walked away, getting into the Maserati, and speeding away.

I took a few steadying breaths and attempted to step away from the car that I was still leaning against. My body screamed as I moved, but I didn't care, it was nothing I couldn't handle. I managed to stumble back to my car and climb into the driver's side. My hands were shaking, and my head was spinning. What the hell had just happened?

I shook myself off, I hated him, he hated me, and that was all just adrenaline fuelled stupidity. I glanced around the car park, apart from the Audi and the unconscious man half hanging from it, it was empty. I looked at the building in front of me and blew out a long breath. It was only when I remembered what was on the side of the building that I tensed again. The camera.

I yanked my phone from my pocket, thankful that it hadn't been damaged in my fall, and bought up Lorenzo's number. I pressed call and listened to it ring out. Seconds turned into minutes where I couldn't breathe, all I could do was press call, over and over again. He didn't answer. I tried Cooper next, but nothing. I chewed on my lip until it began to bleed. He had seen, hadn't he. He was going to kill me, us.

A few minutes later a message popped up on my phone.

Cooper
Stay away from the house, let him come to you. Stay safe. X

I winced, what the hell was going on back there? I pressed call one last time on Lorenzo's number and when I reached his voicemail, I left a short message. "L, I need to clear my head, but please call me back." I sighed, unsure what to say, "Please." I repeated softly. Then hung up.

I checked my face in the mirror, there was blood drying on my skin and a few tiny scratches that I'd guess had come from gravel flicking onto my face when I had been on the ground. I looked a mess, but I didn't care. I needed to clear my head like I'd told Lorenzo, and I knew there was only one way to do it tonight.

30

Lorenzo

"Play it again." I demanded for the ninth time. Cooper did as I asked, and I paced the room. We were in the computer room where Cooper and Amore mio had spent the day working. We'd had such a lovely day, we'd had lunch together, me and her, and we had discussed dress options if she decided to join me tomorrow evening. She didn't seem completely against it this afternoon, but now, I wasn't sure what the fuck she wanted.

I leaned on the back of Coopers chair and glared at the screen. My stepson held my woman's face so delicately, and she didn't pull away straight away. Did she want him? Had their hatred for each other been a lie this whole time.

When I'd called Adonis earlier today to tell him he would be tagging along to her job he hadn't kicked off. Previously he had argued with me over working with her, in fact he made out that he couldn't stand to be around her. Had I missed something?

"Again." I snapped as we watched him walk away from her. Cooper hesitated and looked over his shoulder at me.

"Are you sure?" he asked. She had tried to call him after I'd ignored her, and he hadn't answered, but I was well aware that he had text her after. He was on her side; he always would be.

"Don't question me Cooper. I could have you replaced in a heartbeat." I threatened. It was a lie, but I was angry, and he was here.

He blew air out of his nose but did as I said. Once he pressed play, he rose from his chair. "I can't watch it again Boss, I'm sorry." He gave me a pained look and stepped aside. I softened slightly and nodded, then took his place in his chair. My hands balled into fists at the sight of them. She was *mine*. Who the fuck was he to be touching what was mine?

"Where is he?" I spun the chair around to face Cooper, who was facing the back wall with his hands pressed against it. He pushed off from the wall and faced me.

"I don't know, but I'll find him." He assured me, and I got up.

"Send me that clip." I said, and left the room,

storming through my house towards my office.

Once I was inside the room, I pulled my phone out. I tensed at the amount of missed calls I had from her, but not a single one from him. I then noticed the voicemail notification. I pressed the button to listen to the message.

""L, I need to clear my head, but please call me back. Please." Her voice was full of tension, but the second time she said please I heard it, the softness in her voice, a tone that she rarely used. She felt awful.

I ran my tongue over my lower lip and threw my head back. Damn right, she *should* feel awful. She had assured me that there was no one else, then went and behaved like this.

My phone pinged, notifying me that I had an email. I removed my suit jacket and unbuttoned the top couple of buttons of my shirt before sitting down and firing up my computer to open the email, knowing it would be the video clip from Cooper. When I opened the email, I saw that he had written a message too. 'He's dropped the wolfs car back to The Hellhound, if he's heading here, he won't be long.' Good, I had no idea if Charon would be at his bar tonight, but some of his men would definitely be there. The only good thing to come from everything that happened was that we would manage to send a very clear message to our rival with the two men left unconscious and bloody in their cars.

I replied to Cooper. 'Good, go home.' I'd put him through enough tonight. He had enough going on in his life without all of this on top of it. He swore he was fine, and that he didn't need a break, I wasn't so sure. But I wouldn't push him, if he wanted to carry on as if nothing was going on that was up to him.

Watching the video clip again I sighed. Why was I torturing myself with this? I should just call her and talk about it. But I wasn't ready to hear what she had to say. I pushed my finger and thumb to the bridge of my nose and rubbed hard circles, pushing away with incoming headache. When would my life get easier?

I heard the front door slam closed and heavy footsteps drawing closer to my office door. Cooper hadn't been wrong.

Adonis didn't knock, he threw my door open and marched inside. In a flash I jumped up, leapt over my desk and threw myself at him, backing him against a wall and wrapping my hand around his throat. He didn't react. He just held my gaze with an impassive stare.

"Explain yourself." I bellowed in his face.

He didn't speak. He didn't move. He just stared. "Parla, sei un pezzo di merda." I snarled in our native tongue.

"Liberare." He breathed, and I dropped my hand from his throat, and slammed it into the wall beside his head.

He didn't flinch. "Anger and adrenaline, there was nothing else to it." he said, his voice rough and his accent stronger than usual. It only ever came out this way when he was angry. Who was he angry with? Himself? Her? Me?

"Bullshit." I growled.

"The job got done, your precious little *tesoro* got hurt, would you rather I just left her there to die at the hands of that bastardo? Neither of us meant to end up in that stupid position after. I still despise her. Shit happens Enzo, get the fuck over it." he ducked under my arm and strode over to the small table on the other side of my office and poured us both a large measure of Angels nectar from the crystal decanter.

He walked back over to me where I now stood with my arms folded. He handed me a glass and fixed me with a stern look on his face, "Are we over it?" he asked.

"Not a chance in hell." I ground out and sank the entire glass in one long gulp. "Welcome to my shit list Don. Now get the fuck out of my office." I snatched the other glass from his hand and gestured to the door.

He paused in the doorway and turned back to face me. "I'm surprised you didn't hit me." he smirked.

"I need you looking your best." I said simply.

"Don't worry Don, I have other ways of hurting you."

31

Tobias

A flash of red hair caught my attention as I stepped out of the office and into the lobby. "Meg?" I shouted and hurried in the direction the girl had gone. I rounded the corner leading to the locker rooms just as she threw the ladies door open. "Meg." I shouted again and she paused in the doorway. As I approached her, I noticed her black leather jacket was covered in dust and her loosely braided hair was a complete mess as if she'd been rolling around somewhere dirty.

I placed my hand on her shoulder and she jolted slightly, then hesitantly turned to face me. My jaw dropped at the sight of her. Blood was splattered over her face and neck. I scanned her body, taking in the not so subtly concealed weapon under her jacket, and the array of knives strapped over the top of her leggings.

She swallowed hard and pushed loose strands of hair away from her face. "I'm fine." She said firmly before I could ask. "I need to shower and change, then I'll be out, please tell me you aren't busy?"

I was frozen on the spot, but managed to speak, "I'm not busy." I confirmed in a small voice.

"Good, I won't be long." She said, her voice slightly wobbling. She straightened her spine, wincing slightly.

"Are you sure you're -." I began, but she cut me off.

"I'm fine Toby." She glared at me, her deep green eyes turning emerald with fierce anger.

I stepped back, and shook my head, then blew out a long breath. "I want an explanation." I said and turned to walk away and wait for her in the gym.

"You won't get one." She muttered so quietly that I almost didn't hear her.

I looked over my shoulder at her and raised my brows in a challenge. She sighed and headed into the locker room.

Once I was in the gym I began pacing, the large room was quite busy, but would soon begin to clear out. I had no idea what she needed, she didn't look like she would be able to do a lot, she looked like she might collapse in all honesty. Combat training was definitely out the window. She looked stressed, yoga would probably be perfect for her, but I was no yoga instructor, and she would probably slap me if I ever suggested it as a serious idea. *Or stab me?*

"I'm ready Tobias, do your worst." She said as she slowly approached me. I raised my brows at her again, and then looked her up and down.

"Where did you get those?" I asked, waving my hand up and down at her body. She was now dressed in a bright purple and turquoise matching shorts and bralette set and had nothing on her feet. I'd never seen her in anything so, colourful.

"Doesn't matter." She huffed and pushed past me, heading over in the direction of the punch bags and grabbed a set of gloves from the shelf. "Come on." She urged.

I stood and watched her for a moment as she cracked her neck and rolled her shoulders. "Do you really think *that* is a good idea?" I asked, placing my hands on my hips and staring her down.

"I'm fine, but I'm getting sick of repeating myself." She snarled and began to rapidly pound into the hanging sack. I surveyed her for a while, not giving her any direction or motivation, just watching, and giving her my best 'you're an idiot' look.

"Argh." She screamed as she stepped back a fraction and slammed her bare foot into the bag. A couple of girls over on the treadmills turned to look at her. She shot them deathly glares and they quickly went back to focusing on their workouts. She cursed under her breath and sagged to the floor beside the gently swinging bag.

"Are you done?" I asked in a clipped tone and made my way over to her. She looked up at me and tears filled her eyes. I sat down next to her and tilted my head to one side, "Come on Vixen, tell me what happened."

She blinked back the tears and cleared her throat. "No Toby, I can't." She looked torn though, as though she desperately wanted to tell me something, but was what? Scared?

My mind whirled through various reasons for her turning up here in the state that she had, and it kept falling back to one thing. "Did he do this to you?" I asked quietly and her eyes snapped up to meet mine.

Her brows pinched in confusion, "Who?" she asked.

"Lorenzo?" I whispered and leaned closer to her.

She sucked in a sharp breath as she realised that I knew they were together. She tugged the gloves off of her hands and sighed, "Not here." She said rising to her feet, then held her hand out to me. I hesitantly took it, still not completely sure if I could trust myself around her. I cared for her, I wanted her, and I needed to hear whatever she was willing to tell me, but the second her skin touched mine I felt it, that instant pull that made me almost forget the consequences and say fuck it all.

She towed me out of the gym and down the wide corridor towards the double doors that led to the pool. She opened the door and searched the room; I didn't bother to tell her that I'd known it would be empty. James had closed it off from the public half an hour ago, but I also knew he would still be around somewhere.

She pulled me through the doorway and dropped my hand as she went to go and sit at the side of the main pool. I moved past her and headed towards the door at the end of the room, it was just a storage cupboard, but I'd found James in there before, binging on chocolate. He was mortified, but I promised I'd keep it a secret. I, on the other hand, didn't care who knew what I ate. I may be in the best shape of my life, but I still liked to indulge.

Once I'd ensured that the cupboard was empty, I sat down beside her and slipped off my trainers and socks. We both lowered our feet into the warm water, and I leaned back onto my elbows and waited for her to speak.

She gazed into the water, watching her feet as they kicked gently back and forth and eventually opened her mouth, "It wasn't Lorenzo." She said quietly, then turned to face me, "Why did you think that it was?" she frowned down at me, but it wasn't in anger.

I wrinkled my nose, trying to decide how much to say, "You and him, you're dating or something?" I said, more as a question than a statement, I wasn't actually sure, when Grey had come to warn me off, he had referred to Meg as Lorenzo's girl, that could've meant anything now that I thought about it.

"Or something," she agreed with a tight smile before turning back to face the water.

I pulled out the elastic that had held my hair in its usual topknot, and ran my fingers through it, unsure about how far to push her, but I was worried about her. "How the hell did that even happen?" I blurted and she twisted sharply back to face me.

"How the hell do you even know?" she snapped back, clearly irritated, but not at me, that was obvious. I was just a potential punching bag right now.

"Doesn't matter." I muttered, "What matters is that he's a bad guy little one," her eyes flashed with some emotion I couldn't pin-point, but I continued, "I'm worried about you. You come in here tonight in that state," I felt my voice wobble slightly and I sat upright, "Megan, you were covered in blood." I knew worry was etched deeply on my face, but how did she think she could come in like that and *not* worry me?

"Not my blood." She said, but it wasn't

enough,

I scoffed at her, "That's not the point, what the hell is going on?" I reached over to her and twisted my fingers between hers, she let me, and she sighed heavily.

She looked down at where our hands sat in her lap and her hand tightened around mine before she spoke, "I know he's a bad guy Toby, but so am I, you don't need to worry about me, and I'm sorry for scaring you like that."

"What do you mean you are too? You're not giving me anything here Vixen." I pushed gently, running my thumb over the back of her hand.

"I'm one of them." She said quietly and looked up at me, her bottom lip dragged between her teeth as she anxiously watched me for my reaction.

What? She was what? "You're, you're a Brother?" I asked, almost certain that I wasn't understanding her properly.

She nodded, still chewing on her lip and I released her hand. She bit harder, but I lifted my hand to her chin and gently tugged her lip free.

"Stop that," I gently chastised, "and explain. Properly."

She looked around the pool hesitantly. I stood up and walked over to the entrance and locked the door, "All of it Vixen, no one will hear." I sat back down beside her and dropped my feet into the pool again.

"I'll give you the short version." She decided and I nodded, I'd take any version so long as I got even a tiny piece of the truth from her.

She reached her hand over to me then pulled away. I grabbed her hand and gave her a stern look.

"Okay," she breathed, "I joined The Brotherhood when I was 19, Lorenzo offered me protection if I joined them, I'd done something that had caught his attention, but the consequences weren't going to be good if I didn't get help, Jason had tried to talk me out of it, but one meeting with Lorenzo was all it took for him to decide to join me instead," she smiled sadly as she spoke about him and I felt a stab of sadness for her, "Jason died," she looked up at me, "as you know, and I was a mess, as you also know," I grimaced at the memory, she tried to hide it, but she was a mess. In the end she got stronger, she was not that same girl anymore. "I went after the guy who killed him, and I thought I'd avenged Jase, I was on such a high, and I ended up in Lorenzo's bed, well, not his actual bed," she blushed, "but you don't need details," she was right, knowing he'd had his hands on her, had done every filthy thing that I longed to do to her, it irritated the shit out of me. I still wanted her, no matter how badly I tried to convince myself that I didn't.

"Lorenzo wouldn't hurt me, not on purpose, as my boss he has to put me in dangerous positions, but it's also my choice to be there too," she grinned,

"Toby, I am really fucking good at what I do, and a lot of that is down to you, I have quite the reputation in certain circles," she squeezed my hand, "you don't have to worry, tonight didn't go to plan, but I survived it, and my bad mood, that's mostly down to some complete arsehole who insists on pissing me off."

"What did they do?" I asked, curious about what pisses this girl off enough to have her screaming at a punch bag.

"He saved my ass then almost kissed me." she spat. And I choked on a laugh.

"Fuck Vixen. This is *a lot*." I threw my head back and stared at the ceiling. "Things are starting to make sense now though."

She hummed in agreement, "Most accountants don't take combat classes do they." She said. I'd meant that Grey's threat made sense now, but I was glad she'd presumed I'd meant something else. I didn't need to be telling on her Brothers.

"Are you even an accountant? Or is that just some big cover story?" I asked.

"No, I'm actually an accountant, being in a gang isn't as fulfilling as you'd think. Oh, and my name isn't Megan Clarke, It's Megan Fields." She laughed lightly, and I smiled. That wasn't news to me, Grey had already dropped that bombshell on me, it hadn't made sense at the time, but now it did. Apparently opening up a little had diverted her bad mood, and although I was still attempting to process it all, I was happy about it. I'd do anything to see that girl smile.

"Do you feel better now?" I asked as she began to play with my fingers.

"I do," she admitted, "I didn't think I would, and you're taking it really well." She sighed and a flicker of sadness crossed her face.

"Did you not want me to?" I asked, confused.

"I guess seeing as I'm being all open and shit with you tonight, no, I've been convincing myself that you'd never understand my life, it's been my way of making your rejection sting less." She looked away, and my stomach knotted. I hated that I'd hurt her. I hated that I was hurting myself. "Now that I know you wouldn't have freaked out, it makes it suck so much more."

"Vixen," I whispered, and she looked at me from under her lashes.

"You were lying, weren't you?" she asked.

I removed my hand from hers and ran it through my hair, "You're a smart girl, make smart choices." I told her. "That's what I've done."

I removed my feet from the pool and grabbed my trainers, making my way towards the door. My fingers hovered over the lock, and I turned back to her, she was staring at me with narrowed eyes, like she was trying to work out what I'd meant.

"I don't want to." She said.

"Three men want you Vixen, you can't have them all, so you make the smart choice. Please." I unlocked the door and walked out, leaving her sat by the pool, in her clearly stolen gym clothes, and cursed under my breath. *Why the fuck did I push her away, again?*

32

Meg

Make smart choices. Toby's words echoed in my head as I sat by the pool. I had no idea how long I'd been here. Toby had left me a while ago though, and the skin on my feet was beginning to go wrinkly.

I huffed and got up and made my way back to the locker room. Hopefully whoever this hideous work out set belonged to wasn't in there to kick off at me. The lockers in this place were far too easy to break in to, but I wished I'd found a better one. I supposed I should've just been thankful that the set had fit, otherwise I'd still be wearing my blood and dirt covered leggings and top.

I opened the locker in the far corner where I'd stuffed my ruined clothes and threw my jacket on and stuffed my still damp feet into my heavy boots. I looked ridiculous, but I'd parked on the curb out the front of the gym, so I didn't have to worry too much about being seen.

I hurried out of the gym, pushing though the aching pain that had spread from my back to my arms, and was shocked to find my car still waiting for me, no tickets, no clamp, nothing. Although in this city the police have more interesting things to deal with than illegally parked cars.

My phone buzzed in my jacket pocket, and I winced as I looked at the notifications on the screen. Seven missed calls from Cooper, and one text, from Lorenzo.

Lorenzo
I'm coming over.

Shit. I checked the time stamp on the message, luckily it was only from a minute ago, so I should have enough time to get to my place before he did. Depending on his driving tonight.

I pulled up Coopers number and pressed call, putting him on speakerphone, then shoved my phone into the cup holder and started my engine.

"Where the fuck are you?" he shouted when he picked up.

"Gym." I said, "Heading home, are you ok?" I pulled away from the curb and drove in the direction of my apartment.

"I'm fine, of course I'm fine. What the hell were you thinking?" he was still shouting; I'd never heard him so angry before.

"Cooper, chill the fuck out. Why are you so angry?"

"Because I'm worried about my best friend you fucking idiot!" he softened a little now, then bit again, "I'll ask you again, what the *hell* were you thinking?"

I blew out a frustrated breath, "I wasn't, but nothing happened, and nothing has changed. Lorenzo is on his way to mine now, I'll make this right, I'll be smart." I said, and rolled my eyes, *Make smart choices.*

"Tread carefully, I don't know if he's calmed down or not." He said.

"I will, and Coop," I smiled to myself, "Thanks for worrying."

I ended the call and sped up, the roads were empty, and I found myself pulling into the underground car park in no time at all.

Stepping out of my car I noticed the steel grey McLaren parked a few spaces away, and waited as the stunning, terrifying man stepped out. He looked flawless as always and I cringed as he cast his gaze over me.

"Boss." I said as he approached me slowly, his deep brown eyes fixed on mine. He looked like a predator hunting his prey, and I knew I was in more trouble than I'd bargained for. How the fuck was I going to get out of this.

"Don't '*boss*' me Amore." He growled and walked past me towards the elevator. I followed him and apologised quietly as we waited.

We travelled up to my floor in uncomfortable silence, the tension in the small elevator was suffocating. He stepped out first then stopped by my door, I opened it and unzipped my jacket as I walked in. Lorenzo entered behind me, then grabbed my wrist as the door closed. He pulled me back and held me tight against him with my back pressed against his firm torso.

"You said you'd try," he snarled in my ear, "you told me there was no one else, you are mine. No one touches what is mine." his hands moved to my shoulders, and he pulled off my jacket before spinning me to face him. "Mine." he said in a dark voice as his hands looped around my back, and I tilted my head to look up at him.

"Yours." I whispered and pushed up onto my tip toes. *Smart choice*, Lorenzo was the smart choice, I knew it, I didn't want Adonis, I couldn't have Toby, Lorenzo could give me everything. Yet a small part of me questioned if I was about to walk into something that I should've been running away from. No, this was the direction my life should take. "Lorenzo, I'm yours."

He glared at me, our lips a breath apart, but he didn't close the gap. His hand slid up my back and pushed into my hair, fisting a handful, and pulling hard, my head jolted back, and I couldn't stop the rush of heat that instantly ignited between my legs. "You wanted him." He said angrily and I tried to shake my head, but his grip held me still.

"I want you." I insisted.

"I saw the way you looked at him." The fury in his eyes intensified.

"I pulled away Lorenzo, I hate him." I snapped. He searched my face, looking for a lie that I was certain he wouldn't find. "I'm telling you what I want, it's *you*."

He tilted his head, then raised his brows. I knew what he needed from me.

"The gala, I'll go with you." I offered my answer to his question from this morning, "Everyone will see who I belong to." I added, giving him exactly what he wanted.

His mouth twitched as he struggled to hide a smile, and he pursed his lips to cover it up. "Amore mio," he murmured, then his lips found mine, his hands pulling me into a brutal, possessive kiss that left me breathless and desperate.

"Mine," he said as his hands travelled over my body, "For the whole world to see."

I nodded and let out a shuddering breath. Everything was fine. We were fine. And we were now properly *we*. Tomorrow evening everything will change. The lives that I'd worked so hard to keep separate would collide, everyone would know who I was, who I was with, and what I was a part of. My Brothers would find out our secret, how would they react? My head spun as I realised what I'd agreed to, and my legs went weak.

"Woah." Lorenzo exclaimed as his arms wrapped around my waist and my hands reached up to grip his shoulders.

"Fuck." I breathed, "I need to sit down." He agreed and lifted me into his arms.

"Which door?" he asked, and I realised that Lorenzo had never been inside my apartment.

"Straight ahead," I gestured down the hallway to my lounge door and prayed that it was tidy. I'd spent so little time here recently that I couldn't remember how I'd left it the last time I'd stayed.

Luckily, as Lorenzo pushed open the door, I saw that the room wasn't too bad. There were a couple of cups sitting by the sink in the connecting kitchen and an empty Chinese takeout box on the counter, but the lounge was in its usual, simple state, the only mess being a scatter of sheet music on the coffee table.

Lorenzo placed me down on the sofa and paced the room. "You only said it to stop me being mad at you, didn't you?" he said, a slight harshness to his tone. "You don't want this, do you?" he paused and looked at me.

"I do," I said quietly, "I'm not taking it back Lorenzo." I raised my voice a little as I felt the panic begin to calm.

"Then what?" he began to pace again, "why do you look like," he waved his hand at me, "that?"

"It all changes." I said and took a long breath.

He moved to sit on the coffee table in front of me, pushing the sheet music to one side, and placed a hand on my leg. "Are you scared?" he asked.

"Yes." I admitted.

"Then I'm failing before we've even begun." He sighed.

My hand fell on top of his and I squeezed, "You can't stop me from being scared Lorenzo."

He frowned, and I leaned forward to cup his face in my hand. This incredible man had no idea how to help me. "Distract me," I prompted him, "I'll calm down if you distract me."

His face softened, then turned dark, and I instantly knew what he had in mind. "We really should be celebrating." He said in a low voice and his hand slid up my thigh. I licked my lips and pushed myself to focus on to his touch and away from my thoughts. I could deal with them later, internally.

"Let's get you out of these," he said and tugged on the waistband of the shorts. I lifted my ass from the sofa, and he pulled them off, taking my panties with them. His eyes fixed on my bare pussy, and he pushed my knees wide apart. He dropped from the coffee table to the floor, getting on his knees and looking up at me. His finger brushed my entrance and he groaned, "Is this for me?" he asked as he lifted a wet fingertip for me to see. "Am I the only man who gets you this fucking wet?" I should've hated it, the subtle dig at what had almost happened tonight, but I didn't, the more possessive he got, the more turned on I became.

"Yes. You are the only one Lorenzo." I lied, completely unashamed.

"Good." He growled and pushed his face between my thighs. His tongue pushed into me, and I let out a whimper. He was rough and frantic, the perfect distraction. His teeth grazed my clit and he sucked and lapped at my pussy. I could feel the residing anger rise up in him and he used his mouth to let it all out, his hands pushing my legs wider and his fingers digging hard into my flesh. The pain mingled with the pleasure, and I cried out as I chased a violent orgasm, feeling myself release onto his tongue.

He raised his head as I collapsed back into the cushions in a panting mess. "That worked." I said between heavy breaths, and he hummed his agreement.

"Go get changed." He said, "We're going home."

I opened my mouth to correct him, but as he stood up and offered me his hand I closed it, I didn't need to ruin this evening again. Instead, I accepted his hand and disappeared to my bedroom, trembling slightly on my post-orgasm unstable legs.

Once I was dressed in my own clothes and had grabbed a few items to last me a couple of days I headed back to my lounge. Lorenzo was sitting on the edge of my sofa, and I noticed that he had placed the papers from the coffee table in a neat pile on the stand on my piano.

"Ready?" he asked as he made his way over to where I was stood in the doorway.

"Almost, I just want to straighten up the kitchen." I said and he shook his head.

"Leave it, I'll get one of the girls to come and clean up for you. You don't do housework anymore il mio tesoro." He said and ushered me towards my front door.

I frowned but once again, chose to keep my mouth shut. This was a battle I'd fight later when he was in a more stable mood. I was in no way ok with anyone doing basic household tasks for me, not when I was completely capable of doing them myself. It was the one part of being at Lorenzo's house that I couldn't get comfortable with, but it was *his* house, so I had to respect his ways. But I wasn't going to allow it in my apartment. No chance.

Lorenzo held the door open for me and I passed through, then locked up behind us. As we travelled back down to the parking garage, he eyed me up and down, then took my bag from my arm. "Tomorrow we will go shopping," he began as we stepped out of the elevator, "We can start with a dress, then head to the salon, and then to the jewellers."

"I have dresses, and jewellery." I protested weakly.

"*My* woman deserves the best, accept the treat Amore mio." He said in a voice that screamed 'do not argue with me'.

I rolled my eyes as he walked a pace ahead of me and opened the passenger door for me. "Fine." I said and squealed as his hand cracked against my ass before I stepped into the car.

"Good girl." He whispered as I sat down, and he closed the door.

"Fuck you." I muttered into the empty car, and as he climbed into the driver's seat, he gave me a heated look, and I knew he knew, and I knew I was in trouble. "Shit."

33

<u>Meg</u>

"Which one? The black or the red?" I asked as I emerged from the dressing room wearing an emerald green dress that swept across the floor.

Lorenzo looked up from his phone and his gaze turned dark and dirty. "Neither, *this* is the dress." He said and rested his chin on his fist, "Turn." He commanded, and when I faced him again, he was biting down on his hand. "Fuck." He growled.

I turned to face the mirror and cocked my head, I looked pretty good. I'd never considered this shade before, but the store assistant had selected it and Lorenzo had demanded that I try on every item that she had suggested. I still had two dresses left.

"I like it, put in on the maybe pile." I said and turned back to him. He was shaking his head.

"No, this is it." he said firmly.

"You said I had to try them all, I still have two more to go." I said and went to walk back into the dressing room. He jumped up and grabbed my arm.

"I don't care what I said, we're done here. This was made for you il mio tesoro." His gaze was heated, and he pulled me close. His hands skimmed my bare back and I shivered, then gasped as he pushed his solid length against me.

"Ok, this one is clearly working for me." I said and pressed a swift kiss to his lips before running my hand down to his trousers and gently squeezing his cock through the fabric, then strutting away, swaying my hips dramatically.

I heard him groan and smiled to myself, loving that I could get away with teasing him so publicly. It was a fun part of the change. I'd not let my thoughts dwell on the fear I felt over how this evening would go though. Lorenzo hadn't allowed there to be enough time for me to do that anyway, he had woken me up, sent me off to shower and dragged me out for breakfast before we arrived at the extravagant dress shop.

I slipped out of the dress and neatly placed it back on the hanger. The other two dresses were short, one blue and one black, I supposed the black might have looked nice, but I didn't really want a short dress for the gala. If I had to face all of those people tonight, freshly on the arm of Lorenzo D'Angelo, I'd do it looking classy as shit in a floor length gown.

Tugging on my jeans and t-shirt I smiled into the mirror, the store assistant had given me the most disapproving look I'd ever received in my life, and Lorenzo had openly threatened her if she dared to even glance in my direction again. It was ridiculous, but I appreciated him doing it, on some level. It was sweet, in a psycho way.

I handed the dress to Lorenzo along with the strappy black heels that I'd picked out when we had arrived. They would go with any dress that I chose, and he didn't try to change my mind about them, apparently that was one thing I was trusted to pick for myself.

He took the items and I wondered off while he paid, feeling suddenly uncomfortable about him buying them for me. I'd never had anyone buy me such expensive things. I'd treat myself to expensive clothes and shoes all the time, but it felt different when someone else was paying.

"I think you should wear your hair up tonight." Lorenzo said as he approached me from behind. I had been mindlessly running my fingers over a pile of satin scarves, "Do you want one?" he asked, and I removed my hand from the pile.

"No," I said, snapping back to the present, "You want my hair up?" I asked and turned to face him, "I was hoping to get a fancy blow out, all bouncy and sleek."

He shook his head at me, "You'll look beautiful with it up, let's go, our appointment is in twenty minutes, and I'd like to make sure they know exactly what we want."

I followed him out of the shop and sighed. I'd never been to an event like this before though, so I supposed he knew what would help me fit in a lot better than I did. I'd been to nice dinners and exclusive parties, but tonight would be a whole other level of fancy.

Once Simon had styled my hair into an intricate updo and set it with a crazy amount of hairspray I was feeling pretty good about the evening ahead. Simon had been extremely chatty and threw so many compliments at me I was concerned my head might explode. Lorenzo admired my hair and thanked Simon for following his vision so perfectly and I rolled my eyes at how serious he was acting over hair. Not even his hair, *my* hair.

I left the salon and headed straight for the McLaren, but Lorenzo took my arm and looped it though his and guided me away from the car. "One more stop Amore mio." He said and pointed across the street to a jewellers. I'd forgotten about him wanting to accessorise me too.

"We don't have to." I began, but he walked us across the street and into the glittering shop. He headed straight to a cabinet at the back and pointed down at it.

"Which one?" he asked, and I dropped my gaze to where he was pointing. The cabinet was filled with shimmering diamond necklaces, and I gasped as I took them all in.

"I can't, Lorenzo it's too much." I protested.

"I promised you diamonds; you will get diamonds. If you don't choose one, I'll buy them all." He threatened and my eyes widened.

"You wouldn't." I exclaimed.

"Watch me." he said darkly and beckoned over a tall woman in a navy blue suit. "We will take these." He said to her and ran his hand over the top of the cabinet.

"Which one's sir?" the woman asked and began to open the back of the cabinet for us,

"All of them," he replied, and she paused.

"All of them? Sir, are you sure?" she said carefully.

"Are you going to pick one now?" he directed his question to me, "or shall I let this lady ring up every item in there for you?"

The woman looked at me and waited for my response. "Fine," I snapped, "can we have a minute." I asked her and she locked the cabinet back up and stepped to one side.

"Go on then il mio tesoro." He pushed and I scanned the selection of necklaces.

After a few minutes I pointed to a simple silver necklace, it had three teardrop shaped diamonds hanging in a line from the centre. "That one." I said.

Lorenzo admired it for a moment, "It's quite simple." He said finally.

"Yes," I agreed, "I like simple." I said pointedly. Making it clear that this was not the way to my heart. Something that I was sure he was already aware of.

"Then it's yours." He said and nodded to the woman who returned to us immediately. He showed her which necklace I'd chosen, and I watched her face drop slightly. She had clearly been hoping for a large sale, and I could guess that the necklace I'd selected was not in the price range that she had hoped for. Oh well, I like what I like.

We left the shop and Lorenzo took me back to his car. We made our way back to the house and once we were inside I instantly relaxed. Lorenzo handed my bags to Clive who assured him that they would all be taken care of for this evening, then lead the way to the dining room.

"Quick lunch," he said, "then Claudette will be here."

"Who?" I asked. I'd never heard of anyone named Claudette.

"She will take good care of you, once she's finished with you, you'll feel like a princess." I cringed slightly at the word, then realised who this woman must be.

"I can do my own makeup." I said in a slightly fed-up tone. I was not even slightly used to any of this and was getting a little bored of humouring him to keep him happy.

"She will do more than just makeup Amore, please just relax and enjoy yourself."

I puffed my cheeks and blew out a long breath. I'd messed up last night though, I wasn't out of the woods, so I needed to do what he wanted. "I'll try." I said, "what's for lunch?"

After we had eaten Lorenzo excused himself to attend to business. Overall our morning together had been quite nice, he hadn't been glued to his phone, in fact he had barely glanced at it. Maybe he had handed everything over to Grey to handle this morning instead. I smiled to myself as I considered this, Lorenzo had given me his full attention. And I hadn't been naked. *Good start.*

Lorenzo had told me to treat this place as my own now. It sounded a hell of a lot like he was wanting me to move in, but I was in no way *there* yet, fuck, I'd only just opened up to the idea of us being together, and I still had to worry about how everyone else in our lives would react to that. I supposed I was starting to get comfortable already, but not with the entire house. There were so many doors that I'd never opened.

I walked down the corridor and picked a door at random. Behind the door was a games room, it had a typical man cave vibe about it, and I noticed the pool table in the centre of the room, I'd never played, but I reckoned I could beat Lorenzo if he let me try. My aim was near perfect with a gun, so why not with a pool cue?

I closed the door and made a mental note to challenge Lorenzo to a game soon, then wondered back the way I'd come, making a beeline for the stairs, but as I reached the bottom step Clive appeared out of nowhere and cleared his throat, "Miss Jones has just arrived and is setting up in the guest bedroom." He announced, and I turned and frowned at him in confusion.

"Who?" I asked.

"That would be me," a voice came from the top of the staircase, and I looked up to find a stunning blonde woman standing in a white tunic and matching trousers.

I looked back at Clive, still confused, and he nodded and gestured for me to go to her, apparently knowing who she was.

"Claudette," she said with an outstretched hand when I ascended the final step. I took her hand and searched my mind, quickly trying to place this woman. Of course, she was the woman Lorenzo had booked to do my makeup. But the gala was hours away, surely I shouldn't have my makeup done this far in advance, but I suppose I'd thought the same about my hair and I'd been assured that it would hold up until at least the early hours of the morning.

"M," I said, and her brows pinched slightly, "or Meg," I offered, but her brows just tightened, "Megan." I gave in, and her face relaxed, apparently she wasn't going to be comfortable calling me by anything other than my full name.

"Lovely to meet you darling," she said with a saccharine smile that made me a little uncomfortable. She placed a hand on my back and gently guided me towards the guest room door, "Shall we get started, we have a very busy afternoon ahead of us."

I nodded a little dumbly and tried not to let on how confused I was. *Busy afternoon?* I could do my own makeup in less than half an hour, how much was she planning on caking onto my face for it to take an entire afternoon?

She opened the door and I paused in the doorway, taking in the guest room. The room that I knew so well didn't look even slightly the same as it had the last time I'd been in here. It looked like a freaking spa.

"Claudette, what exactly are we doing this afternoon?" I asked, turning to face her where she was stood beside me looking impatient.

She nudged me into the room and locked the door behind us. "Everything darling, when I'm finished with you, you will be the picture of perfection. Now strip down and lay on the table," she instructed and handed me a large white towel, "place this over you if you want."

I did as she said, still feeling a little stunned. I'd really thought this woman was just going to slap some makeup on me and be done with it. I'd never had any of these kinds of treatments done before, Shelly had taught me how to do everything for myself when I was younger, so I'd never bothered to let someone else do it.

"Chocolate or strawberry?" Claudette asked from a table on wheels that she had set up by the door.

"For what?" I asked, confused as all hell? Am I getting snacks? I've only just had lunch, but sure, I could squeeze in a few chunks of chocolate.

"Wax, or you could have unscented, but personally I like to go for something tasty, if you're lucky the scent will linger on your skin." I laughed in response, but she didn't join me. When I looked over at her she was frowning again.

"Oh, oh okay, this isn't a joke, erm, strawberry I guess." Great, I was going to have a fruity fanny.

"Great choice," she said, and I laid down on the table and draped the towel over myself. I was pretty confident with my body, and if I wanted it or not, this woman was going to be getting all kinds of intimate with it, but I didn't really want everything exposed when it wasn't necessary. "Are you looking forward to the gala?" she said, beginning the small talk thing that I wasn't a huge fan of.

I indulged her with mindless chatter for hours as she plucked, pruned and prodded me from head to toe. She had listened to my requests a lot better than I had presumed she would. Lorenzo had given her a guide, but luckily his vision for me tonight had a little wiggle room and I was able to select the shade of lipstick I wore and the shape of my brows and nails.

I stood in a fluffy white robe as Claudette circled me like a vulture, "Open." She commanded and I unwrapped the robe. She stood in front of me and slowly looked me up and down, "Perfection." She said with a wide smile, and I felt myself relax a fraction. "Let's go and get you dressed. You'll be leaving soon."

I wrapped the robe back around myself and followed her along the hall to Lorenzo's room. She hovered by the door and then knocked.

"Come in." Lorenzo's voice came from behind the door. I hadn't expected him to be in his room, but why shouldn't he be? He would have to get dressed too.

Claudette opened the door, and I entered the bedroom behind her. "Good evening, Mr D'Angelo," she said with a slight purr to her tone that made my jaw clench.

Lorenzo looked up from where he was stood buttoning his shirt and looked straight past the woman to me. "Amore mio, you didn't want a different colour lipstick tonight?" he asked with a disappointed frown.

"I like red Lorenzo." I said with a shrug.

Claudette's smile dropped from her face in an instant and she spun to glare at me, "If he doesn't like it, we will change it, Megan." She hissed.

"*He* doesn't have to wear it," I smiled at her sarcastically, dropping the nice act I'd been putting on since I met her, then drew my attention to Lorenzo, "Is there a problem with me wearing this shade?" I asked.

"I wouldn't have picked it amore." He said as he ran his gaze over me, "but I suppose it looks fine."

"Good," I said and gave him a sly smile before turning back to Claudette, "The red stays."

She pursed her lips but didn't argue, "Shall I take Miss Fields to get dressed now?" she asked Lorenzo and I rolled my eyes at how she looked at my man with unashamed come-fuck-me-eyes. *My man.* That felt a little weird.

"Yes, please Claudette, *Miss Fields*' dress is through there." He pointed towards the large walk-in wardrobe, and the woman walked across the room, grabbing my arm, and towing me behind her.

"I'll see you downstairs in twenty minutes." Lorenzo said and placed a passing kiss to my cheek as I was dragged into his wardrobe.

Inside the wardrobe I was shocked to see that my dress was the only one hanging on the rail on the left of the room. I had presumed Selene's dresses were still in here since Clive had found one for me not that long ago. If they weren't in here, where were they? There wasn't a single sign that the woman had ever had any place in this room, just like the bedroom showed no hint of her either.

Claudette opened up the expensive looking box that sat on top of a black velvet chair in the corner of the room and handed me a scrap of black lace fabric, "I'm not sure that this will look right under that dress." She said thoughtfully, "maybe we forego underwear tonight?" she raised a perfectly shaped brow at me, and I shrugged a shoulder.

"Sure," I agreed, "but Claudette, I don't need help putting on a dress, I manged it fine by myself in the shop this morning. I'll be fine now."

"I am aware that you can dress yourself," she said, pulling the dress gently down from its hanger, "but I need to ensure that you look perfect, and that the bruises on your back aren't visible." She handed me the dress then pulled a small compact from her pocket and opened it to reveal pale powder. "I've already hidden them quite well, but no harm in making sure it's set properly."

I dropped the robe and stepped into the emerald dress, pulling it carefully up my body and slipping my arms into the thin straps. Claudette stepped behind me and began patting powder on to my back where my bruises from last night were. Once she was done, I turned to examine her work, you'd have no idea that there were large purple marks covering a large amount of my back with how well she had worked on me. "Thank you, you are very good at what you do." I said honestly, I may not like her, but she was talented.

"I know. Now go and sit down, I'll find your shoes." She said and I pushed the underwear box onto the floor and perched on the edge of the velvet chair. I glanced at my reflection behind me in the mirror and smiled, feeling crazy levels of confident in this dress, Lorenzo was right, it really was made for me.

Claudette left me after she had helped me into my shoes and given me her final approval. I politely told her I hoped to see her again sometime, but if I was being honest, I prayed I never had to endure another minute with her again. Next time I'd put my foot down and do it all myself. Except maybe the facial, that part was relaxing as hell. But we could find someone else to do that.

I grabbed my small clutch bag and checked that everything I needed was inside. Phone, lipstick, pocketknife. Best to always turn up prepared. I took a deep breath and stepped out of the bedroom and headed towards the stairs.

Adonis' appeared from behind the door just past the guest bedroom and I guessed that was where his bedroom was. He walked towards me, and I frowned at his attire. He was dressed in a black suit with a white shirt and black bowtie. Suits were his choice of clothing quite often, but not like this, not with any kind of tie, and *never* a white shirt.

"What are you all dressed up for?" I asked coldly. I hadn't seen him since he had almost kissed me last night. I'd pushed the thought out of my mind, but it all came flooding back as he stood before me. I needed to keep hold of the hatred I felt towards him. Lorenzo needed to see that no matter how deliciously tempting his stepson was, our feelings towards each other hadn't changed.

"Same reason as you Nutmeg." He said with a dark smirk and pulled a small silver flask from inside his jacket and took a long swig.

"*You're* coming to the gala?" I scoffed, "Why the fuck would you be coming?"

Adonis gave me a smug look and licked his lips, "Didn't Daddy tell you? We're both moving up in the world, you'll be stepping out as his new piece of meat, and I'll be networking, preparing for when he retires. He's getting on a bit, so I doubt it'll be long before I'm taking over The Brotherhood."

My mouth fell open and I spluttered a cough.

"You're joking?"

"Do I look like I joke?" he deadpanned. "Don't tell me you thought *you* might have been the one to take over. Oh little Nutmeg, you'll be lucky to even stay a Brother now that you're publicly his. I really thought it might have been a challenge to get rid of you, but apparently you've just walked straight into your exit."

Before I could stop myself, my palm collided with his cheek, and he chuckled a low laugh. How did he manage to go from almost kissing me and worrying about me being hurt, to this?

"Nice to see you two are back to your usual bickering selves." Lorenzo's voice carried up the stairs to us and we both looked down to find him leaning against the banister. "but we're going to be late, so get your asses down here now."

I shot Adonis a deathly glare and descended the stairs, he held back, but I refused to look back. I plastered a smile on my face and made my way down to my man.

"Amore mio, you look lovely." Lorenzo said as he took my hand and twirled me around. "Don't you agree?" he asked, directing his question at Adonis, who was coming down towards us at a lazy pace.

Lorenzo was clearly testing him, all three of us knew it.

"You've done well for yourself Enzo." He

said, boosting Lorenzo's ego and avoiding giving me a compliment, smart man.

Lorenzo gave him a satisfied look and turned away from us and headed to the front door.

"Non sembri adorabile però, sembri una dea mandata direttamente dall'inferno a tormentarmi." Adonis murmured to me as he pushed past me to follow after Lorenzo. What the hell had he just said, and why had his words sent a tingle through my entire body? I shook myself off quickly and tried not to let the fact that I couldn't understand him bother me. Knowing Adonis he had probably told me that I looked like a swamp slut and that he hated me.

Outside the front door was a sleek black Ducati, and Lorenzo's McLaren. I eyed the bike and looked down at my dress. Damn, if I didn't have to wear this thing and my hair wasn't looking all fancy I'd happily shove Adonis into the McLaren with Lorenzo and take the Ducati for an extra long ride.

Adonis swung his leg over the bike and mouthed something that looked a hell of a lot like 'hate you', before pulling the helmet down over his head. I pushed my tongue into my cheek and narrowed my eyes at him as he roared away. Lorenzo pushed the passenger door of his car open from inside and called me over. When I was sat inside, he placed his hand on my thigh and gave me a soft smile.

"Are you ready amore mio?"

"As I'll ever be," I said with a small smile, and blew out a long, slow breath, "This doesn't change my place in The Brotherhood, does it?" I asked. Adonis' words at the top of the stairs had struck a chord and I couldn't help but wonder if things would change *that* drastically.

"No amore, please ignore Adonis, you are far to valuable to all of us." He reassured me and I felt my shoulders sag with relief.

As he drove, he kept his hand on my thigh, rubbing his thumb back and forth in a soothing motion, and with each passing minute I felt more ready for what we were about to do. I was safe with him. Nothing bad would happen to me tonight. My man wouldn't let it.

We pulled up out the front of the large hotel where the gala was being held and a young guy rushed around the car to open my door for me. I thanked him and told him he was doing a great job, then made my way round to Lorenzo where he was having a stern word with the valet about how expensive his car was. I stepped in between them and passed the keys from Lorenzo's hand to the valet. Lorenzo frowned at me, but I just smiled up and him and looped my arm through his elbow. "Let's do this." I said confidently, and he spun me to face him, dipped me low and pressed his lips to mine in a passionate kiss.

Once I'd found my balance again, we walked

up the steps towards the main entrance and through the foyer to the extravagant ballroom. There were tables laid out all around the room where we would eventually sit down and eat. A long auction table ran down one side of the room, and on the other was a stage where a band was playing beautiful classical pieces. Everyone in this room looked incredible and I was glad I'd let Lorenzo choose this dress; I really did fit in here wearing it.

Across the room I spotted Adonis talking with a couple of men, he was smiling at them and talking animatedly, and I couldn't help but laugh.

"What has amused you, amore mio?" Lorenzo murmured in my ear, then placed a quick kiss to my shoulder.

"Your stepson, he's smiling, it's funny." I said, and Lorenzo followed my gaze.

"Clever boy, sucking up to the big shots in the room." He said proudly, then looked down at me, "but amore, please don't give him too much attention." He warned, and I bit my lip.

Lorenzo dragged me over to a large group of people who I didn't recognise and introduced me to each of them. I shook hands and pretended to follow conversations, I wasn't dumb in any way, but the subjects these people wanted to discuss didn't interest me at all.

I excused myself from a small group of women who had crowded around me, clearly curious about the mystery woman on the dangerous man's arm, and made my way over to the small bar. The barman placed a flute of champagne in front of me and I looked at it with disappointment but raised it to my lips and took a long gulp.

"You look as bored as I feel." A familiar low voice said next to me, and I turned to find Adonis leaning his back against the bar. I turned to look out at the people enjoying themselves and groaned.

"I am."

We stood in silence for a few minutes, until my eye caught on something across the room, and a low growl left my throat.

"What the fuck was that?" Adonis said in shock.

My grip on my glass tightened and I searched the room for Lorenzo. I found him and his eyes met mine. I mouthed for him to come over and he held his finger up to me, indicating that I should wait a minute.

"What's got you all growly?" Adonis said with a slight laugh.

"My brother, Jason, he was murdered ten months ago, and being in the same room as the piece of shit who was responsible for taking away the only family I had left makes me feel sick." I told him as my eyes locked on the man with the deformed face sitting in a wheelchair next to Charon. I knew Charon would be here, and I had avoided him all evening, not that we would usually talk to each other, but after last night, it seemed like a good idea to keep our distance. But why had he bought that worthless piece of shit with him?

"Jason, as in *our* Jason? He was your brother?" Adonis asked and I flinched, he wasn't his Jason, but I knew what he meant. A Brother.

I nodded sharply and pushed back the tears that threatened to come forward.

"If you feel sick being in the same room as him, why are you with him?" Adonis said quietly, and my head flew around.

"What did you just say?" I snapped. I must have heard him wrong.

"Why are you with him?" he repeated, "Kinda messed up that you'd start a relationship with the guy who killed your brother. I had no idea you and Jason were related…" he trailed off as I felt my entire body turn cold. His eyes widened in shock, and he inhaled sharply, "You didn't know?" he gasped.

34

Don

Her face turned ghostly white, and she swayed where she stood. I reached out and grabbed her arm, "Shit Nutmeg, you really didn't know?"

"No." she whispered in a pained voice and tears filled her deep green eyes. My throat went dry, and I pulled her closer to me, holding her up so she wouldn't fall to the floor.

I'd known about what Lorenzo had done, I didn't know why, I presumed the guy had been a traitor or some shit, maybe he was, but I had no idea what she had been to him. When she had said about him being her brother my first thought was that she was using Lorenzo, playing him so that she could hurt him. It's what I would've done. Messed with the guy who killed my family, got close, and then killed them myself when they thought they were safe. But she'd had no idea.

Her body was trembling against mine and I had to swallow hard to keep myself composed. I could feel her pain, I knew what loss felt like, but I couldn't allow myself to relate to her too much, I couldn't allow myself to stop hating her. I'd been responsible for this though; I'd opened my mouth and the truth had come out. Why the fuck did hurting her like this make me feel so shit?

"What the fuck is this?" Lorenzo snarled as he appeared behind M, and I shot him an apologetic look.

"You," Meg hissed and pushed away from me to face Lorenzo, "You killed him." She said shakily but she held herself tall and closed in on him. I wasn't sure if she was brave as fuck, or a complete idiot.

"I kill a lot of people amore, be specific." Lorenzo said flatly, ignoring how emotional his woman was.

"Jase." Her voice broke into a watery sob, and I fought with every fibre in my body to resist moving closer to her, instead I stood back and watched as my stepdad's eyes met mine and turned dark.

He snapped his attention back to her and placed a hand on her shoulder, "Let's talk somewhere more private." He said, and guided her away from the bar, she pushed his hand away and marched ahead of him out of the ballroom doors and he threw a furious glare back at me. *Fuck.*

I turned back to the bar and ordered myself a large whiskey, then took the drink and left the ballroom. I couldn't stay in there, not knowing that two short tempered killers were somewhere in this hotel possibly attempting to kill each other. I sat on one of the small white sofas in the marbled foyer and undid the buttons of my jacket then sipped the amber liquid in my glass.

People came in and out of the foyer, some leaving, some booking rooms, all of them happy and at least a little intoxicated. A man came over to me after a while and informed me that the meal would begin in ten minutes if I wished to go back into the ballroom. I informed him that the three of us would be skipping the meal, and requested that he tell anyone who asked that we had called it a night due to Meg feeling unwell. I supposed I could do a little damage control; it would be good practice for when I was running things.

I grabbed my phone and scrolled though the numbers, not that I had many, and pulled up Coopers number, smirking at his saved name, *Captain Dickface,* then pressed call.

"Adonis, is something wrong?" he said when he answered, he sounded a little out of breath, but I wasn't going to be asking what he was up to, I didn't care.

"Fucking obviously." I said bluntly, "The boss and your best friend might be dead."

"What? Fuck, what's happened?" he exclaimed, sounding panicked.

"Yeah, I didn't know that Nutmeg didn't know Enzo was the one who killed Jason," I said casually, swirling the liquid in my glass as I began to briefly explain, "so now she knows, and she's not happy about it, they disappeared about twenty minutes ago, I'm presuming they are still in the hotel, but god knows if either of them are alive."

"Hang the fuck on, what?" Cooper said, "Lorenzo killed Jase?" *Fuck. Did no one in this gang know about that?*

"Yes," I said feeling exasperated, "So I need you to do your techy shit and find out where they are."

"Adonis, you can't just drop shit like that on people," he whisper-shouted "Fuck, right, fuck, ok," he rambled on, "I can access the hotel's cameras, I might be able to find them, hang on." I heard tapping coming from the other end of the line and threw the rest of my drink back as I waited. "Got'em," he finally said, "wow she looks angry," *Of course she looks angry, dickwad.* "They are in the ladies' room to your left, looks like they've locked the door from the inside because three women have tried and failed to get inside, how haven't you noticed that?" he asked, and I rolled my eyes.

"I'm a little bit stressed right now pretty boy." I snarled and he growled back at me.

"As am I, and I still noticed, I swear to god Adonis, if anything happens to her, fuck, Adonis you keep her safe." He practically begged.

"It might be too late." I said quietly.

"Don't" he snapped. "Just make sure she's ok. I'm watching." He said and hung up.

I pushed my phone back into my pocket and stared at the bathroom door and waited. A knot was twisting in my stomach, I didn't want her dead. I didn't want him dead either. He wasn't my Dad, but he was the next best thing, part of me felt something towards him.

The door flew open, and Lorenzo came storming out, he ignored me and headed to the ballroom doors, he paused, straightened his tie, composed his facial expression, then pushed through the doors as if nothing had happened.

My eyes snapped back to the bathroom door and a few moments later Meg came walking out, tugging her hair loose and tossing hairpins on the floor. I released a breath that I didn't know I'd been holding and stood up. Her eyes met mine and she shook her head at me then ran to the main doors. I followed after her as she flew down the outside steps and managed to catch her arm as she hit the bottom step. I turned her to face me and a growl tore through my throat.

"He did this to you. He hurt you." blood was trickling from her lip down her chin.

"What does it matter to you?" she shot back with a deep frown lining her forehead.

I grasped her chin in my hand and ran my thumb over her lip, wiping blood and lipstick across her face. "He doesn't get to do this to you." I muttered. "Come on, lets go." I dropped her face and pulled her arm.

She twisted herself out of my grip and made to move away from me. I shot in front of her and was met with the cold metal of her pocketknife pressed against my throat. "Where's the bike?" she asked.

"Nutmeg," I began, and she pressed the blade harder against my skin.

"The bike Adonis," she said, and her eyes filled with tears again.

The voice in my head screamed at me to not let her go, to not let her leave alone in this state, yet when I looked into her eyes, I knew I wouldn't fight with her. I pulled the key from my pocket and directed her to where I'd left my bike. I just had to hope she knew what she was doing. I could not have her death on my conscience.

She dropped the blade from my throat and gave me a grateful look, then grabbed my shirt in her fist, she tugged hard, and her bloody lips collided with mine. My hands instinctively grasped her waist, and I dragged her in closer. She pulled away a breath later and shoved me hard before she turned and ran away towards the parking lot in a blur of fiery red hair and emerald silk.

    I stood in shock, my hands balled into fists, hating what she had done. Hating that I was struggling to cling to any reason for hating her, and hating that I wanted her to come back. She had tasted of blood and fury and grief, and I wanted more. I wanted a woman I'd never be able to have.

35

Meg

I yanked the helmet from my head and shook out my hair, running my fingers though it to try to break up some of the hairspray. I probably looked like I'd been dragged through a hedge backwards, but right now I didn't give a shit. I tossed the helmet onto the Ducati and smoothed down my dress, the green silk was creased where I'd bunched it up around my thighs to straddle the bike.

Unshed tears stung my eyes, but I couldn't fall apart yet. Not until I knew that I was somewhere safe. Lorenzo had shown me his true colours, colours I'd always known were there, but I'd had no idea how vibrant they really were. After an aggressive outburst from both of us he had spilled every truth that he could without showing a hint of emotion and had proceeded to walk away from me and go back to the gala as if nothing had happened.

The way he handled it all terrified me.

I looked up at the unfamiliar building in front of me and prayed that I'd found the right one. I'd never been here before, I don't think I've even been down this street before, and that made me feel a fraction safer. I walked up the path and located the intercom on the wall. I found the number that I vaguely recalled being the one I was looking for and pressed the button.

A rough, sleepy voice came through the speaker a minute later, "Hello?"

"Toby?" I said shakily, "It's Meg, can I come in?"

The door buzzed indicating that I could open it and I pushed through. "Wait there." I faintly heard him say as the front door closed behind me.

I stood in the small lobby and chewed on my lower lip, it stung where it had split and tasted faintly of whiskey. Of Adonis. I'd kissed Adonis. What the fuck had I been thinking. No, I wasn't thinking, I was upset, angry, scared, fuck I was every shitty emotion all rolled into one, and he was there, and he acted like he cared, and I couldn't find the words to thank him, so I acted. But I should not have done that. It was a mistake. *Never again.*

"Up here." I heard Toby's voice echo down the stairs and followed it up three flights. "Shit little one." He whispered and rushed forward to me.

I tilted my head to look up and him and fell

apart. The overwhelming sense of safety that I felt when I looked into his eyes broke me, and my legs wobbled gave way. He caught me before I could crumple into a mess on the landing floor and scooped me up into his arms.

"You're okay, everything is okay." He murmured as he carried me into his apartment.

Toby placed me on a small beige sofa and crouched in front of me, "What do you need?" he asked gently, and I sobbed harder, pulling my feet up and wrapping my arms around my knees.

"I don't know." I sobbed between shuddering breaths. I'd never fallen apart like this before, I had no idea how to calm down from it. When anything bad had happened in my life I'd turned numb and angry. Mum, Jase, I'd shed tears sure, but I didn't break down, sadness never ruled me, vengeance did. But this time it didn't. This time all I could feel was pain.

"Okay little one," he stroked my arm softly, "I'm going to make you a drink, get you some tissues, and find a snack." He made his way to the other side of the room to a small kitchen area and grabbed a couple of glasses from a cupboard. "Whiskey alright?" he asked, as he hunted in another cupboard, and I mumbled a noise of agreement. Right now I'd drink anything. Even if it tasted like a man I shouldn't want. *No, I don't want him.*

He sat down on the floor in front of me, his hands were full, and for a moment I was distracted from my breakdown, impressed that he hadn't broken anything. He placed the two glasses and a half empty bottle on the floor, followed by a plate of brownies, and tossed a box of tissues up onto the sofa next to me. I pulled one out and dried my face as best as I could. Tears were still falling, but I could breathe a little easier now.

"What happened?" he said as he handed me a glass and poured me a large drink.

I tossed it back in one, the burn of the liquid taking the edge of off my emotions slightly, then held the glass out to him. He poured again, but this time I sipped slowly. "Lorenzo murdered Jase." I said out loud. The fact had been repeating in my head over and over on a loop since he had admitted that it was true. My entire body sagged as the words left me, and I tucked my feet underneath me and looked down at Toby.

His lips were parted, and his eyes were wide. He placed his glass down onto the rug he was sitting on and pushed up onto the sofa next to me. He dragged me into a tight embrace, and I melted into him. He pressed his mouth to my hair, "Do you want to talk?" he asked, and I nodded.

He wriggled us around so that he was sitting comfortably, and I was curled into his lap with my head resting on his shoulder. He ran his fingers up and down my bare arm in a soothing motion and I told him about my evening.

"He admitted it, he told me in great detail what had happened and why he had done it, he tried to justify his actions, he murdered my brother because he wanted to leave his wife and be with me, and Jase was so overprotective when it came to me and men. He knew Jase would never approve. My brother died because Lorenzo D'Angelo couldn't have what he wanted." My throat thickened as the tears filled my eyes again, "He died because of me."

"You can't say that. You didn't know. Lorenzo is a psychopath, and that is not your fault." Toby said softly but firmly.

"I know, I know I shouldn't' blame myself, but now I don't know what to do Toby." I confessed, "He's my boss, I've been dating him, he's a huge part of my life, what am I going to do? I can't be around him, but if I refuse to be with him, I think he might kill me." I swallowed hard.

Toby tilted my chin up, forcing me to meet his eye. "He will never hurt you again Vixen, I promise."

"How can you be sure? How can you promise that?" I asked. Jason was far more skilled than me, and he couldn't protect himself. I was more skilled than Toby, unless it was a fist fight, so how could he promise me that Lorenzo wouldn't hurt me. I had no doubt that this kind, gentle giant would do anything to protect the people he cared about, and I hoped I was one of those lucky people, but I couldn't imagine him killing anyone. And in the end, that's what it would come to.

"Just trust me," he said, his eyes burning into mine, "I will do whatever it takes to keep you safe." His gaze fell to my lips, "If you'll let me."

"Is this your way of telling me its all been a lie?"

"Of course it's been a lie," he said, "don't tell me you honestly believed that I didn't want you."

"For a moment, yes." I confessed.

"Fuck." He cursed, and his mouth collided with mine. Tears ran down my face again, but this time they were tears of joy, because in the darkness I'd found a spark of light, and he filled me with so much hope.

36

Lorenzo

"I'm so sorry that your lovely lady wasn't feeling well, I do hope we will get to meet her again soon." Westeroak's chief of police said politely as I announced my leave to the group of people I'd been speaking with. She leaned in to speak to me quietly, "Charon has upped his payments, Lorenzo." She gave me a meaningful look and I rolled my eyes.

"Call me Monday morning and we will arrange something." I said with a tight smile. Her loyalties would always lay with the highest bidder, up until now that had been me. Both myself and Charon had plenty of her men in our pockets but having *her* on side was what really mattered.

"Buonanotte amici miei." I said to the others and turned to leave. Once I'd stepped out of the ballroom doors, I yanked off my tie and tossed it on the floor. Adonis was sitting on one of the sofas in the lobby, his jaw was clenched and as his eyes met mine, they narrowed into a glare that could cut ice.

"I don't know why you're looking at me like that son, if you hadn't opened your damn mouth she'd never know."

He rose to his feet, puffing his chest out, and walked towards me. "You hurt her." He snarled.

I scoffed, "Why would you care about what I did to her? Maybe you don't hate her as much as you say you do. Does little Donny have a crush?" I said with a bitter laugh.

He stopped when we were toe to toe, his eyes still on mine. *If looks could kill.* "You murdered her brother, lied to her, and split her lip, is that how you want us to treat each other? Is that how you want us to treat the people we care about?" he said, avoiding my little dig about his feelings towards my woman.

I don't care what had happened this evening, she was still mine. There wasn't a chance in hell that I'd let her get away from me now. Three years I'd longed for her to be mine, and I finally had her. I'd removed every obstacle that had been in our way, and I'd convinced her that I was the one she needed. I changed, I tried, for her, she didn't get to throw it all back in my face now because she'd found out about some stupid little lie that I'd told.

"Sometimes we have to hurt people to give them a better life. When you find a woman like that, you'll do whatever it takes to give her what she deserves." I said, then pushed past him towards the main doors.

"How can you give her anything when your actions have pushed her away?" he said, following after me. "How do you expect to come back from this? You've lost her Enzo, we've lost her."

I spun on my heels to face him, "She's always known what I am, she can handle it. Her absence is only temporary, she *will* come back." I snapped then gave him a disgusted look, "I haven't lost her, The Brotherhood hasn't lost her, and you never had her in the first place, but go-ahead Adonis, keep telling me that you hate her. It's actually starting to become funny."

I turned away from him again and pushed through the main doors and strode out into the crisp evening air. The valet was waiting at the bottom of the steps, he looked up at me and quickly hurried away. Moments later my car rolled up to the bottom of the steps. I pushed a random note from my pocket into the valet's hand and climbed into my car, I had no idea what I'd handed him, but from the look on his face I'd guess it was a lot more than he'd expected.

The passenger door flew open, and Adonis slumped down into the seat. Still glaring at me like he was tempted to put me in an early grave. "She took my bike." He grunted in explanation and slammed the door.

I winced at the sound as it pushed me over the edge, and snarled at him, "One more shitty move, one wrong word, and I will rip you apart Adonis, you're walking a damn thin line, remember your place."

He glanced at me, a challenge in his eyes, but when they met mine, he blinked it away. The boy tested my patience and maddened me beyond all reason, but I couldn't deny that he was the perfect replacement for me when I stepped down. I just needed to get my woman locked down and then pass it all over. And no matter how much he clearly wanted *everything* that was mine, I'd keep him alive for the sole purpose of taking my place.

When we finally made it home I was more than happy to be getting out of my car. Adonis hadn't said another word, but his anger towards me clung to the air around us like a bad smell. He hung back when I left the garage and entered the main house. I wasn't shocked to see that his bike wasn't back, M wouldn't have come here, she needed time to cool off, and I did too. She had crossed a line when she had attacked me in the bathroom, no real damage of course, but I was not happy about it. Her split lip was a result of me defending myself, Adonis may have been mad that it had happened, but I hadn't done it viciously.

I made my way up the stairs and into my

bedroom, I was exhausted. I checked my phone for any messages, but the only ones I had were from Grey asking if there was anything he needed to take care of. He must have been bored, or maybe Deb had kicked him out for the night, again. I rolled my eyes and sighed heavily, the shit we put up with for the women we love.

I typed out a simple message to M and pressed send.

Lorenzo
I'll see you tomorrow morning once you've calmed down. Sleep well amore.

This would be my strategy. Ignorance. She'd found out the truth, and we wouldn't speak of it again. She would spend the night being angry about what I'd done, and then she would come home to me, and we would move past it. It may take a while for her to fully let it go, but she *would* let it go. I always get what I want.

***

"Mr D'Angelo, Miss Fields is in the foyer." Clive announced as he entered the dining room.

"She's not a visitor anymore Clive, just tell her where I am, and she can come and find me." I said, peering over the top of my newspaper at him.

"I did sir, but she is refusing to move. She says that she will meet with you in your office, or she will leave." He said and a heavy look of concern covered his face.

I sighed and neatly folded my paper. "Why did I have to fall for such a stubbornly demanding woman?" Clive offered me a small smile in response, but the worried lines didn't leave his face. "Tell her I'll be there in a moment."

Clive disappeared from the room, and I rolled my shoulders. She wasn't going to make this easy. Demanding I meet in my office meant one thing, she was here as a Brother. She was going to leave me.

Well, she could try.

The deliciously sweet scent of her hit me the second I walked into my office. She was sitting in a chair with her back to me. She looked tense. I walked up behind her and placed my hands on her shoulders and began to knead her aching muscles.

"Don't touch me." she said in a firm voice and shrugged out of my grip.

I ground my teeth and inhaled slowly before stepping away from her and moving to my chair on the opposite side of the desk. "Still mad at me then Amore mio?"

Her lips parted as if I'd said something shocking, "Yes Lorenzo, I'm still mad. Of course I'm still mad," she searched my face, "did you think I'd get over what you've done?" she blinked rapidly and opened and closed her mouth like a goldfish before she spoke again, "I'm never going to be over it. We are done, was that not clear?" she asked.

"Ok, you need more time. I'll book you in to a spa for the weekend." I said and fired up my computer to make a booking.

"What the fuck," she spluttered, "No. Lorenzo we. Are. Done. I'm here because we still have to work together and I thought we should discuss that." she twisted her fingers together on her lap, "I would like to leave The Brotherhood, but I know I that I made a promise to you all when I joined. If you dismiss me, I promise that I will go quietly and never breathe a word of what any of us have done. I won't run, or hide, you'll be able to find me if I break that promise. If you won't dismiss me, then I'd like to take a short leave to prepare myself to continue to work with you." She pulled her lower lip between her teeth and kept her eyes fixed on the desk.

"No." I said simply, "We aren't done, and you're not leaving, I will not dismiss you, and you will not take leave."

Tears filled her eyes and she bit down harder until the skin broke, and blood stained her lips. "I can't be with you." she said, "I can barely stand to be in this room with you."

"Megan, you are lucky that I love you enough to keep you alive, stop this and let's go and get breakfast." She flinched and met my gaze, and a thoughtful look crossed her face.

"Right, so you won't kill me, because you

love me." the sides of her mouth lifted in a slight smile, and I frowned. She rose from the chair and turned towards the door, "Goodbye Lorenzo." She said and walked away from me.

"Don't you dare walk out of that door Megan." I bellowed and made my way after her. She didn't turn back around, she kept her pace steady and walked down the corridor to my front door. Rage filled me as I watched her go and I snapped, "You stupid fucking slut," she turned her head to look at me and a smug smile fell on my lips, "You can go and fuck your worthless trainer, your pretty boy best friend, and my little prodigy, you can pretend you're getting away with disrespecting me and leaving me, but I promise you Megan, you will end up back here, and you will be with me. You're mine. Whether you want that or not."

"But you won't kill me. If you drag me back ill just leave over and over and over again." She said softly. "I'm sure you'll give up eventually."

37

Tobias

I paced my lounge while shoving brownies into my mouth, barely chewing as I inhaled the chocolatey bites of heaven. Stress eating, I was stress eating. Because my little vixen had gone to speak with her ex-lover slash boss, and I had no idea what he would do to her. If she made it back here, what state would she be in?

My phone buzzed on the kitchen counter, and I rushed over to it to read the message.

Megan
I need coffee.

Was that good or bad? She was alive, clearly, so I guessed that was a good thing, and she wasn't asking to start drinking at 10am, so that was another good sign. But I knew there was no way it had gone smoothly. I wasn't an idiot.

I replied telling her I'd have one waiting for her and switched on my coffee machine. A few minutes later the intercom buzzed, and I let her in and waited by my open door. She made her way up the stairs and a grin lit up her face as she noticed me waiting for her.

"I'm so screwed." She sighed, and fell into my arms, "but I think that I might have the upper hand."

I held her tight and pressed a kiss to the top of her head, "I'm just glad you're back, I made coffee, you wanna fill me in?" I asked and she nodded and nuzzled into my chest. I chuckled and walked backwards into my apartment with her still clinging to me. I kicked my door closed and walked us to the lounge. When the backs of her legs hit the edge of the sofa, she released me and flopped down. I went to grab our drinks and joined her, handing her a pink mug with a fairy princess on it.

"Cute." She smiled as she inspected the mug, then groaned happily as she took her first sip.

"So?" I prompted, desperate to hear what had happened. Last night had been crazy. The last thing I'd expected to happen when I fell asleep on my sofa after stuffing my face with pizza was for her to appear at my door looking like a goddess about to break into a million tiny pieces. I also hadn't expected to end up kissing her, to let go of every part of me that had been keeping her at arm's length. I'd pushed her away to keep her safe, but he had already hurt her, why should I keep denying us both what we wanted? And honestly, if I had to, I knew I could protect her.

After the kiss, we had ended up in my bedroom, I'd helped her out of her dress and had wrapped her up in one of my soft plaid shirts, I wasn't prepared for how incredible it would look on her, and I swear in that moment I fell harder than I ever thought I could. Her hair had been a mess, her face was red and puffy, blood was crusted below her lip, and I felt like the luckiest man in the world. Because she had let down every damn wall for me, and I was allowed to see her in her most vulnerable state. I vowed to myself right there and then that I would never let anyone make her cry like that again.

"He loves me," she began, and I scowled at her, "Don't look at me like that," she laughed and poked me with the toe of her shoe, "It's given me the upper hand. He said he loves me enough to not kill me, he won't willingly let me go, but he can't stop me. Not really."

"But he's a psychopath, he could chain you up in his basement." I half joked, but I wouldn't put it past him after the way she had told me he had behaved last night.

"I just have to avoid him," She said, "that's the hard part though. He could probably find me anywhere I go, and he won't let me leave The Brotherhood, so he's still my boss."

"Are you a blood-in gang?" I asked and she raised a brow at me.

"No, no we're not like that, that's more of a traditional gang thing, like The Wolves, they do that shit." She grimaced.

"So what are the conditions? How do we get you out?" I gave her a thoughtful look, "If you want out that is?"

"I do, Toby I really fucking do. I want a normal life, I want to run away from all of this. Will you run away with me?" she asked with a hopeful glint in her eyes.

"I'll follow you anywhere Vixen," I promised, "Whatever it takes."

A blush flushed her cheeks, and she blew out a long breath as she thought. "I can only leave The Brotherhood if I am dismissed, Lorenzo can do it any time that he wants, and my Brothers can request it if they feel they have a good reason to kick me out. If enough of them want me gone he will have to listen. If he doesn't, he loses all of their respect, he would never let that happen."

"So we play that angle then? Make them feel like you're a threat to them all?" I asked, ideas buzzing in my head, "make you look like a traitor?"

She nodded slowly and narrowed her eyes at me, "Exactly. Why do you look like you have an idea, Toby, please don't tell me you want to be involved? I won't put you in danger."

I stood up and grabbed my phone from where I'd left it earlier, "I do have an idea, they won't be happy about it, but I can guarantee it will help." I said as I sat back down next to her and scrolled through my contacts. I found the number I needed and leaned in to place a kiss to her cheek, "Don't ask me not to get involved though Vixen, it's too late for that."

She sighed in frustration, and I placed my finger on her lips to stop her saying anything else, then pressed call and put my phone on loudspeaker.

"Tobias, well this is a nice surprise." A booming voice echoed down the line, and I smiled.

"Hey Dad, I think you'll be taking that back in a minute." I said. Meg's brows pinched together, and her lips parted against my finger.

"For fucks sake son, what have you done?" he groaned, and I watched Meg's eyes narrow as she moved closer to my phone.

"I haven't done anything, technically, but I need you. Did mum tell you about the girl?" I asked and felt my face heat.

"Of course she did, but that was weeks ago, why have you been so tight-lipped about her son?"

I ignored his question, "She's in trouble, I really need you to help." I dropped my finger from Meg's lips and grasped her hand as I prepared for them both to flip out.

"Go on." He prompted, "If she means that much to you, I'll do whatever I can."

I locked eyes with Meg and took a deep breath, "It's Megan Fields." I said quickly and tears stung the backs of my eyes, "Dad you have to help her."

My grasp on her hand tightened and she stared at me in confusion as we waited for him to speak.

"He hurt her last night, didn't he?" My dad finally said, "That's why she left the gala."

"You were at the gala?" Meg said as she searched my face for answers.

"Megan?" Dad said in a rough voice, "What did he do to you?"

"Who are you?" She asked, ignoring the concern he was showing towards her. The fact he was being so kind had me slightly shocked.

"Toby hasn't told you?" he asked.

"No, You sound familiar, but who are you? and how can you help?" she asked, desperation lacing her words.

"I don't know if I can help. It's a huge ask when we're supposed to be rivals."

Her jaw dropped as the realisation hit her.

"Charon." She said in a cold voice that made me flinch.

"Don't be like that, kid," Dad said with a

slight laugh, "I *might* be the answer to your problems. I have a meeting in an hour, I'll come over after, better that we aren't seen in public together. I'm not making any promises, but we can talk."

I agreed that we would wait at my apartment for him and ended the call.

"Why didn't you ever tell me that Charon was your dad?" Meg asked, but she didn't sound mad, just curious.

"No one knows, Dad didn't want me to grow up in his world, so he kept us separate. Gave me the choices in life that he never got." I explained briefly.

"So he did it to protect you, and here I am, dragging you into all of the shit he wanted you to stay out of. I've just given him yet another reason to hate me." She said sadly.

I pulled her closer and nudged her nose with mine, "He knew I could end up getting mixed up in this stuff somehow, why do you think my combat skills are this good? He gave me the tools and prayed that I'd manage to avoid needing them." I said, and gently pressed my lips to hers, "I'm not too bad a shot either." I added and she chuckled darkly.

"I'm going to need you to prove that sometime." She said in a lust filled voice and I couldn't ignore what it did to me. I'd been the perfect gentleman up until now, but I wasn't sure that I could let her speak to me like that and keep the act up.

"Rumour has it, you know your way around a weapon." I teased and she pushed me away with a hand on my chest as she fell into a fit of giggles.

I smiled at her as she laughed, enjoying the moment, I could lock up my horny ass for a while longer.

"I like who I am when I'm with you." she said as her laughter subsided, and she ran her fingers through my hair. "I want to be this person every day."

I couldn't speak, she was so fucking cute. All I could do was wrap my arms around her and kiss her until I couldn't breathe. I wanted her to be happy, and I was going to make sure that we could have a future. Whatever future she wanted; I'd give it to her.

"Can I stay here?" she asked as we broke away from each other. ". I don't think I should be at my place anytime soon. Lorenzo is probably on the hunt for me right now."

"Of course." I said, and her shoulders sagged in relief. *Like I'd have ever said no.*

"Thank you, I have a bag in the car, I'll just pop down and grab it." she said, and I pulled her in for a quick kiss before she could escape my hold.

She hurried out of my apartment with a promise to be quick, and I headed to the kitchen area to hunt for snacks. Dad would be a while, so I planned on killing some time with a movie. I found a bag of popcorn and emptied it into a bowl before answering the frantic knocking she was doing on my door.

"Calm down little one, keep your panties on!" I said as I flung open the door. But she wasn't there. Instead I found myself face to face with the deadliest looking man I'd ever seen.

38

Lorenzo

Clive rushed into the foyer where I was stood staring at the broken table with my hands fisted into my hair. "Clean this up!" I shouted and stormed away back to my office. Launching the console table across the foyer had done nothing to calm the blazing inferno of my rage.

I snatched up my phone and dialled my second's number.

"What's up Boss." He said, answering my call after two rings, like the good little bitch that he was.

"M's missing." I said, forcing calmness into my tone.

"Ok, what do you need me to do?" he asked.

"FIND HER!" I roared, then threw my phone across my office. It smashed into pieces against the door. *Fuck.*

She didn't get to do this. She was mine. She did not get to walk away from me. But there was nowhere she could hide. She will be found, and brought back to me, and I'll make sure that anyone who stands between us meets a brutal end. I don't care who it is. I love her, and she *will* love me.

"Clive!" I yelled, and my head of household staff quickly appeared in the doorway.

"Sir." He said and glanced down at my broken phone on the floor. "I'm on it." he said and disappeared down the corridor. *This* is why I've kept him around. Clive had had a blatant crush on my dead wife, it was disrespectful, but I chose to ignore it as he was damn good at his job.

I opened my emails on my computer and found nothing of any importance. Grey needed to hurry up his search before I smashed everything in this room. I needed a distraction while I waited for everyone to do their fucking jobs. I pushed to my feet, kicking my chair away from me, and headed out of my office and up the stairs. Once I was in my room, I tore off my shirt and kicked off my shoes before tugging down my trousers and underwear. In the wardrobe I found a pair of dark grey shorts and pulled them on before sitting on the velvet chair to lace up a pair of trainers.

My jaw ticked as I looked up at the other side of the wardrobe. The rails were bare. I'd had this side cleared of all of Selene's clothes a couple of days ago in preparation for when I asked M to move in, a question I was planning on voicing to her last night, if she hadn't gone and had a tantrum over something I'd done almost a year ago. Sure, it wasn't very nice, and I did feel bad. I liked Jason, he was a good Brother, but he was an overprotective arsehole when it came to his sister, he couldn't accept that she could handle herself against the wrong man, or that the right man could protect her far better than he could, and he wasn't going to back down. So I did what I had to. I did it for her.

That's what I'd told myself when I'd tied him up in my garage. I hadn't wanted to do it. I'd sent him away for M's birthday in hope that she would be mad at him and push him away for not being around on her special day, then I'd be able to pounce, but no, he came home, and she didn't give a shit, she was just happy to see him. They needed to be forced apart so that she could be with me, and his death was the only way it would happen. So I did it, I hid him away, fired six shots into his body, then had Grey take him into Wolf territory and leave him to be found by Charon, he would presume one of his men had done it, and the blame would be passed to them. Charon had worked out that it was a set up eventually, but by then it was too late, M had attacked Slash and they hadn't retaliated, he had believed that his man had deserved it. His realisation came too late. But even if he had worked it out sooner, I'd have never let him touch her.

"Sir," Clive's voice grabbed my attention and my gaze snapped from the empty rail to his face. "Cooper is on his way here with a new phone, he will be here in twenty minutes," he pulled his own phone from his pocket, "Grey called me, he has information." He handed it over to me and closed the door, leaving me alone again.

I called Grey and tapped my foot impatiently as the tone rang out, was he deliberately trying to piss me off today?

"I thought I told you to tell him to call me." Grey snapped down the line and my fist clenched. He had no manners.

"*He* is calling you, you disrespectful bastardo." I snarled.

"Shit, sorry Boss, I have a location though, and information that I think you'll find very interesting." He said sounding smug.

"Well, spit it out."

My jaw was clenched tight as he spoke, but as he went on my face slowly split into a menacing grin. This was too fucking perfect. I concocted a plan before Grey had even finished, and I relaxed in the chair as I hung up and dialled another number. Setting it in motion.

39

Don

Thoughts of M had filled my dreams and I'd woken with a feeling of frustration, denial, and a horrific headache. Why did she have to kiss me, and why did I now find myself wanting her blood-stained lips on mine again? No, I didn't want her, nothing had changed, this was just a physical reaction because yeah, she's kinda hot. That's all.

I sat up in my bed and stretched, feeling a slight crack in the centre of my spine and groaning at the relief. I then headed to the bathroom in search of painkillers. I'd left the house shortly after arriving back there last night. A ride would have helped to clear my head, but stupidly I'd given Nutmeg my bike when she'd fled the gala. I knew it had been the right thing to do, She needed to escape, and not having her around would make things so much easier for me, but I wished she'd just hotwired some random guy's car instead.

I'd had to take my car, but the thrill that I was seeking to get out of my own head wasn't there. So I'd come here, to the apartment above the tailors, and had drunk myself to sleep instead.

I found a bottle of aspirin in the back of the medicine cabinet and swallowed them down before climbing into the shower. Once I felt slightly more human, I pulled on a black shirt and trousers from the small wardrobe and got my things together. I wouldn't stay here this morning, I needed coffee and I was fresh out. I slipped on my black leather loafers and headed out of the door. I got into my car and sped off on autopilot. Only realising where I was going when I arrived.

The bubbly woman handed over my coffee and baguette without instruction, having apparently remembered my order from my previous visits, and I made my way around the lake to my escape.

The bench was empty as usual, and I sat and gazed across the water. My mind travelled back to the time that Nutmeg had turned up here and tried to take this place from me. How did she even know about this place? I'd not seen her here since though, so I'd presumed she'd happened upon me by accident and was just being a royal bitch.

My phone ringing in my pocket dragged me out of my calm state and I cursed as I looked at the screen. *What now?*

"Come home Don. It's important." Lorenzo said then hung up before I could utter a single word. I'd wanted to protest, needing more space away from him, I hadn't agreed with his behaviour last night and I wasn't sure If I could look at him without wanting to hit him, but his command was clear, the boss had spoken.

Clive pointed me towards the gym when I arrived back at the house, and I found Lorenzo and Grey tangled up in each other's arms on the floor.

"There are plenty of beds in this place you know, you don't have to fuck on the gym floor." I said with a flat look.

"Hilarious." Grey said breathlessly from underneath Lorenzo. Had he *let* him win that? or was dear old stepdaddy actually able to hold his own without a weapon? I wasn't sure why, but it shocked me. Up until this moment I'd never imagined Lorenzo getting down and dirty in a fight. I was half tempted to go and change into some gym wear and find out for myself, but I was here for a reason, and I needed to find out what it was.

"What was so important then *Boss*." I folded my arms and leaned against the treadmill as I waited for Lorenzo to get up.

"Drop the attitude Adonis," he said flatly as he moved across the home gym and sat down on a bench where he had left a bottle of water. "I have a treat for you, not that you deserve it." he glared across at me,

I kept my mouth shut, but rolled my eyes and raised my brows at him.

"Keep this shit up and I'll send Grey to do this instead." He warned and I glanced at Grey who was doing press ups and pretending not to listen to us.

I unfolded my arms and crossed the room to sit next to Lorenzo. "Okay, what's the treat."

His face lit up with a cruel smile, "I have just been informed that your mother's killer has a son." He offered this information and every muscle in my body tensed.

"So you *know* who did it then? Tell me who and where I can find him," I said slowly, attempting to hide my anger over him keeping this from me, because, well I knew I was on thin ice.

"No Don, I don't want you going after him, your target is the son."

"Why? The Bastardo killed my Mamma, that's nothing to do with his son. Is it?"

"If you go after his son he will know how you felt. Kill his son, and it will hurt him so much more than if you went straight for him. You want him to suffer, don't you?" So he *did* understand that killing people's close family members was a hurtful thing to do. Interesting. He placed a hand on my shoulder. "He deserves pain."

"Then I'll torture him before I kill him, I can cause him pain and suffering," I argued, desperate to get my hands on this man.

"I know you want him dead, but trust me, take away the people that he loves first, make his life so miserable that he practically begs for death. Don't give it to him so easily Don. Start with the son." He squeezed my shoulder then stood up and made his way over to where Grey was now doing sit-ups.

I thought it over for a moment, an eye for an eye, except I wouldn't stop at just one. He had stolen away the only person who had ever mattered to me. Lorenzo was right, I needed to take away everything that matters to him. Except...

"I won't hurt a child." I said quickly, and Lorenzo spun around to face me.

"Of course not, he is not a child."

I nodded sharply, "Good, ok, I'll do it, just tell me where and when?"

Grey paused and looked at me, "I have an address, he's at home right now."

I exhaled slowly and cracked my neck, "I better get going then."

***

The front door to the building had been propped open with a woman's shoe and I took that as a sign of good luck. I didn't need to force my way in or tell some elaborate story to one of this bastardo's neighbours. I walked straight inside and began my journey up the stairs.

Apartment number 11 didn't take long to get to. I shrugged my jacket off and slung it on the banister on the landing, then rolled my shirt sleeves up. I'd left my gun in the car for this, I doubted I'd need it. Instead I pulled a shiny new butterfly blade from my pocket. It had been a little treat that I'd given to myself for finishing my initiation, I'd not used it yet, and now felt like the perfect time to christen it.

I pounded my fist into the door manically until I heard his voice approaching the door.

"Calm down little one, keep your panties on." The bastardo said as he swung the door open. His face dropped the instant he saw me.

There was something vaguely familiar about his face, but I couldn't place him. Not that it really mattered, he was still going to die at my hands within the next ten minutes. Five if he didn't fight back too much.

I raked my eyes over him, slightly taller than me, broad, shirtless, showing off heavily tattooed golden skin, pretty, but not in the same way that Cooper was, no, this guy was a rough rugged kind of pretty. I bet it's all for show though, but a small part of me hoped that it wasn't, a fair fight would make this even more satisfying.

"Little one?" I asked in a voice like ice, "Hardly." I smirked and advanced towards him.

He pushed the door closed on me, but he wasn't fast enough, my body was already inside his apartment. I smashed the door into the wall behind it and he shot away from me at an unexpected speed, stopping in a kitchen area and rummaging in a drawer. I moved slowly towards him, enjoying the way his eyes widened in fear as he fumbled, unable to find whatever he was searching for.

I raised my hand with the blade in it and pounced, aiming for his bare arm. His arm shot up and deflected my attack, knocking my hand away as he grabbed a random item from the drawer and slammed it into the side of my head. I stumbled slightly on impact and let out a low groan as pain shot through my head. He was stood with a half-smile on his lips as he examined the cheese grater in his hand. I winced a little as I noticed it and lifted my hand to my head. My fingers came away with specks of blood on them. My eyes narrowed and locked on his, but the fear had left them and all that I saw staring back at me was a mirror of my own expression.

"Who are you?" he asked with a deep growl.

"I'm the bringer of death." I smirked and he laughed, it was a loud booming laugh that mocked me and sent a fresh bolt of rage through me.

"I'm going to carve up that pretty face so badly that your Daddy won't ever sleep again for fear of it haunting his dreams."

His face twisted with confusion then he sighed heavily, "So you want to send a message to the big bad wolf? He disowned me; this won't mean shit to him." He said in a tone that felt rehearsed. Whoever his Dad was, he had trained him to say this. Smart man protecting his son like this, except I could see straight through it. This would hurt his Dad even more than I had initially realised.

"Bullshit." I snapped and lunged at him; he was prepared though. His fist flew into my chest as my blade slashed across his stomach. He threw me to the floor and held me down. I thrashed around beneath him, striking out with my arms and legs until I managed to free myself. I pulled myself to my feet as he did the same, blood was trickling down to his waistband, but he didn't seem to notice. I sliced towards him again, this time with more precision. My blade connected with his cheek and dragged down, causing him to cry out. His hand caught my wrist and he twisted me around and pressed my chest onto the kitchen counter. I released my knife and it clattered against the hard wood floor. His hand fisted into my short hair, and he yanked my head back sharply. Before he could push it down onto the counter I kicked out and his legs buckled beneath him. He wobbled and lost his grip on me, I shot beneath him to where my knife had landed, grabbed it and plunged it deep into his thigh. He yelled and fell to his knees. I pulled the blade from his flesh, scratched a thin, shallow line from his collarbone to his navel, then thrust the blood coated knife into his stomach.

I pushed him to the floor, my knife still buried in his stomach, and rose to my feet. Standing over his shaking body I sneered down at him. "This is for my Mamma."

"What the fuck!" a voice came from behind me. A voice I knew all to well.

Before I could turn to face her, she was on my back, her thighs gripped around my waist and her hands on my neck, squeezing tight and blurring my vision.

It was only when I spoke that she released me. "Nutmeg, stop."

40

Meg

"Adonis?" I whispered as I fell from the man's back, my bare feet thudding onto the floor. What was he doing here? What had he done to Toby?

He spun around to face me, blocking my view of Toby. I could hear him groaning, I knew he was hurt. I needed to get to him. I shoved Adonis to one side, but he grabbed me and pulled me closer to him, his hand reaching up to cup my jaw tightly and force my focus onto him.

"What are you doing here?" he asked me, his accent thicker than I'd ever heard it.

"Me? What are *you* doing here? What have you done to Toby?" I yanked my face out of his hold, "Adonis what the fuck is going on?!" I yelled.

"You know him?" he asked, and his eyes

widened with understanding, "*this* is where you ran off to." He exclaimed, disgust lacing his words.

"Explain this all, now!" I pushed.

"Your *friend* here is the son of the man who murdered my mum." He raised his head high, "this is just a little bit of revenge, you should understand that."

I blinked at him in disbelief, where had he got that idea from? Charon hadn't been the one responsible for Selene's death.

The pieces fell together in my head in an instant though and before I could stop myself, my palm connected with Adonis' face. "You idiot!" I screamed, "You complete and utter fucking moron! His dad didn't do it, you've been played." I pounded my fists against his solid chest in frustration.

His hands wrapped around my wrists, and he pushed me away from him, "You don't know anything about it, you can't protect him." He spat.

"I know *everything* about it Don, why do you think I ran last night? Why do you think I couldn't be around *you*?" I threw my arms up in exasperation, but he was blocking me out. He turned his back on me and I snapped, reaching into my pocket for the blade that I'd held against his throat last right, and launched it, it flew through the space between us and sank into his shoulder. He let out an agonised shout and turned back to me, reaching to the place where my knife had pierced his skin and yanked it out. Adonis' eyes turned darker as they landed on mine, a breath later he was coming towards me. I backed up slightly before his hand wrapped around my neck and he threw me up against the wall.

"Leave, before I kill you too." He said through gritted teeth.

"No. I won't let you make a mistake like this Don, just listen to me." I gasped and his grip tightened. "Don please."

His grip loosened for a moment, then tightened again. He pressed his body hard against mine, "Just because you can't get your revenge, doesn't mean I can't get mine."

"It was Lorenzo." I choked out.

His eyes narrowed, then he let out a sharp laugh, "Nice try."

Of course he wouldn't just believe me, It hadn't even been twenty-four hours since he said the same thing to me, but he needed to know that I was telling the truth. He needed to know what Lorenzo had told me in the hotel bathroom.

With a burst of strength I fought him off of me, tearing his hand away from my throat and kicking his legs out from beneath him. He crumpled onto the floor and shock flashed in his eyes. He had honestly believed that he was better than me. Toby had taught me well; I could get myself out of almost anything.

Toby let out a whine of pain and Adonis turned quickly, with determination in his face, as he attempted to move to where the noise had come from.

I kicked him onto his back and straddled his chest, pushing my knees down on to his arms to hold him down, "Stay away from him, you *will* listen to me Adonis Knight," I screamed at him, and he pushed his tongue into his cheek.

"Are you going to make me little Nutmeg?" he smirked.

I clenched my jaw then nodded before grasping his face firmly in my hand and leaning down, pushing my face so close to his that I could almost taste him, "Last night Lorenzo told me he was the one who killed Selene, he told me that she had found out that he was the one responsible for Jase and that she was threatening to tell me, he called her an obstacle Don, an obstacle to getting what he wanted, so she had to go. I'm sorry, I am so fucking sorry, he was only going to leave her at first, until she found out his secret, and he's insane Don, can't you see that? It was not Charon, he doesn't have any motive, can't you see what Lorenzo is doing? Sending you after Toby straight after I tell him that we are done, he's using you and your grief to get what he wants." I backed up slightly and waited for his reaction, his eye twitched and he shook his head, *Idiot.* "You need to understand how his mind works, he knows that I want someone else, so he's eliminating them, he thinks I want you too, so he's making sure that you are the one who does it, he's removing obstacles. You're being used as a threat to me." my voice broke as the words came out, and tears filled my eyes.

Concern flashed on Adonis' face, followed by anger, "How do I know you're telling the truth?" he asked, and I released his face.

"Why would I lie? You know it makes sense." I moved my knees from his arms and let my body slump heavily. Adonis didn't attempt to push me off of him, he just looked up at me and ran a hand over his face.

"He told me exactly what he did to her, Don. I don't want to repeat it, but I will if it helps you to see that I am telling the truth. We all believed she had just been shot because *you* made sure of that, you and Sal made sure that no one knew how fucked up her murder had been. If I was lying, I wouldn't know that you'd done that, would I?" His lips parted.

"Fuck."

41

Don

She was telling the truth. Sal had been visiting Mum when she had been murdered, I'd stayed home to keep on top of business and to take the pressure off of Aunt Rosa. She hated running things when Sal wasn't around. Sal was the one who had found mums body lying in a pool of blood by the front gate of my stepfather's property. He had called me before anyone else and sent me a video of what he had found. The images still haunt me, her body barely recognisable, swollen, bruised and sliced apart. He asked me what I wanted to do. I told him I wanted to hunt down the pezzo di merda who had done this, but he had meant what did I want to do with her body.

I'd had no idea what he meant, too stunned and full of anger to think, so I left it up to him to decide. Uncle Sal, ex leader of The Brotherhood, was the smartest man I knew. I trusted him with anything. He didn't think anyone should know the truth about it, he said he wanted people to remember her for how she lived, not how she died. I agreed.

So we hid it all, Sal took her body and made sure no one would ever find it, he hadn't told me how, and I didn't need to know. He told Lorenzo that he had found Selene out by the front gate with a bullet hole in her head and that he had gone hunting for the person responsible and when he had arrived back, a failure, her body was gone. Sal destroyed the camera footage from the front gate and blamed it on 'stupid unreliable technology'. Lorenzo hadn't questioned it; he had just updated his security system and hired a guard for the gate.

Lorenzo had played along, and we'd had no idea. He hadn't been fooled by any of it, because he was the one responsible. He had vowed to Sal that they would find the person who had taken my Mamma from this world, and it had all been a lie. We had done him a favour, covered up his crime and given him an easy opportunity to pin it on whoever he wanted.

Bile rose in my throat, and I swallowed hard as the truth of his betrayal hit me.

"Fuck, fuck, fuck!" I pushed my hands into my hair and pulled, squeezing my eyes closed, praying that when I opened them, I'd have made it all up. That Megan wouldn't be sitting on top of me, that I'd not attacked the son of an innocent man, that my stepfather hadn't been the one who had taken away the only person I had ever cared about.

    When I opened my eyes they landed on her, but she wasn't looking at me. All colour drained from her face, her eyes turned wide, her mouth fell open, and I watched her heart shatter into a million pieces.

    She pushed off of me and flew across the room, a distressed scream falling from her lips. "Toby!"

    I sat up, hissing at the pain in my shoulder, and watched her. She fell onto him, tears streaming down her face, and blood soaking her hands as she pushed down onto his stomach. His skin was pale and sweaty, his breathing ragged and his eyes glassy. My knife sat between us on the floor, the fucking idiot had pulled it out.

    Without thinking, I rushed to her side, ripped off my shirt and shoved her out of the way. I packed the wound as best I could and yelled at her to call an ambulance.

    "What have you done?" she said shakily as she stared from her blood-soaked hands to me.

    "Ambulance Nutmeg, Now."

To be continued....

Hello Reader,

We made it! I wrote my first book, and you've read it.

How crazy is that? Well, for you probably not very crazy at all, but for me, wow, I can't actually believe I did it.

I'm so thankful for every single one of you who has taken a chance on an unknown author and read my little story.

If you love these naughty characters (they can be really quite frustrating at times) and want to know what happens next, then do not fear, book two will be coming your way very soon.

Will Toby survive? Will Meg and Don learn to get along? Will Lorenzo get what's coming to him? He's a pretty smart guy, so I doubt it. But who knows. Maybe he'll get a happily ever after.

There has to be a happily ever after for at least someone right? Maybe multiple people, depends who makes it to the end. Currently, there is only one person guaranteed to make it, and that's because I made a promise.

Love, Addy

Books In This Series

Love and Lies

The Truth

The Promise